Carla started writing when talking to... after having
flirted with musical theatre and occasional writing in her youth.

Since then she has written and produced several stage plays, has four self-published books, has acted in several independent films and is currently in the final stages of production of her feature horror film, *Penny for the Guy*.

She now writes full time as well as co-owning a film, photography and video production company located in the heart of Redditch town centre.

www.carlakovach.com

ALSO BY CARLA KOVACH

Her Final Hour
Her Pretty Bones

THE
NEXT
GIRL

CARLA KOVACH

sphere

SPHERE

First published in 2018 by Bookouture, an imprint of StoryFire Ltd.
This paperback edition published in 2019 by Sphere

1 3 5 7 9 10 8 6 4 2

Copyright © Carla Kovach 2018

A CIP catalogue record for this book
is available from the British Library.

ISBN 978-0-7515-7746-4

Printed and bound in Great Britain by
Clays Ltd, Elcograf S.p.A.

Papers used by Sphere are from well-managed forests
and other responsible sources.

Sphere
An imprint of
Little, Brown Book Group
Carmelite House
50 Victoria Embankment
London EC4Y 0DZ

An Hachette UK Company

www.hachette.co.uk
www.littlebrown.co.uk

This book is dedicated to all those who are suffering in abusive relationships. You may not yet see it, but you are worth so much more. x

PROLOGUE

Saturday, 14 December 2013

Same height, same hair colour. She could almost pass for Deborah from behind. But as the woman turned, he could tell she was no more than a cheap imitation. Her leggings were riding up between her butt cheeks, and she was wearing a short puffy jacket and spiky heels, further going to prove she was no Debbie. His Debbie wouldn't be seen out looking this trashy. She looked up and down the main hill through the town centre before walking over to his car. He pointed to the right and pulled over beside the chip shop, past the busy bar. Redditch was certainly alive with people, all partying the night away in the run-up to Christmas. She dutifully followed, as if in a money-induced trance – or was it drugs?

He'd only ever come looking for company once before, but it had been a disaster and long before Debbie had entered his life. He'd only wanted to talk, but that woman had been corruptive, trying to encourage him to do things his mother would never approve of. He'd been willing up to a point and that point was his release. She couldn't have it.

The woman tapped on the window and winked as she spoke in an Eastern European accent. Where was she from, he wondered – Romania, maybe, or Bulgaria? Now she was close, he could see her dark roots and the slight wonkiness of a nose that he guessed had once been broken. She wasn't his Debbie, but he could pretend.

The woman smiled. 'Looking for something special to end the evening?' she asked. He glanced in the wing mirror and noticed a group of drunken revellers jokingly pushing and shoving at the entrance to the bar, not one of them taking any notice of what was going on just down the road. As they shivered in their short-sleeved shirts and Santa hats, he turned his attention back to the woman. 'Well? I haven't got all night, mister. It's cold out here.' She exhaled a stream of white mist into the icy air and began shuffling on the spot to keep warm.

'Get in.'

'You know how to treat women. Is good job I know how to treat a man.' She licked her teeth and stared into his eyes. He looked away. 'First you show me the cash, and after, I get in.' The woman stumbled alongside the car, banging into it as she made her way around. She opened the passenger door and leaned in. 'Cash first, mister.'

He took his wallet from the centre console and held up two ten-pound notes.

'Cheap, but I can work with. Don't expect brilliant.' She filled his airways with the smell of cheap perfume as she fell into the car, snatching the cash as she landed on the seat. 'Okay, not too far.'

'I need to go somewhere quiet. Can we go for a walk – like a date?'

'Quiet is good. You didn't expect me to see to you here, did you?'

'Of course not.' He placed the car into gear and began to drive. *See to him*, that's all she was going to do. He wanted so much more. He needed to talk, to think, to feel something – anything.

His mind was a whirr with what his mother would say. 'Going with dirty girls makes you a dirty boy. My boy is better than that.'

'Take a left, just down there. There's quiet car park, by the chemist. Pull in there.'

He began to tremble as he passed the illuminated fountain and took a left as instructed. The road was still too public. Three women wearing reindeer antlers staggered past. It wasn't right. He needed to be somewhere else, somewhere peaceful where they wouldn't be disturbed. Maybe where he walked their dog, Rosie, along the river, up by the locks of Marcliff, just past Bidford. His heart quickened as he passed the chemist and put his foot down to reach the ring road.

'Stop. Pull over,' the woman said. 'Where the hell you taking me? Stop.'

He did an emergency stop at the side of the road, trembling as the car jerked. 'Have I done wrong?'

'You drive too far. I say the chemist and you do this.' The woman opened the door.

'Wait. I just want some company, that's all. I've had a bad day. You see, my mother died today and I don't want to be alone. I have no one else.' In his mind at least, his mother was dead. Since her diagnosis, she'd been walking around like a carbon copy of her former self. He shivered. He'd just told this woman that his mother had died today. What kind of person did that make him? 'Sorry, Ma,' he whispered.

'I'm sorry. Must be hard for you.'

He stared into the lamplight ahead without blinking – just a little longer and there might be a tear. As predicted, his eyes watered. He sniffed and wiped his eye on his sleeve. 'I miss her. Please don't leave me alone.' He was too good, tears were now falling, one after another. Even his nose began to fill up as he inhaled the frosty air.

'Look. I will come for drive but you must pay me now and I want to be back here in a couple of hours. I know you're upset but I am not head doctor. Two hundred and I am yours. I give you distraction or you can talk. I listen, whatever you want.'

'Thank you.' He took her cold, bony hand and kissed it. 'Thank you for being so kind.'

'Money?' She held her shaky hand out as he opened his wallet.

'Half now, half after.' She nodded as he passed one hundred pounds to her. She folded the notes up and zipped them into her pocket.

'Deal. Two hours.' She reached into her other pocket and pulled out a pill. 'Do you want one? Ten pounds and we both have good time?'

'No, but you go ahead.' The woman tossed the pill to the back of her throat, head twitching as she leaned her neck back and swallowed it whole. Closing the passenger door, she rested back into the seat and closed her eyes as he drove out of the town, heading along the Alcester Highway towards Warwickshire. A few miles past the small industrial town of Cleevesford was his destination – Marcliff, to be exact. It was one in the morning; he had until three. They would walk, he could talk, and then he would drop her back.

You could drop her back now. Do the right thing, he thought.

His heart fluttered as he glanced over at her. There was only him and the sleeping whore in the car.

'Are we there yet?' The woman stirred as she wiped a trail of saliva from the corner of her mouth.

'Nearly,' he said as he put his foot down, weaving through the country lanes.

As he pulled up alongside the river, he watched her sleeping. Maybe it was the warmth of the car, the hum of the engine or whatever was in the pill she had taken. The fields stretched ahead for miles, and except for the light of the moon, there was nothing but darkness. He opened the door and the woman stirred. She smiled and leaned closer to him, massaging his groin over his corduroys. He leaned back, allowing her to unzip and stroke him. He felt himself harden as she released him from his clothing and expertly placed a condom over his penis. She leaned down to take him in her mouth. He wrenched her hair.

'Ouch, tosser.'

'Not that. Don't do that.' He paused, listening to the blood coursing through his temples. 'Bitch.'

'Take me back now. Call me bitch, grab me like that. Weirdo, that's what you are, you bloody weirdo.'

He gasped for breath, wanting to shout, to scream, to smash the dashboard up into hundreds of tiny pieces. He wasn't a weirdo, he was just confused. Why couldn't he be here with Debbie instead of this cheap whore?

'Take me back. What are you? Deaf?'

'Sorry. I didn't mean to hurt you, you just caught me wrong and made me jump. You hurt me.' He forced a smile. 'Please, can we start again?' She looked at him and sighed. 'Could you just touch me with your hands?' He removed the condom and dropped it by his feet.

'Whatever, but don't grab me again.'

'Sorry. I'm truly sorry.'

As she continued to caress him with her warm hands, he closed his eyes and thought of Debbie. In his fantasy, the candles always glistened in the background.

They were in the barn and they'd just had dinner. She walked towards him and slipped off her dress to reveal her naked body. Her nipples glistened in the candlelight as she bent over on the sofa with her legs apart, begging him to take her. He kissed the small of her back as he slapped her buttocks. He couldn't wait any longer, he needed to be in her. As he thrusted back and forth, his desire heightened. Almost there.

'Come on, you do it, just do it, mister,' the woman said as she stroked him vigorously.

'What? What the— Stop! Stupid whore – get off me!' He shouted as he pulled away and gasped for air. 'I'm so sorry, Debbie, so sorry.' He stumbled out of the car and zipped his trousers up, taking the keys with him.

'Prick!' she shouted.

He'd betrayed Debbie, the only woman he'd ever loved. 'Stupid, stupid, stupid,' he said as he paced the riverbank and slapped himself across the head. What if Debbie were to ever find out what a dirty man he'd been?

The sound of the River Avon gushing through the weir brought him back to the situation in hand. He realised he was shivering to the point his muscles were in pain. Cold, it was so cold.

The woman staggered over to him and lit a cigarette. 'You want puff to calm the hell down? Then you take me back and don't forget my other hundred. I think I bloody well earned it with you.'

He shook his head. Was she mocking him and his inability to respond to her charms? He detected a grin on her face. Was the grin aimed at him? They walked until they reached the lock. He stared into the calmness of the water, then his gaze darted across to the violent gushing of the weir next to it.

He shook his head again. 'What have I done? What the hell have I done?' He continued pacing. A curl of the woman's cigarette smoke filled his nostrils. Along with his churning stomach, it made him want to spew. He watched as she walked over the lock's bridge, staring at the water below. He couldn't let her tell anyone. If Debbie ever found out… He shuddered. It wasn't going to happen. She turned as he reached her.

'By time you take me back, will be two hours.' She dropped her cigarette into the water and started walking back down, almost tripping over the stones on the pathway. As she turned, he gripped her arms. 'Please let go of me,' she said, her eyes glassy. When he didn't, she began to struggle. 'Let me go!' she yelled as she tried to grab his face and poke at his eyes.

He forced her back towards the bridge, and then with what seemed like no effort at all, he pushed her slight frame into the ice-cold water below. He listened as her body cracked the thin layer of ice coating the top of the water. With a head first, fifteen-foot drop into freezing cold water, she wouldn't stand a chance. He watched as she gasped for air, her voice echoing in the lock, 'I can't swim! Help!' She gagged on a mouth full of water. He stared down and caught her distorted features as the moonlight lit up one side of her pained face. His heart was beating so fast he was sure he'd have a heart attack – then the splashing finally stopped. Ten minutes he waited. There had been no noise, no more thrashing and no shouting.

'I'm so sorry, Debbie. I love you and I'm so, so, sorry I betrayed you.' He frantically searched around, making sure he was alone, and hurried back to the car. The passenger door was still open. He leaned in to tidy the seat belt, which had snagged around the chair, and noticed a driver's licence in the footwell. She was Romanian. Nicoleta Iliescu was only twenty-four years old. He stroked the outline of her photo on the small card. He was right: she wasn't Debbie. What had he been thinking? He took a duster from the glovebox and began wiping down the passenger seat. Her perfume still hung in the air, making him gag. Although he could barely feel his fingers, he knew he'd have to leave the window open while driving home to get rid of the stench.

He walked down to the riverbank and went to throw the card, then hesitated. He'd touched it. Would his fingerprints stay on it if it were immersed in water? He rubbed it against his trousers and held it with the tip of his fingers. Placing it in his pocket, he decided that disposing of it now was too risky. If the body were found, they might also find the card, then they'd know who she was. Maybe she'd remain in the river until she was unidentifiable, but he wasn't going to leave any further evidence behind. Maybe if they knew who she was, they'd know her whereabouts, where she lived. Maybe they'd have him picking her up on CCTV in Redditch. He couldn't take the risk. He'd take it with him, away from the scene.

He gazed up and down, trying to spot her body – nothing, except for a rustling in the bushes. He flinched, following the sound. Was it the breeze catching the bare branches? Was it just an animal? Foxes and badgers were common around these parts. The bushes opposite him rustled once more. His heart hammered against his ribcage. Had someone seen him?

'Who's there?' he asked in a quivery voice as tears streamed down his face. He gasped until he almost passed out. Who'd seen him?

A fox darted from the trees and ran off into the distance. An owl hooted, making him flinch. He ran as fast as he could, back to the car, almost slipping on an icy puddle. Mother would be awake soon. She'd need her breakfast and the bread was in the car. He was going home, then he was going to watch Debbie – just another normal day.

CHAPTER ONE

Friday, 1 December 2017

Albert belched as he supped the last of his ale and placed his cap on his head. Another would've been grand but he knew his pension wouldn't stretch that far. His mouth watered as he thought of the homemade steak and kidney pudding his neighbours Mark and Jean had promised to make him for supper. He gripped the table and hauled himself up, flinching as he straightened out. It wasn't easy being old. Once the ageing bones had set in the same position for more than a few minutes, they rebelled at being moved.

Partygoers drank, yelled, and played darts and pool. They danced as another pop anthem started on the jukebox. It was the run up to Christmas and he loved every minute of it. As he straightened his tie and buttoned his overcoat, he gazed through the leaded window, into the darkness. In a moment, he'd be out there getting drenched, leaving the warmth of the roaring fire behind. Grabbing his stick off the back of the chair, he shuffled through the crowd, thanking anyone who moved as he neared the door.

'Bye, old Albert,' shouted Jeff, one of the bar staff, as he pulled a pint for a man in a light-up Christmas jumper.

'Less of the "old",' Albert replied with a smile, winking. He watched as Jeff wiped his forehead on his sleeve before continuing to serve the revellers. He pushed the door open and gasped for breath as a gust of wind hit him face on. Water soaked his shoes as he waded through the puddle that had gathered at the doorstep. He knew his shoes were cheap, but they were all he could afford and they looked smart. A real man needed a collar and a shiny pair of shoes. He was amazed at how many youngsters would go out in tracksuit bottoms and T-shirts. That attire was for exercising in, not for making an impression. He smiled as he remembered the night he first cast his eyes on his Lillian.

Cleevesford Village Hall on the seventeenth of December 1954. It was the first Christmas without rationing for as long as he could remember. Wearing his only suit, he entered the hall and paid his fee. The room was filled with bodies dancing to 'Shake, Rattle and Roll'. His heart fluttered as he searched for a place to stand. Every man seemed to have a girl on his arm or be on the dance floor. He watched as they rock-and-rolled and lindy-hopped.

At eighteen, he'd had a couple of dates but he hadn't been lucky enough to find someone to see again or go further with. He was the skinny, spotty boy that most girls avoided. He grinned, remembering his mother's warning when he'd left earlier that evening: 'Don't you go getting some poor girl into trouble.'

The dancers moved closer as a woman stepped forward to sing 'Secret Love' by Doris Day. Albert bit his bottom lip and began nervously twiddling his fingers. He placed his empty glass on the table and turned. As he looked up, his gaze locked onto the most beautiful girl he'd ever seen in his life. She looked like an auburn-haired Marilyn Monroe. Well, the rest was history. He'd married his Lillian a year later, and they had two beautiful girls soon after.

He inhaled and all he could smell was pie as he squelched across the road, passing the chip shop. Steak and kidney pudding, he thought as he smiled. His socks were waterlogged and it began to bucket down once again. Raindrops bounced off the gurgling gutters and pummelled the windows of the terraced houses opposite. Water dripped off his cap and drizzled onto his nose before dripping off his chin. He shivered and scooted past the car park, towards Cleevesford Library – or Cleevesford Village Hall, as he'd always refer to it. Once again, his mind was filled with the music of that night.

Back then, he'd had his first real dance with Lillian to 'I Saw Mommy Kissing Santa Claus'. How his Lillian had loved The Beverley Sisters. The night ended with him having his first proper kiss. He'd brushed lips with a girl before, but hadn't felt anything special. Kissing Lillian had been real. He remembered the moment her soft lips first touched his.

Her rose-scented perfume filled his nostrils. He wanted to hold her tight and caress her smooth skin, but he'd been brought up properly. He held his arms out behind her, not daring to touch her back. She broke away from their kiss, reached behind and pressed his hands onto the small of her back before letting a little chuckle slip as she continued kissing him. Fifty-eight years later, any mention of Lillian still made his heart flutter. There would never be another.

He crossed the road, heading towards the library. One quick look, for old time's sake. He placed his stick on the kerb and stepped up. The street lamp above flickered before finally staying off. He stared at the door as he adjusted his focus. Back in 1954 he'd seen a sign on that very door advertising the local dance, the only local dance that year.

'Love you always, Lillian,' he whispered as he smiled. He squinted at the small white bag of rubbish that lay on the doorstep, sheltered by the canopy above. 'Damn litterbugs. Why use the floor when you have a bloomin' bin right there?' He placed his stick against the door and held his back as he bent down. His knees creaked and crunched as he reached for the rubbish. Why was there a red sash tying up the bag? He leaned further down until his fingers reached the mass. It was a towel. He reached again and tugged at the material. Whatever it was, it was going in the bin. He was sick of his streets and community being disrespected by the youth that congregated on the streets.

He grabbed the mass and the material fell open to reveal a doll. He squinted again and reached down. His trembling hand trailed across the head of the doll. It didn't feel like plastic. It felt like skin – cold skin. His tremble turned into a full-on shake as he stepped back and tumbled into a puddle, wetting his backside. He tried to yell for help but his heart felt as though it was beating out of his mouth. Tears fell as he thought of the little bundle that lay before him. If only it was a doll. It should've been a doll. He rubbed his damp backside and crawled open-mouthed towards the bundle as he reached out once again. It was the tiniest and coldest baby he'd ever seen. The streetlight above hissed and flickered back on, revealing the baby's delicate facial features. He had to get help. It might be too late to save the poor mite but he'd damn well try his best. As he steadied his frail body against the doorway, he managed to stand and grab his stick.

'Help,' he whispered. He tried again and again to call out. 'Help!' he finally yelled, hitting the doors of the terraced houses with his stick. The light behind the third door came on and a woman answered. 'Call an ambulance and the police,' he said as he panted in her doorway.

'What's happened? Here, come in. You'll catch your death,' said the woman as she assisted the soaking-wet man through the front door.

'There's a baby. You have to check on it. Get something warm. Please,' he replied, grabbing her arm for support as he caught his breath.

'A baby? Look, are you okay?'

'Yes. I've just found an abandoned baby in the library doorway. Please go and help it,' he said as he collapsed on the sofa, wetting all the cushions. The woman grabbed her mobile phone and ordered her teenage daughter to sit with Albert. The girl placed a blanket over his shoulders before heading over to the window and watching her mother from the comfort of their lounge. Albert shuddered at the thought of the stone-cold baby. It reminded him of the same stony coldness he'd felt after finding Lillian's body in bed, back in 1985, after she'd passed away in the night from pneumonia. His heart missed a beat as he gasped for breath again and wept.

CHAPTER TWO

Gina combed her damp brown hair with her fingers. As she stepped out of the car, she pulled an elastic band from her pocket and scooped the tangled mop into a ponytail. Another bath disturbed by the job, another emergency that would more than likely be followed by another sleepless night. She spotted Detective Sergeant Jacob Driscoll's slim, tall figure. He was talking to a woman under the canopy outside Cleevesford Library. Curtains twitched, hallways cast light onto the street and people began to migrate towards the scene. A paramedic held the tiny parcel, wrapped in a towel. He stepped into the ambulance and closed the doors. Gina shivered. That towel might be all the little one would have when they grew up. A scrap of material, holding secrets that might never leave the closely knitted fibres.

Jacob turned to face her as she approached. His thin, fair hair stuck to his wet forehead, making him resemble an Action Man figure. 'Mrs Craneford, this is DI Harte. Mrs Craneford looked after the baby until the emergency services arrived. The paramedic stated that the baby is suffering from hypothermia and a low pulse rate.'

'Oh, that poor baby was freezing. What an awful state of affairs. There's an old guy in our house. He found the baby and knocked at our door. He was frantic. He's not in a fit state for much though, seems in shock. My daughter's making him a cuppa,' Mrs Craneford said.

Gina looked up and down. She watched as the fine droplets of rain crossed the lamplight. Her ponytail stuck to the back of her neck, wetting her shirt. She shivered and turned to Jacob. 'Right, ask PC Smith to knock on the doors along this street and get statements?'

'Will do,' replied Jacob.

Gina glanced up at the library. 'We need to secure the library's CCTV. Call the out-of-hours number at the council and get someone onto it? Mrs Craneford, would you go and wait with the man who found the baby? I'll be there in a moment.' The woman nodded and padded back towards her house, almost tripping up the step as she entered.

'Anything to go on so far?'

'PC Smith hasn't found any witnesses as yet and a lot of people are out,' said Jacob. 'The ones that were in had their curtains shut and their TVs on. Are you alright?'

Gina shivered and wrapped her arms around her body. 'Yes, just cold. I was in the middle of a bath when you called. Nothing new there. I hope the mother's okay. Did the paramedics give any indication as to the age of the baby?'

'Yes, newborn and slightly premature looking. They won't know any more until she's been properly examined. I did notice a slight smell of diesel on the towel.'

'Diesel, interesting,' said Gina, gazing at the scene around her. Her bath was now a distant memory. 'What a way to spend an evening.'

'You're telling me. Not that I'm complaining, but I had to break a date with Abigail, the one I was telling you about who works at the café in town.' He paused. 'Anyway, at least the baby's getting the best possible treatment now. Our only objective is to find the mother and see if she's okay. Sounds straightforward.' Jacob wiped the rain off his face and swept his damp hair back.

'Let's hope so. I best start thinking about a press statement too, see if anyone's seen or heard anything. I'll go and ask our chap in there some questions. Can you get the items that the baby was wrapped in before the ambulance leaves? Bag and tag them, and send them to Keith in forensics. We need them to check for anything that might help us find the parents. Ask them to test for the usual – hair, blood and traces of anything else that may help. And diesel, too. You never know.'

'Will do,' DS Driscoll replied as he pulled his hood up and walked towards the ambulance.

The rain began to pelt as Gina stepped away from the canopy. She rushed towards Mrs Craneford's house and knocked as she entered the slightly open door. She shuffled through the cluttered hall. 'Hello. DI Harte,' she said, almost knocking a pile of coats off a stand before entering the cluttered lounge. The electric fire radiated a cosy warmth and the flashing multicoloured Christmas lights added to the chaos of the room. An elderly man was sitting on the settee, staring at the wall.

'Oh, Detective. This is Mr Thomas, the man I was telling you about who found the baby. Can I get you a cup of tea?' the woman asked as she stepped backwards towards the kitchen.

'I'm fine, thanks,' Gina replied, sitting down beside the frail man. His hands trembled as he pulled the blanket over his shoulders.

'My neighbours, Mark and Jean, will be wondering where I am. They do worry,' the man said as he checked his watch.

Gina took out her phone. 'Shall I call them for you?' Albert nodded and replied with their home number. She called and explained that they were asking Albert a few questions and they would drop him to theirs shortly. 'Jean said she'll put your steak and kidney pudding in the microwave. Mr Thomas—'

'Albert, you can call me Albert.'

Gina smiled and took out her notebook and pen. 'Albert, tell me what happened in your own words.'

'I came out of the Angel about seven thirty. It was rainy and horrible. Well, I crossed the road and headed alongside the houses towards the library. I stopped at the library for a look. It used to be Cleevesford Village Hall, you see. Lillian and I used to dance there. I wanted to think about those times. You understand?' Gina nodded and smiled. 'Only, when I stopped, I saw something and thought it was rubbish. I went to pick it up and realised then it was a baby. I managed to get this kind lady to open the door and she went out and tended to the baby thereon. Is the baby alright? It was so cold when I touched its head. Is it, you know…?'

'The baby is receiving treatment now. You and Mrs Craneford did a good job.'

The man took a deep breath.

'It's hard to believe a mother could leave such a helpless little baby on its own,' Mrs Craneford said as she bit her bottom lip. 'I mean, if she didn't want it, there are plenty of people who can't have kids and—'

'We don't know this woman's circumstances – that's what we're here to find out,' Gina replied kindly. With her experience in child protection and domestic violence, she knew things weren't always as clear-cut as people assumed. The mother may have been underage or abused, or might even be under some kind of threat. It was her job to unravel the mysteries and solve the case, and in her experience, jumping to conclusions wouldn't help. Only the facts helped. She glanced at the frail man beside her. He looked down and wiped his nose with the back of his hand. 'Here's my number, should you remember anything else. I'll get someone to drop you home.' She called PC Smith who arrived within moments.

'Thank you,' Albert said, as he dropped the blanket onto the settee and left with the police officer.

Mrs Craneford smiled as she tapped her foot on the floor. Her daughter entered from the kitchen carrying a drink. The girl smiled and went upstairs.

'Did you see anything or anyone suspicious when you went out to tend to the baby?'

'No, I can't say I did. The old man told me where it was and I found the little one straight away. I called you lot and held the baby until the paramedics came, hoping to keep it warm. It didn't even cry,' the woman replied, staring at the wall.

'The baby's in good hands. I'm sure your help paid off. Did you see anyone hanging around?' Gina asked. She wondered if the mother had waited until someone found the baby. Maybe she had been standing at the end of the street or around the corner. Gina's face began to glow from the fire's warmth. Even her hair had stopped dripping.

'No. There was no one in sight. Just me.'

'If you remember anything else, please call,' Gina said. She handed the woman her card and walked to the door.

'Can you let me know how the baby is?' Mrs Craneford said as she saw Gina out.

'Yes, of course.' As she left, the press release ran through her mind. An appeal for the safety of the mother and witnesses would be their best hope. She'd need to pass all the details to DCI Briggs so that he could get the information to the press before the morning news went out. Rain pelted down and the drains gurgled as they flooded. The ambulance splashed water over the pavement as the paramedics pulled away. Jacob Driscoll jogged towards her.

'As requested, I've bagged and tagged all the garments for the lab,' he said as he wiped his wet face and removed his latex gloves. 'We'd best get back and process everything that's happened. There appears to be no witnesses. We've asked everyone along this road – well, the ones who answered. I think we should get back. Oh, and one last thing – not good, I'm afraid. The CCTV hasn't been on for over a year due to funding cuts. It's just been left there as a deterrent.'

'Damn.' Gina wiped the rain from her face and watched as the lights in the houses started switching off and curtains were closed. All the action was over, leaving the public to go back to their books, television programmes and nice warm baths. She sloshed through the gutter towards her car. 'I'll see you back at the station,' she called as she closed the door and started demisting the windscreen. She would find out to whom the baby belonged and how it arrived there. In her experience, the truth always found its way out. To start with, she'd organise the appeal. She released the handbrake and followed Jacob back to the station.

As she drove, she stared hard into the darkness of the street and imagined a figure. At the moment it had no face, it had no size, it wasn't a woman or a man. Whoever placed the baby there had chosen carefully. The library entrance provided some shelter to protect the baby from the stormy weather. The road was densely populated and was crossed by passers-by with frequency. The figure would've been aware of this, and therefore they'd have left the baby quickly. Were they local? Was it a relief to leave the baby or was it the most heart-wrenching moment of their life? Was there violence involved?

CHAPTER THREE

As Luke sipped the last of the wine in his glass, he watched Brooke twisting her blonde curls between her thumb and finger. Their gaze met. He couldn't look away. He didn't want to look away. He leaned across and stroked the side of her face before kissing her. She tasted just as he'd imagined. A hint of wine lingered on her breath. As his tongue reached further, caressing hers, she ran her fingers through his hair and pushed her body closer to his. The fire crackled as he reached up her jumper. He wanted her; she wanted him.

'Stay the night,' she whispered.

'What about the kids?'

'I'm sure they'd love a sleepover.'

He smiled as they continued kissing. She reached back and unclipped her bra. He stroked her soft back as his desire increased. The firelight glinted off his gold wedding band, and he moved his hand out of sight. Tonight, he wasn't going to wallow in his sorrows or keep reliving the past. Her hand moved along his leg and continued upwards. Maybe it was the wine, or maybe it was the wood gently burning, but he wanted her. He had to move on and now was as good a time as any. Now was the perfect time. He leaned across and pushed his groin into hers, relishing the moans she was making in his ear.

Then Joe barged through the living room door, forcing them to part. 'I hurt my finger,' the little boy said, tears falling down his face.

Luke's heart was beating like mad. He straightened his hair as Brooke pulled her jumper down. Glancing down at his ring, he shivered as he thought of his past, his children.

A thunderous noise filled the house as Max and Heidi ran down the stairs. 'Daddy, she hit me,' Max shouted, as he jumped into Luke's lap.

'I did not. He started it,' Heidi replied, her face reddening. As his nine-year-old little girl stared up at him with her hazel eyes, he was reminded of the only woman he'd ever truly loved. She resembled her mother more every year.

'She did!'

'Do you two always have to argue?' Luke shook his head. 'Damn it! I suppose we should make a move.' He stood up.

Brooke hugged her son and looked up from the sofa. 'Blooming kids,' she replied with a smile. 'Is that a no to the sleepover then?'

'I forgot, their nan's coming over first thing. I really need to get back.'

'Do you really?'

'Kids, go and get your things.'

'I'm going to stamp on your dinosaur if I get up the stairs first,' Heidi shouted.

'No,' Max yelled, racing his big sister back up the stairs.

'Joe, can you give Mummy a minute to talk to Luke?' She kissed his little finger and then stood up. 'There, all better.' The little boy wiped his face and nodded as he left the room.

Luke kissed Brooke on the head and held her in his arms. 'Thank you for a lovely evening. I think I've had a couple too many anyway, so I'll head home. I really enjoyed tonight though – really.'

'Really?' She began twisting her hair in her fingers once again as she bit her bottom lip, allowing the slightest of smiles to escape.

'Really.' He forced a smile as he headed towards the door, meeting Max and Heidi with their coats.

'I'll call you tomorrow about picking the kids up together from Jake's birthday party,' she said as she returned his smile. He waved as he closed the back gate and began the short walk home with the children.

'I'm tired, Daddy,' Max said.

As they walked past a row of houses and neared their road, he thought back to happier times. A tear slid down his cheek as he thought of his wife and all she had been. But she was gone. Brooke was in his life now and he liked her, a lot. *Move on, Luke. She's not coming back.*

CHAPTER FOUR

Gina tapped the light switch and the strip lights flickered in her office until they settled. The dank air still smelled of the takeaway burger she'd eaten earlier that afternoon. She shivered as she pushed the window open to allow the odour to escape. Her in tray was precariously balanced on the edge of her desk, and she slid it back into place, perfectly angled in the corner. She stared at it, then shook her head and shoved it askew again.

'Whoa. It's rank in here,' DS Driscoll said as he wafted his hand in front of his nose.

'About which I make no apologies,' Gina replied. 'Tell me what we have.'

'We have a few things, guv. DCs O'Connor and Wyre will be assisting with anything we need on the case. They're just pulling up some seats in the main office. We can update everyone at the same time. DCI Briggs called and he's at home, awaiting the press report.'

'I'll be there in a moment,' Gina replied as she slid her damp coat off and hung it on the back of the chair. Jacob smiled and left.

She turned to face the window and stared into the darkness of the station car park. The guttering above spilled over and flooded into a pool below. Budgets and cuts were the cause, she knew it. The guttering was nothing more than a growbag for moss, a gatherer of dried twigs from the tree that grew alongside the wall.

She grabbed a grey suit jacket from the back of the door and pulled it on before entering the bustle of the station.

Detective Constable Harry O'Connor passed around a packet of chocolate biscuits. 'Just maintaining my energy for my big bike ride,' he said as he patted his belly.

Gina grabbed one and bit into it. 'Bike ride?'

'It's a charity thing. I'll message you the details. Maybe you can sponsor me?'

Four machine-made coffees sat on a tray in the middle of a paperwork-covered desk. 'O'Connor, the biscuits are lovely but I have to insist that you keep the case files in order,' Gina said. She couldn't understand how he managed to work in such chaos. Some of the reports had even fallen to the floor and cruddy plates and cups covered the surface. She knew her office could get messy but O'Connor's desk was in a state. Even his mini Christmas tree was threatening to throw itself to its death from the edge of the desk.

O'Connor fumbled for the reports with his chubby fingers and placed them in a folder, his shiny head reflecting the strip light above. 'All sorted, ma'am,' he said, as he grabbed a coffee before sitting on the edge of his desk, knocking the mini tree flying.

Gina cleared her throat and began. 'Right. I'll give you what I know so far. A baby girl was found by a Mr Albert Thomas after he left the Angel pub at approximately seven thirty this evening. He stopped by Cleevesford Library and spotted the bundle. Thinking it was litter, he went to pick it up to place it in the bin, whereupon he discovered it was a baby. In an attempt to get some help, he banged on a couple of doors before Mrs Craneford opened her door and let him in. We were called and the baby was taken to the Cleevesford General Hospital by paramedics. DS Driscoll smelled diesel on the towel the baby was wrapped in. The towel has gone to the lab for testing so hopefully we'll get that confirmed.' Gina bit into another biscuit and grabbed a coffee.

'Alan Cummings, council security, confirmed that the CCTV on the library hasn't been active for way over a year,' said Jacob. 'PC Smith had a walk around and couldn't see any further CCTV cameras amongst the residential roads. There appears, at first enquiry, to be no witnesses either, but we are hoping for callbacks and we will continue to canvass the area.'

Gina wiped a crumb from the side of her mouth before taking a swig of coffee. 'So we don't really have a lot to go on as yet. Did you follow up at the hospital?' she asked, looking at Wyre.

'I did. I spoke to the consultant in charge, ma'am, a Dr Nowak,' replied DC Paula Wyre in her usual soft tone. The petite woman cleared her throat and took a step forward, brushing her straight black hair off her shoulders. O'Connor held the packet of biscuits under her nose. 'No, thank you,' she replied before clearing her throat once again. 'The five-pound female baby has mild hypothermia. Their initial assessment tells them she's premature. She'd been fed within a couple of hours as she brought up a lot of milk on the way to the hospital. She is currently being hydrated and nourished through a nasal tube. They estimate her to be no more than a day old. The cord had been clumsily cut, definitely not by anyone who knew what they were doing.' Wyre took a step back and nodded.

'Thank you,' said Gina. 'What does that tell us, O'Connor?'

'It tells us someone—' O'Connor began to cough as he tried to dislodge a rogue crumb from his windpipe. Gina shook her head as he took a gulp of coffee.

'It tells us,' she said, 'that we have a distressed parent out there. The fact that the mother and/or father kept her for a few hours says that there was some hesitancy. Did she consider keeping the baby? She must've fed the baby quite well before they parted.' Gina stared as O'Connor continued to cough and splutter. 'I can't think with this racket going on.' Rain bounced off the roof and she heard a distant rumble of thunder.

'Sorry, ma'am. It's all gone now,' he said, and he clapped his hands and jumped off the desk, landing with a thud on the tiled floor. Gina flinched as a roll of thunder vibrated through the building. Her hammering heart almost made her gasp.

'Are you alright, ma'am?' Jacob asked.

She forced a smile and looked up. 'Yes, I'm fine,' she said, as she undid the top button of her shirt and stepped backwards towards her office. 'Driscoll, chase up forensics on the items that were bagged – we need those analysed, see if they can tell us something. Wyre, I'll pass the press release over to DCI Briggs when I'm done. Can you monitor the responses? I'm sure we'll get a fair few. We need to continue with the door-to-doors, see what PC Smith comes back with. O'Connor, when you've tidied those biscuits away, investigate whether there's any CCTV at any of the establishments along the high street? Try the chip shop. I doubt the person who left the baby would've gone that way as it's so public, but you just never know,' Gina said as she continued along the corridor and closed her office door.

She walked towards the window and shivered as the wind howled through the room. A line of water had gathered under the open window. The blinds rattled as the breeze whipped up. She pulled the window closed, fell into her chair and took a deep breath. Thunder clashed and the lights dipped then flickered. The combination of thunder and seeing the helpless baby had dug up her memories. Memories she'd rather forget.

Twenty years ago, it had been a thundery night, just like this. Her own child, Hannah, then only two years old, had been screaming. In darkness and half asleep she'd staggered from her bedroom to comfort her. As the toddler's wailing continued, she'd hurried along the landing before colliding with her drunk husband, Terry, at the top of the stairs. Just like back then, her heart quickened and the walls seemed to be closing in, showing no mercy. She wanted to fall to the floor and curl up in a ball, closing her eyes until it was all over and she could breathe again.

*

There was a knock at the door, bringing her back into the moment. Jacob entered. She turned and took a few deep breaths as she wiped her watery eyes and massaged her throbbing head

'The items have arrived at the lab. They'll let us know when they have something for us,' said Jacob. 'Are you sure you're alright, guv? You look a bit pale.'

'I'm fine. Just a headache.' She shook her head. 'I think I'm coming down with a cold or something. Anyway, enough of me. We have a baby's mother to find. The poor woman is probably feeling a lot worse than I am.'

'Let's hope the public don't scare her away. There will be slagging off galore in the Facebook comments and Twitter feeds in the morning. Are you sure you're alright? Is there anything I can get you?'

'Bloody Facebook. Full of sanctimonious trolls. I'd love another coffee if you're getting one, and then we can go over the case together. I'll email DCI Briggs while you're gone.'

'On it like the proverbial car bonnet. Whoever came up with that pile of nonsense?' Driscoll replied, tucking a section of overhanging shirt into his trousers as he left to get the drinks.

A combination of finding the baby, a thick head and the stormy weather had turned her into a wreck. She inhaled and exhaled slowly before straightening her jacket. She turned on her computer. Time to start writing the press release to send to Briggs. It needed to be done quickly if it were to make the morning news programmes. As she'd reminded Driscoll, they had a baby's mother to find. Thunder clashed once again. She inhaled slowly and exhaled. She was in control. Nothing a good night's sleep wouldn't fix.

CHAPTER FIVE

Saturday, 2 December 2017

Debbie shivered as she pulled the coarse blankets over her shoulders. Lying on her side in a pool of sticky wetness, she thought of the small life she'd pushed from her body a day ago. The kettle whistled as he stomped across the wooden boards of the loft to the camping stove. As the kettle's whistling stopped, his whistling began: 'You Are My Sunshine'. That song that made her want to vomit. Tears trailed over her nose, down her cheek and gathered with the others on her lumpy pillow.

'Tea, dear?' he asked as he opened the door, flooding the room with battery-powered light. She flinched and cried. 'Don't cry. Don't you dare cry,' he said, staring into her eyes.

She inhaled, held her breath and let it out slowly before forcing a smile.

'When you smile, you make me the happiest man alive. Make me happy and I make you happy. Do you trust me?' She nodded. 'Good. Breakfast will be served in a minute.' He pulled the door closed as he continued to whistle. She listened as he took the plates from the cupboard and slammed them onto the countertop. He then turned the portable television on and she heard the sound of a morning news show. As he turned up the volume, the cries she'd suppressed burst out. Sobbing, she clenched the blanket and silently screamed into it. As she drew her legs towards her chest, her body leaked more liquid. She lifted one leg off the other and yelped as pain seared through her body. The ankle chain clattered as she moved her other leg. Shivering, she curled into a ball, trying to warm up.

'Here we are,' he said as he burst through the door, smiling, wearing a chef's apron. He placed the tray on the side table. 'I've made your favourite, honey on toast. Are you happy?'

Through chattering teeth, she smiled.

'Are you happy?' he asked, as his smile turned into a frown.

'I'm happy,' Debbie stammered. She hated honey; she'd always hated honey. How he ever thought that honey on toast was her favourite thing to eat was beyond her. In the beginning, she'd rebelled, thrown the food against the wall and screamed, but she'd soon learned that no one was coming; she'd learned that she did love honey. And if loving honey kept her alive another day, she'd continue to love it.

'Well, I hope you aren't going to be this disobedient all day. You know you must sit up if you're to get your honey on toast,' he said as he looked down at her quaking body. 'Sit up,' he yelled.

She clenched her teeth as she forced her legs straight and attempted to throw them over the side of the bed to sit up. Pain shot from below and through her abdomen as she tore her tender area a little more. To hide her yelp, she grabbed the blanket and held it over her mouth, only pulling it away from her body as she reached a full sitting position. There was no point saying she wasn't hungry, just like there was no point expressing how much pain she was in. He refused to see or care. She was there to service him and his delusions, and the last thing she wanted to do was antagonise him. She grabbed the hem of her soiled nightdress and pulled it over her knees.

'I knew you'd do anything for your honey,' he said with a grin as he watched her eating. She chewed on the toast, almost gagging every time she swallowed. Once finished, he passed her a cup of lukewarm black tea. He hadn't given her hot drinks since she'd flung one at him in the early days. 'You love your tea warm. I make it just how you like it. You really are my sunshine,' he said, whistling again. He stared into her eyes as he whistled the melody. She coughed and spluttered the brown liquid over his knees. 'Filthy cow!' he yelled, leaping up and slapping her once across the cheek. 'You seriously need to clean yourself up.' He grabbed the cup and plate before slamming the door and leaving her in darkness once again. Clean herself up? With what? He left her in filth, in dirt, in her own secretions.

She stared into the suffocating darkness. She used to stare into nothing and see her family, she used to be able to dream about them, but now she'd resigned herself to never seeing them again. She shuffled on her bottom until her back was against the wall, then she dragged the blankets back over her shivering body. She yelped as she turned. For a moment, she allowed her mind to wander back to the day before.

'You know you mustn't yell. Little Florence is on her way. This is what you and I have been waiting for all this time. The fruit of our love. You do love me, I know you do.' She dreaded the thought of the baby being a boy. He didn't want a boy and she knew exactly what he was capable of. Thankfully she'd pushed out a little girl. A light but healthy little girl.

A few minutes was all she'd been given to hold her daughter. She was left empty as he dragged the screaming infant from her arms and closed the door to her cell. The baby screamed and screamed. The sound echoed through the building.

'Take the feed, you bloody little runt,' he shouted. Her weary heart beat ten to the second as the sounds of her distressed newborn emanated through the building. 'I can't have you scaring mother with your wailing. You will take the feed. You will take the bloody feed! Shut up!'

*

That was a day ago, and she was reliving it continuously. Her heavy breasts began to trickle and she wiped the milk away. What had he done with her baby? She gasped for air as she sobbed. She thought he'd hurt her all he could, but this hurt like nothing she'd ever experienced before. That little life had been the only reminder that she was still alive. For years she'd felt as if she were dead, but that baby, her baby, had awoken something in her. She grabbed the smaller blanket that lay on the end of the bed, rolled it up and placed it between her legs. She'd remove the soiled blanket she was lying on later, when she had more energy, but for now she needed to recuperate and think. She needed her body to heal, just in case – but in case of what, she didn't know. She needed to remember her baby. There was nothing more he could take from her now. She yelled into the dusty blanket and hit the wall before taking a few deep breaths.

He turned up the volume on the television and she listened in. The weather passed and the local news came on. Rain, more rain, and it would be cold. That was no surprise. It hadn't stopped raining for days. That question ripped through her heart again. What had he done with her baby? Isobel. Her baby was not called Florence and she wasn't his. She wasn't evil like him.

'It's been reported that early last night a newborn was discovered in the doorway of Cleevesford Library. Anyone with any information—' He turned the television off and bounded down the stairs. She heard the main door slam shut and his car start up outside. She smiled. Her baby was safe; the police had found her. As she sobbed hard and loud, her tears soon turned into manic laughter. Her baby was alive and free.

CHAPTER SIX

Gina entered the hospital and followed the signs to ward six, where the baby was being treated. The good night's sleep she'd hoped for hadn't materialised. 'Excuse me, you can't go in there,' a nurse called, stepping in front of Gina.

She pulled out her identification and held it up. 'DI Harte. I'm investigating the abandoned baby case.'

The nurse examined her identification, smiled and stepped out of the way. 'You can't be too careful. I'll show you through. Doctor Nowak will be coming round shortly.' Gina followed the nurse through the long, sterile corridor, past several smaller rooms. She caught a glimpse of a couple sitting beside a baby. Tubes, beeping monitors and the father's ashen face all left an imprint in her mind. 'Here we are. If you want coffee, there's a machine just there.'

'Thank you. I might just be in the market for one of those. What time did you say the doctor was coming around?'

'He's due in about half an hour. I'll let him know you're here though. He'll probably finish up with the patient he's with and come and see you,' the nurse replied as she left. Gina felt around the rubbish in her pocket, moving receipts and crumpled tissues aside before finding a few coins to buy a coffee with. As she fed the coins in the machine, she noticed another liver spot appearing on the back of her hand. Her forty-six years were beginning to show and the stress Hannah was putting her under certainly wasn't helping. Her reflection in the coffee machine revealed that she also needed to dye her roots.

She lifted a plastic chair from the pile and placed it next to the baby's cot and sat. Steam arose from the cup, warming her cold nose. She gripped the warm cup with both hands and looked at the baby. 'Who left you there, little baby?' she thought as she took another sip of coffee. The infant slept peacefully, a feeding tube neatly inserted into her nose.

Gina had been twenty-three when her daughter Hannah was born. She'd been a sleepy baby, just like the little one in front of her, except for the night of the thunderstorm, the night her mind kept getting drawn back to. Despite trying to move on from the past that haunted her, Gina's bad memories were as tattooed in her mind as every gruesome crime scene she'd ever attended.

Despite Hannah's most recent demands, attending her husband's memorial service was out of the question. He'd been gone a long time, too long for any memorial service but Hannah had arranged it and insisted on having it. Gina didn't want to remember. She was being forced to remember a past that would never leave her alone.

'Good morning. DI Harte? Doctor Nowak.' An older gentleman entered the room, holding his bony hand out towards her. Standing, Gina shook his hand. 'The baby is doing fine. It may all look a little scary with the tube and monitors, but her weight dropped and we wanted to make sure she was well nourished. We'll be removing that in a few hours. She isn't sedated, just sleeping.' Gina detected a slight accent as the doctor spoke. 'How can I help you? We gave all the information we had to your DC Wyre last night.'

Gina brushed her creased trousers with her hands and scraped away a stray hair that was stuck to her face. 'I know, and thank you for your assistance. The news of the baby has been released on the local news this morning. I'm just asking that you and the hospital staff keep an eye out for anyone acting suspiciously. The mother may come to the hospital to catch a glimpse of her baby and we are worried – as I know you are too – about her physical and mental health.'

The doctor lifted his glasses from the chain that hung around his neck and put them on. He grabbed the chart and scanned it as he spoke. 'And I totally understand that. We will do everything we can to assist you with your enquiry. I will send out an immediate memo to all hospital staff.' He clipped the chart to the end of the cot and walked towards the door. 'I best get on with my rounds,'

'Yes, thank you for your time.' Gina listened as his footsteps disappeared down the long corridor. A chorus of babies cried in the distance. Gina turned to look at the infant in front of her. This baby hadn't cried; this baby had barely moved; this baby had been deprived of her first moments to bond with her mother. The girl brought her little legs towards her chest, removing the blanket as she did so. Gina crept over towards the cot and pulled the blanket back over the baby. Although the hospital was kept at a warm temperature, she still felt a chill coming from the winter air as doors were opened and closed. She brought her hand gently towards the little one's head and stroked her fine hair before leaving.

As she reached the nurses' station, she searched for the nurse she'd spoken to on her arrival. The young dark-haired woman appeared from a side room. 'Doctor Nowak's sending a memo around shortly,' said Gina. 'Could you please be extra vigilant of anyone loitering or visiting? Here's my card, should you need to report anything.'

The nurse smiled and took the card. 'Will do,' she replied. She left Gina standing alone as she continued with her duties. Gina pressed the release buzzer and left the ward, leaving the crying babies behind. As she turned onto the main corridor, she watched a man trailing a drip and wearing pyjamas. The two women and the child walking beside him bore a familial resemblance.

Who was she looking for? Someone who was alone, someone who looked scared, someone who was anxiously trying to find a way of checking on the baby without looking suspicious. The corridor was dotted with people.

Two nurses wheeled a man on a bed into a lift. A woman with a child got out of the lift, followed by a tall man wearing a woollen hat and wrapped in a scarf. He bumped her arm as he passed. She turned to see him rubbing his neck, but he didn't look back. 'Sorry,' Gina called. The man continued walking without acknowledging her apology. She turned and watched as he slowed down outside the ward. She hadn't caught his features as he passed. He bent down and tied a shoelace before continuing towards the coronary ward.

She shook her head, checked her phone and picked up the pace. There's no way she could vet every passer-by in the next five minutes. The man with the woollen hat had gone, and another man wearing a huge smile, carrying a box of chocolates, walked into view from the other direction and entered the maternity ward.

She looked at her watch. Hannah was bringing Gracie, her granddaughter, over that evening for a visit. Her phone beeped as she left the hospital and her signal returned. It then rang. 'Jacob,' she said, as she snatched the car keys from her pocket.

'Are you on your way back? Wyre has had a mass of calls to process.'

'Sure am. See you in a few minutes,' she replied, as she started the engine up and headed straight back to the station.

CHAPTER SEVEN

'Are you sure you don't want me to stay? I can put lunch on for you,' Cathy called up the stairs.

Luke hung up his shirt and slipped his blue jumper over his head. He slapped a bit of aftershave on his chin and smiled at his reflection. His teeth were clean, he still had most of his fair hair and all the coffee he'd consumed earlier in the day ensured that he still looked awake. He'd made it home from the house viewing just in time to pick Max and Heidi up from Jake's birthday party, but he needed to hurry. He glanced once more at his reflection. He had to make an effort to move on. Brooke was good for him.

'Luke?' she called again. He swallowed as he took the photo of Debbie from his bedside table and placed it in the top drawer.

'Sorry, I was in a world of my own. You should get off home and have some rest. You do too much for us. There's a box of your favourite chocolate truffles on the side,' he said as he ran down the stairs and grabbed his coat. He checked his watch. Brooke would be knocking in several minutes. He was early, and he was staring at the door. It wasn't like he'd never been on a date before. After all, he was thirty-eight years old. And walking to another kid's house to collect their respective kids was hardly a date. After being friends for almost two years, he hadn't been sure he was ready to risk it all and try for a relationship, but things had just happened. He listened as Cathy put the plates away in the kitchen.

He'd found it hard to focus that day, preoccupied with thoughts of their kiss the previous evening. They'd spent the rest of the night texting each other. Awkwardness had turned into a natural fondness. For the first time since… He looked down and ran his fingers through his hair. He couldn't live in the past any longer.

He didn't know what had happened or where she'd gone, but it had been four long years and Debbie hadn't tried to contact them at all. No one had seen her and initial police investigations and appeals had come back with nothing. He flinched as his fist hit the wall and a tear escaped down his cheek. He'd spent weeks, months even, drinking in the Angel Arms, scrutinising everyone, but he'd come up with nothing but a continuous hangover. He'd watched her workplace as the men arrived and left until it had become all-consuming. Cathy had eventually pulled him out of the gutter, and she'd been there for him and the kids every day since.

Everyone told him that it was time to move on. Even Cathy, Debbie's own mother, had encouraged him. 'Brooke's a nice young lady,' she'd say. He shrugged it off every time. But he'd been lonely since Debbie's disappearance, and while he'd never stop thinking about her, he needed to live, he needed a life. His children needed some normality back in their lives and Brooke represented that normality.

Cathy trudged into the hall, holding the chocolates in one hand and her overcoat in the other. 'I love these but you didn't have to. I know money's tight and you have my lovely grandchildren to bring up. The washing-up is all put away.'

He took the coat out of her arms and held it up for her. 'I've sold some expensive houses this month, Cathy. And I want you to always know that we're grateful for everything you do. I don't know how we'd manage without you. Thanks for everything.'

Cathy smiled as she buttoned her coat up. 'I see you took my advice.'

'What advice was that?'

'Brooke. I think she's lovely. I'm happy for you. Max and Heidi love her, and they love little Joe. Really, I'm happy for you.'

Luke scratched his neck. He felt a warm itchiness spreading over his shoulder and climbing up his face. He knew Cathy could see the redness forming. She'd always sensed his anxiety with uncanny precision. Her slightly trembling hand reached for his cheek. She stroked it as if to stroke the redness away. Her serious expression turned into a smile, and he forced a smile back. He had Cathy's blessing, his friends all liked Brooke, his kids liked her, too – so why did he feel so guilty? He twisted his wedding ring around. He'd lost weight since Debbie's disappearance. The ring would slip off easily. He pulled the ring up his finger and felt a lump forming in his throat. Anything he did would have to happen slowly. Whatever his future might hold, he still had a past that was hard to let go of. He didn't want to let it go.

His years with Debbie had been the best of his life. Cathy, an older version of her daughter, was a daily reminder of what he grieved for. Her tiny nose and large hazel eyes made him think of Debbie. Her voice was slightly more hoarse than Debbie's, but he could still hear the similarities. The way she poured tea, walked, tended to the garden and hugged the kids was so like Debbie. He pushed the ring back down. Brooke understood that things were difficult for him. They were difficult for her too. As a young woman who'd lost her husband to cancer only three years earlier, she still wore her ring. They didn't need to explain it to each other; they just knew. They'd both been very much in love with their past partners.

Cathy wiped away the tear that was rolling down his cheek. 'She wouldn't want this, you being unhappy.' She paused. 'We might never know what happened. In fact, the more time that passes by, the more I lose confidence that we'll ever know—' Cathy placed her hand on her forehead and closed her eyes. 'She would want you and the children to be happy. I want you to be happy too. Damn it, this is hard. I love you like a son and I love those children with my life, and you have my blessing. You're a good man, Luke, and you deserve all the happiness in the world. I'm always here for you.' She opened her eyes, stood on the tips of her toes and kissed him once on the cheek. 'You smell lovely, and that new jumper is really you.' She opened the door and left, waving as she reached the gate. 'Give the munchkins a kiss from Nanny.'

'Will do, see you tomorrow. We love you too – and thanks for putting the Christmas tree up!' He closed the door and fell against the wall. Cathy was right. He loved Brooke's company, and he was going to try and make it work. He paced up and down, waiting for the knock on the door. He glanced at his watch again. A couple of minutes to go.

He ran to the kitchen, grabbed a packet of mints from the drawer and crunched on one. He stared into the garden. Max's goalpost leaned upright against the back fence. The sandpit the kids were too old for was filled with murky water.

He looked at the family photo that was perched on the windowsill. Debbie was holding baby Max while he was holding Heidi. He remembered that Heidi had been a little terror during that photo shoot. The more they'd tried to placate her, the worse she'd become. They'd put it down to jealousy. He remembered picking her up and hugging her, explaining that Mummy and Daddy loved her 'more than ice cream and chocolate sauce'. For one moment, he'd got her to smile. The photo in front of him had been taken at that exact moment. The rest of the day had continued as a tantrum fest. He picked up the photo and traced Debbie's outline. She hadn't been sure of the photo shoot and had spent the morning complaining about her baby weight. She looked a little puffy in the face, but he loved her puffiness. He loved everything about her. She'd given him two beautiful, healthy children. She had made their family and for that he'd given his whole self to her.

There was a knock at the door. He placed the photo back on the sill. 'I'll always love you, Deb,' he whispered as he pulled the blind down over the photo, shutting out the drizzly weather and the memories of a long-gone chapter in his life.

He grabbed an umbrella from the stand and opened the door. Brooke smiled and leaned forward to kiss him. He placed his arm around her waist and kissed her back. 'So, you don't regret last night?' she asked.

He stroked her damp hair and looked into her eyes. Debbie would always be in his heart, but his heart was big enough to give more love. He shook his head and smiled. 'I've been looking forward to seeing you all day.'

'Me too,' she replied as she took his hand and led him towards Jake's house. He knew the other parents would talk, but he didn't care. He'd been a devoted husband and Brooke had been a devoted wife. They were both just two people with a lot of love to give and they'd found each other. The rain fell heavier. He put the umbrella up and pulled Brooke closer to him. She bit her bottom lip, brushed her curly blonde hair away from her face and smiled. Maybe he was ready to finally say goodbye to Deborah.

CHAPTER EIGHT

A cockerel screeched in the distance. Debbie smiled, savouring the sound of the outside world. She placed her ear against the wall, hoping to hear it a little clearer. Occasionally she'd hear vehicles rumble by. She knew she was by a road and that it was likely a minor one. It was probably only an access road, given the number of vehicles that used it. On a still day, she was sure she could hear the hum of traffic. Maybe there was a dual carriageway or a motorway in the distance. She had no idea where she was, except that it was rural and she was being kept in a cold, two-storey outbuilding.

The night she'd been taken haunted her. At six thirty that evening she'd left work for the bus stop. She normally finished at five but she'd been making up time after watching Heidi's Christmas play earlier in the day. Luke had nagged her for years to take her driving test again, but earlier failures and her near miss of an elderly man crossing the road on a mobility scooter had rendered her phobic of driving. She pondered the 'what ifs' over and over again, until they'd driven her crazy. That Friday, the twentieth of December, was the beginning of what was to become her nightmare.

The orange glow of lamplights led Debbie through the deserted industrial estate. Rain bounced off her umbrella as she passed a factory and scurried alongside the closed snack van. A cat darted across the path and a small van narrowly missed hitting it. Water seeped into her shoes; her toes had been numb for a good five minutes already. Then the van stopped in the road beside her, the driver like some sort of hero in a warm vehicle. As his window came down, the sound of Christmas filled the air. Mariah Carey sang, 'All I want for Christmas is you.' The scent of his vanilla air freshener travelled with the breeze, filling her nostrils.

'Hop in. I've just got to collect something from the electrical unit around the corner before they close. You look like you could use a lift,' he said with a warm smile.

Although she didn't know him well, she'd always thought him to be polite in passing. Did she know him well enough to get in the van? She thought of the things she would say to her own children. She always told them never to get in anyone's car, familiar or not. 'I'll be okay,' she called. He scrunched his brow and placed his hand by his ear as he beckoned her over. The music overpowered every sound around them. She stepped closer to the open window and leaned in, shouting over the noise. 'I'm fine, but thanks for the offer. I'm heading to the shop and it's only a few minutes down the path. I have a few bits to do first. It was really kind of you to offer though.' But before she had the chance to stand upright, he leaned across the passenger seat and up towards her. The sharp prick in her neck made her wince. 'What? Why?' she managed to mumble as the drug began to take effect. She stumbled away from the car. The orange glowing lamps seemed to fall from the sky and block her way. She staggered, trying to avoid them, one step after another. As she pushed further, her legs felt like they were slowly being

filled with cold sand, until she could no longer run. She fell to
her knees, landing in a freezing cold puddle. He grabbed her
from behind. She tried to yell but no sound came out.

'You need to get in the van where it's warm. I'll look after
you, keep you safe,' he said as he kissed her head. He dragged
her unresponsive body across the rough pavement. Her shoe
– she was losing her shoe. She tried to clench her floppy feet
but gave up and her loose shoe slipped off. The heaviness, the
lights, even the stars were blurring into a strange light beam.
She gasped as he bundled her helpless body into the back of
the van. Wizzard sang 'I wish it could be Christmas every
day' – one of her all-time favourites. The overpowering smell
of his vanilla air freshener left a lasting memory before the
darkness filled her mind and ended the ordeal.

That was a long time ago. Now, she stared into the darkness
of a cold room, which is what she'd done every day since.

Her heart hammered as she heard his car trundling up the
bumpy road. Her aching body tensed up. 'Don't upset him,'
she repeated several times as she heard the slam of his car door.
'One, two, three…' She continued counting until she reached
twenty and he reached the bottom door. He stomped up the
stairs before unlocking the door to her prison. He yelled and
cried, then kicked a chair across the room. She flinched. Her
body stiffened as her wide eyes locked onto his. She glanced away.

He dashed to her side and grabbed her hair, yanking her
back. 'I didn't get to see Florence. I wanted to so badly but
the ward door was locked and there were people there, there
were people everywhere. They were looking at me… I'm sure

they were looking at me. Why me?' As she struggled to catch her breath, he let go of her, bouncing her head off the wall. He removed his woollen hat, revealing his flattened hair. He paced and began muttering under his breath, as he always did when he was stressed.

A tear trickled down her cheek. Her baby was safe, but her thoughts had now moved on to her baby's future. With no mother coming forward, her little one would end up being fostered, then adopted. She wanted her baby. She wanted her baby to know she was her mother. She wanted to hold her, feed her, love her, take her to school and watch her grow up. At the start of the pregnancy, it had been easy to think that she wouldn't bond with the life inside her because of the horrific circumstances in which she was conceived. But as that life grew, as it hiccupped and turned, she'd felt hope, a connection. After the birth, she'd wanted nothing more than to hold and nurture her baby. Her daughter needed to know she had a brother, a sister and a grandmother who would all love her. 'Please, you have to get her to my mother. Let my mother look after her. Your ma would want that too. She's also a grandmother. Don't do this to her. Please help me. Help Florence.'

He looked into her eyes, staring deeply. The battery-powered light and his stare almost blinded her. She looked down before he could get angry.

'We could have her back when things get better,' he whispered. Pacing up and down, he continued to mutter to the shadows while banging the side of his head with a loose fist. 'What should I do?'

'I can't lose her forever. Please. Do something, I beg you. Just tell the police she's mine. You can do it anonymously.'

He stopped pacing and turned to face her. 'Ours. She doesn't just belong to you. I made her too.'

She wiped his spit from the corner of her eye. 'And would you want our baby to be lost forever and be sent to live with strangers? My mum will love her, care for her and look after her,' she cried.

'What the hell should I do? She's gone.'

'She didn't have to go. You made her go and you can fix this,' Debbie yelled.

'You couldn't shut her up, could you?'

'You didn't give me a chance. Babies cry. Please help me, please. I can't lose her. We can't lose her. Your ma can't lose her.' Mucus dripped from Debbie's nose as tears poured from her red-rimmed eyes. He kneeled on the bed beside her and kissed her forehead. She clenched her teeth to fight the pain as he sat and pulled her into his embrace. 'I love you. You know I love you, don't you? I love Florence too. I don't know what to do. Florence wouldn't shut up. Mother goes mad when she hears noise. I can't have Ma upset. What do I do? I don't know. I just don't know,' he said, rocking her back and forth, dragging her broken body with every movement.

'You do. You could tell them to check her DNA. They'll link her to me. Please just call them. It's our only hope. You will lose her forever – you know that, don't you? You will never see your baby again. Is that what you want?'

She knew the police had her DNA on file. Just after she'd been taken, she'd heard talk on the news about a body turning up in the River Avon, by the Marcliff Weir. The local papers had initially linked the body to her. He'd enjoyed taunting her, telling her that people would think she was the decomposed river corpse and they'd never look for her. He'd sneered as he told her how he'd watched the 'dirty whore' gagging on the icy river water until her dying breath. She shuddered at the thought.

She'd heard another newsflash soon after the incident. DNA had been used to eliminate her. She knew her DNA was on file, and could be matched to her baby's.

'I can't lose her forever. You're right,' he said. 'I shouldn't have left her.'

Blood pumped through Debbie's body as she pressed him harder. 'You will lose her if you don't make the call. Imagine never seeing her little face again or her perfect little fingers and toes. Imagine never knowing where that life you created ended up. Please make the call before it's too late, or you'll never see her again.'

'I don't know what to do.'

If he called the police, they'd look for her. Were they still looking? Had he slipped up in any way before this? This was her chance. She imagined the reunion after the police saved her. She'd run into Luke's warm arms and see her two beautiful children. Her mother would turn up with her baby and they'd all be a family. That was the tiny glimmer of hope that would keep her going.

'I don't know what to do!' he yelled. As abruptly as he'd grabbed her, he let her go, propelling her forward as he moved.

'Please. Make the call. Not for me, but for you. You'll never know where your baby is if you don't make that call. Don't lose her forever. They'll match my DNA. We know they have it on file, from when the body turned up in the river, remember?' Debbie reached out and touched his hand.

'Why did you bring that up?' He removed his hand. 'She was a whore,' he said, looking away.

Debbie removed her hand from his.

'She was a whore. I wanted you. You! How dare you ever bring that up!' He spat in her face and pushed her away. Without so much as a glance back, he left and locked the door, leaving her once again in darkness, with only the outside noises to occupy her.

'Please make the call,' she yelled, as she burst into uncontrollable sobs. 'What did you do?' She rocked back and forth and closed her eyes. 'Make the call. Please!' She heard the bottom door slam.

*

'Damn it, damn it,' he said as he locked the door. He stared at the grey skies above as he stood outside the main house. The curtains were still closed. He'd not got round to opening them.

'Have you got my bread?' the old woman asked as she opened the front door, letting the dog out.

The little black spaniel jumped up around his legs. 'Get lost, Rosie,' he said, giving it a kick and brushing past his mother.

'Where's my bread?' she yelled.

'You've had your breakfast. I gave you bread. Honey on toast, you wanted.' He began pacing the hallway as he ran his fingers through his hair. 'Where have you put my other phone?'

The old woman stared at him blankly. 'Are we going to the shops?' She walked over to the coat stand by the door and began putting one of his old coats on inside out. Her illness was taking a toll on him. The dog bounded back in, shaking its wet fur off against the wall. 'Dog – get out,' his mother shouted. 'Get out. Get out. Get out.'

He hurried over to her and grabbed her arm. The woman yelled in pain as he shoved her outside and slammed the door, shutting her and the dog out. He bent over and stared through the letter box. She was still standing there, wearing his inside-out coat, waiting. For what? He had no idea. He wasn't taking her shopping today. He wasn't taking her shopping ever.

The kitchen. He'd last seen the phone in the kitchen drawer. He ran and opened it, smiling as he grabbed the phone, the one where he kept all the old photos he'd taken of Debbie before they'd got together. He grabbed the charger and plugged it in. Just a couple of minutes' worth of charge would be enough to make the phone call. He couldn't lose Florence forever. He needed to call the police. He opened the top cupboard and a straw hat fell out. He grabbed his mother's old scarf, which had been folded up underneath it. It would be useful to distort his voice. His Debbie phone had never been registered and he'd bought it with cash. It was safe to use. He'd drive out, into the middle of nowhere, make the shortest call ever, destroy the SIM card and head back.

There was a knock at the door and the dog barked. He dashed to open it, letting his mother in. The woman was shivering and crying. He took her hand and led her to her chair in the living room. 'Sit there, Ma. I won't be long.'

'I want to go to the shop.' She began to sob as she rocked back and forth. He grabbed one of her chicken pies from the sideboard, opened it and handed it to her. The dog lay by her feet, waiting for crumbs.

'I'll be back soon.' He kissed her on the cheek and left, locking the door behind him.

CHAPTER NINE

Gina threw her bag into the corner of her office and turned her computer on. It was almost lunchtime.

Several emails pinged up as her computer finally came to life. As expected, a mass of calls had been made to the helpline in relation to the baby. Jacob and the team had sifted through a handful of them and only come up with one that was meaningful.

She picked up the phone and dialled his extension. 'Jacob, I'm back in my office. Pop through and we can talk through these calls,' she said, searching in her drawer for some paracetamol. She placed the receiver back in its cradle and massaged her temple as she popped a couple of pills onto her desk.

Jacob knocked and entered with a steaming Styrofoam cup. 'Coffee. You are my saviour,' she said, taking it from him. She placed the pills in her mouth and took a gulp, flinching as the heat from the coffee burned the back of her throat.

'You're welcome. Feel more human yet?'

'I will do in a minute. My head has been pounding since I left the hospital.' She swallowed and grimaced, realising that her throat was starting to feel like sandpaper.

Jacob grabbed the chair opposite her and placed his notebook on the desk. 'How were things there?' he asked as he loosened his tie.

'Just routine. I spoke to the doctor in charge, a Doctor Nowak.' Jacob scribbled the name under the rest of his illegible notes. 'I asked him to circulate a message requesting that the staff keep an eye out for anyone coming to the hospital and acting suspiciously.' Gina scrolled through her emails and came across a flagged email from Jacob. 'What's this? Must be important if you've flagged it.'

He leaned forward. 'We had one call that struck a chord. It just came in a few minutes ago. The rest are still being sifted through, but they were basically descriptions of the many people that had been in the area that day. We have tall, short, fat, thin, workmen and women, wearing yellow jackets and suits – the usual. There wasn't anything that really stood out on the first scan except the one I've highlighted. The officer who took the call said the man sounded distressed. The recording is very crackly. It sounds like the caller had a piece of cloth over his mouth. He appeared to be mumbling to himself, taking about a baby and his love. To cut a long story short, he basically begged us to run a DNA test on the baby. He screamed and yelled before bursting into tears.'

'I can see why you flagged that one up. Why would someone call and request that we do a DNA check on the baby? I wonder if he's the father. Or maybe it's another crank.'

Jacob looked into her eyes. 'He also said that the baby had a birthmark on the back of her right leg, just above the knee.'

Gina took another gulp of coffee. 'Have you verified this?'

'I called the hospital immediately and spoke to the nurse in charge. She confirmed the presence of the birthmark.' He began to chew the end of his already worn-down biro as he stared at his notes.

'We need to get that baby's DNA sample to the lab. I'll get it cleared with Briggs. There's more to this story. Where's the mother, for heaven's sake? Have we traced the call? It sounds like our suspect was on the phone for a long time?' Gina swigged the last of her coffee, pulled a cereal bar from her bag and began eating it.

'Not as long as we'd hoped. He blurted everything out at speed then hung up. The only thing we managed to get was that the call came from an unregistered phone. We tried to call him back but the line was dead. He's probably ditched it already.'

'That's a bit of a pain but not unexpected,' she replied. The intensity of her headache began to reduce. She cleared her dry throat and smiled. 'Right. I'll arrange the DNA sample. Go through the recording again and listen for anything that may help us. Something's really off about this case.'

Jacob stood and walked towards the door. 'If you want a sausage roll, there's a bag in the main office. O'Connor brought them in. Apparently, his wife made them yesterday.'

'What would we do without O'Connor and his talented wife?' Gina asked. Jacob smiled and closed the door as he left.

This wasn't a usual request from someone involved in this type of case. If he were the father, he'd more likely be asking if the baby was safe and well. Where was the mother? A man had called, but a woman had recently given birth and she certainly hadn't been assisted by anyone with any midwifery skills, given that the cord was cut so badly. Somewhere, there was a woman in pain, in distress, yet this man was calling and begging for the baby to be DNA tested. Something didn't compute. This wasn't a typical abandonment.

There was no way it could be a crank call, as the caller had given them a description of the birthmark. What if there wasn't a match? In that case, their only hope of making any progress with the case would be to wait for another call.

She opened up a new email and addressed it to Briggs. Even though she was more than fond of him, his new tight-fisted approval process on anything that ate into their measly forensics budget was wearing her down.

CHAPTER TEN

An email from Briggs popped up on her screen, requesting her immediate attendance in his office. She swallowed as she stood and made her way through the main office and along the corridor. She took a deep breath, scooped her messy hair up into an elastic band and knocked. She heard Briggs bellowing down the phone as he ended his conversation. Her stomach grumbled and she felt a wave of nausea sweep through her. As soon as their conversation was over, she needed some lunch.

'Come in,' Briggs called.

'Sir,' she said as she entered. Briggs finished texting and placed his phone on the table. She watched as he tidied his suit jacket and rearranged his tie.

'I hear some congratulations are in order. The CPS says the robbery case you passed to them is watertight. Good result.' He paused and smiled. 'It's good to see you again, Georgina.'

She grimaced as he said her name in full. He was the only person in her life who called her Georgina since Terry had died. It sounded different when it rolled off his tongue though. 'Thank you. It certainly was a cause for celebration.'

'And that we did,' he replied, before his gaze moved towards his computer screen. Gina felt her face flushing as she stared at her feet and tried to forget that night.

'Anyway, I didn't call you in just to massage your ego, Harte. What's this about a request for more DNA tests?' He stared at his computer screen and clicked his mouse.

At least he was back to calling her Harte. She began to pick her fingernail as she spoke. 'We had the strangest call relating to the abandoned baby case. As I explained in my email—'

'The email,' Briggs repeated as he clicked his mouse and began reading what was in front of him. 'Yes. Call from a wack job asking us to run a DNA check on the abandoned baby. Right, here's where I stand, Harte. This department has already gone over its forensics budget by twenty-six per cent and the financial year isn't over yet. Looking at your history, a lot of this budget has been wasted. We've had forensics go out to standard car break-ins where we already knew the owners had contaminated the crime scene. You see where I'm coming from? I just have to make sure it's justified,' he said as his hand hovered over the keyboard, occasionally tapping as he continued to read.

'But sir, this case is different. Whoever called is definitely connected to the baby. It may be our only clue as to who left her.'

'But is it crime of the century? No one is in danger. We can still continue with the public appeal.'

Gina felt a fluttering in her chest as the pressure began to build up. She knew there was more to this case. 'There is a mother out there somewhere. A man called, basically pointing us in the right direction. He made an attempt to disguise his voice, and used an unregistered phone to call us, which has now gone off the radar. This is no ordinary case of abandonment, with all due respect, sir.'

'I sent the press release out. We should wait a bit longer, at least until everyone has seen the news. The baby is safe. No one has died and no one is in immediate danger.'

'I know, but I also know there's more to it. Why would this person call? Why? He knew about the birthmark.'

Briggs looked up at her for a second, then back to his computer screen. 'If this turns out to be a waste of resources, it's on you, Harte. I've just sent the approval through.'

Taking a deep breath, she smiled. 'Thank you, sir. It won't be a waste. I'll get on with it right away.'

'Georgina? Are we okay?'

An uncomfortable silence filled the room. She felt the redness creeping up her neck as she thought back to the other night. At that moment, he knew where her mind was and she knew exactly where his was. She cleared her throat. 'We're okay, sir.'

'Sir. It sounds so ridiculous now.'

She gave him a slight smile as she left his office.

As she walked down the main corridor, she scratched her hot neck. She didn't know whether to smile or mentally slap herself. What had she got into with Briggs?

A bucket caught the rain that dripped from the ceiling. They'd needed a roofer for a while. It was becoming impossible to do the job properly. They needed more available officers; they needed a larger forensics budget; they needed more people everywhere, in every department. An abandoned baby probably wasn't crime of the century, as Briggs said, but it needed resolving like any other and that's what she was going to do.

As she passed the main office, she spotted one slightly damaged sausage roll on O'Connor's desk. 'Thank you,' she said as she grabbed it and scurried into her office. She picked up her mobile phone and began texting Hannah. There was no way she'd make their appointment at teatime. She had the DNA sample to organise. She took a bite of the sausage roll and tried to swallow, but guilt won. The lump in her throat was saying no. She spat the pastry in the bin next to her desk and threw the rest of the sausage roll in there too. Letting Hannah down was going to be hard. She'd probably been expecting it, which made it worse.

> *I'm so sorry, my love. Something really important has come up and I won't be able to make our teatime date. Send my love to Gracie. I will make it up to you both. Xx*

She could picture Hannah's expression when she read the message. Her face always went a little red when she was flustered. She'd inherited her fair complexion and white-blonde hair from her father, and with that came redness while expressing any emotion. She flashed back in time, seeing Terry's flushed face as he reached the top of the stairs in their old house, the face he made just before… She sucked in a burst of air and began to hyperventilate.

The sound of pumping blood travelled through her ears. Feeling light-headed, she rolled back on her chair and opened the window, letting the wintery chill fill her office. As she shivered, the memory of Terry and that night began to fade – for now.

Several minutes had gone by, and Hannah hadn't replied. She was officially being ignored. She blew her nose and took a couple of painkillers. The ones she'd taken earlier had worn off and her head was thickening once again.

Grabbing the file she'd marked up as 'Library Baby', she began to pull out the scene photos and make her own notes on the call that had been logged.

Her phone beeped. Her heart threatened to fly out of her mouth as she grabbed it and read the message, but it was just another piece of PPI-related spam, destined for deletion. Hannah wasn't going to answer. Then, a message from Briggs pinged up.

Can I call you later?

Where the hell was all this going? She knew they needed to talk at some point but it wasn't going to be easy. They'd made a mistake, that's all it was. It had meant nothing. Or had it?

CHAPTER ELEVEN

She drove home just after eleven, along the country lanes just outside Stratford-upon-Avon. The fog blanketing the fields had an eerie look about it in the moonlight. Her heart jumped as a fox darted in front of the car. The creature made its safe escape through a hedge before completely disappearing into the gloom. She reduced her speed to below thirty as she continued with the treacherous journey.

She pulled in off the country road and parked outside her little cottage. As she stepped out of the car, Ebony, her little black cat, ran over and began purring at her ankles. She followed the cat into the house and filled up the feeder. As Ebony crunched her food, Gina threw her coat onto the kitchen table and checked her phone. Still no text from Hannah. Her stomach flipped when she reread the last message from Briggs. She popped her phone in her pocket, turned off the light and headed upstairs.

Standing in front of the washing basket on the landing, she stripped off and threw her clothes at it before entering the bathroom. A damp smell hung in the air. She turned on the light. She badly needed a shower after getting home late the previous night and rushing out in the morning.

The bathwater from the night before stared back at her in all its murky glory. She'd been in such a hurry, she hadn't even emptied the bath. She reached into the scummy water and yanked the plug. As it emptied, she sat on the toilet and watched the water slowly sinking away. Walking over to the washing basket, she pulled her phone from her trouser pocket and checked for messages. Nothing. It wasn't as if she was expecting Hannah to respond, but she had hoped Briggs would call.

She logged onto Facebook and searched for her daughter. Her last status was a rant about how people say they love you but just continuously let you down and how they put themselves first all the time. Her friends' comments were what really hurt. Gina felt a tear slip down her cheek as she read them. 'Don't waste your time on people who treat you badly'... 'Why the hell do you put up with people like that in your life?'

She wasn't selfish. Hannah had no idea why she wouldn't fork out the money for Terry's memorial service or why she always worked late. Her job was important and she needed it, she loved it. It kept her sane. And even if Hannah did know about her reasons for not wanting to pay, would she believe her? The treatment that Hannah's father had forced on her had turned her into a fighter, and now she needed to continue fighting for those who couldn't fight for themselves.

The first domestic violence case she'd dealt with had been a success. The suspect had been found guilty and imprisoned because of the evidence she'd collected. She'd since thrown her life into making sure that other perpetrators didn't get away with it.

The plughole gurgled as the last of the water escaped. She grabbed the untouched glass of red wine that was sitting next to her shampoo and took a swig, grimacing as the day-old liquid swirled around her mouth.

She dropped the phone onto a pile of towels and turned the shower on. She needed to wash away the dirt of the day, ready to begin again. As she lathered up her hair, her phone began to ring. She turned the shower off and stepped out of the bath, snatching the phone in her soapy hands.

'Sorry it's late,' Briggs said.

'Don't be sorry,' she replied. She didn't know what to say next. Should she mention the previous week? Was he trying to forget it? It had been easy to forget – until she'd been in his office earlier that day. 'Any news on the case?'

'No,' he replied.

Her teeth began to chatter as the coldness of the bathroom enveloped her soaking body. She reached for her bathrobe, sat on the toilet seat and pulled the material over her knees.

'About the other week, sir—'

'Sir, sir, sir. Just call me Chris when we're not at work.'

'Are we not at work?'

'You make it hard, don't you? If you want me to end this call, just say. I'm not into staff harassment.'

'Sorry. I'm not good at this.' Gina shivered again. What did she want? It was one night, not a relationship, not even planned, but the thought of it made her smile. 'I'm glad you called.'

'That's a start. About last week, I don't think it should become common knowledge, you know what I mean?'

Through her shivering, she felt her face flush with an uncomfortable hotness. Ebony ran up the stairs, licking her legs as she wrapped her body around Gina's dripping ankles, depositing fine black hairs all over her feet. 'Me neither. I won't say anything, no need to worry about that.'

'That doesn't mean I didn't enjoy it or wouldn't like to do it again some time—'

'Stop. You don't have to say anything else. It shouldn't have happened. Really, it doesn't matter.'

'I like you, Gina. Think about things and we'll have a pint or a coffee or whatever you want.' He fell silent. She didn't have any issues sussing out the perps, but when it came to her personal life, she felt like a clueless teenager again. She didn't want to admit that she'd enjoyed the night, that it had been the release she'd needed after so many years. Flashes of her desperate hands running through his sweaty brown hair and gripping his buttocks tight raced through her mind.

'I might take you up on a coffee. A pint would be too dangerous,' she replied.

'I like danger.' With that final comment, he ended the call. Gina grinned and leaned back on the toilet seat. The soap suds from her hair dripped into her eyes, stinging. She dropped the robe onto the floor then stepped back into the shower to finish what she'd started.

CHAPTER TWELVE

Sunday, 3 December 2017

Gina yawned as she grabbed the three coffees from the side. She placed one on Jacob's desk. 'Let no one tell you I don't care,' she said as she placed O'Connor's coffee beside him. 'Give the lab a call and see if they've run the DNA test yet? If not, tell them to get a move on. I need it yesterday.' O'Connor nodded and continued to munch on his bacon butty. Gina hurried along the corridor, closed her office door and sat in front of the computer. Jacob wasn't exaggerating when he said they'd received a lot of irrelevant calls about the baby case. Her inbox was bursting at the seams with what the service desk had forwarded to her.

There was a tap on the door and Jacob entered, holding his drink. 'Thanks for this,' he said. She leaned back in her chair. Jacob swigged his coffee and ruffled his other hand through his messy hair. 'That call yesterday has certainly thrown up something odd with this case. The quicker we get the results back the better.'

'I've nudged O'Connor to chase up forensics. I did mark them as urgent so I'm hoping to hear soon.'

One of Jacob's eyebrows lifted slightly. 'That'll be a nice bill.'

'It certainly will be, but how the hell are we meant to do our job without forensics? Our budgets over the past few years have been pathetic and I doubt the next few will be any better. I'm sick of being told we're overspending, that we need to cut back and save it for the crimes that matter. An abandoned baby matters, crime of the century or not.' She felt a familiar itch in her nose and grabbed a tissue off her desk just in time to catch a sneeze. 'I'm not feeling at my healthiest today. Damn Smith for bringing in the lurgy last week.'

Jacob's phone beeped. He smiled as he picked it up and scrolled down the message. 'Looks like Abigail's giving me another date opportunity.' He tapped on his keys while staring intently at the screen. 'That's that sorted.'

Gina's phone lit up and a text popped up from her daughter.

We're coming round this evening. If you're not there, that's it. I'm sick of you cancelling. Can't you put us first, just this once, instead of your stupid job?

Gina turned her phone over and stared at all the emails that had been sent. She'd deal with Hannah's text when she had a moment. 'I thought they filtered the crank calls out before forwarding them to me,' she said to Jacob. 'The first one I open says that the person reporting saw flashing lights in the sky before a beam of light shone from some sort of flying craft. Apparently, a package was sent down from the Lord. Where do these people come from?'

Jacob laughed and looked up. 'I sense you're working with a closed mind, guv.'

'Closed mind, my arse.'

The door burst open and O'Connor stood in front of them, panting, his face red. 'Ma'am, the results weren't what we were expecting. I think you need to put your coffee down before I say another word.' Jacob put his phone in his pocket and looked up at O'Connor.

She took another swig of her coffee to lubricate her dry throat and tossed the empty cup in the bin. 'Okay. We're ready for it.'

'Remember the Deborah Jenkins case, four years ago? The disappearance?'

'Just about. It was when I first started here as inspector.' It had been the first case in her new role and she'd failed to solve it. Maybe this was her second chance. Gina stared into space and then clicked her fingers. 'Don't tell me. Young woman. She leaves work late. It's close to Christmas. She vanishes without a trace. The only thing we have in evidence from that night is a shoe we've confirmed to be hers. The shoe, from what I remember, was found by the roadside. What has that got to do with the baby case?'

'That's the thing, guv. Her husband provided us with her toothbrush and razor back then, which allowed us to obtain and log her DNA on file. Her DNA is a match for the baby's.'

Gina stared at O'Connor. She'd been promoted to inspector at the start of the case and had been transferred from Birmingham to Cleevesford, where there was a post. She remembered the investigation all too well. It had haunted her for months afterwards. She could still see the look on Deborah's husband's distraught face. Luke Jenkins.

She was there when they found the body of a woman in the river, down by the Marcliff Weir. That had been a few weeks after Deborah's disappearance. She'd been the one to ask Luke for something that may contain his wife's DNA, for elimination purposes. She remembered him holding his children and sobbing into the little girl's hair. After obtaining the DNA and cross-matching it to the victim, it was found that the woman's body was not that of his wife, Deborah.

From what she remembered without opening the file, the body had never been identified. No one had been reported missing at the time. She remembered the hours they'd spent going through missing persons, trying to find a match. Appeal after appeal brought no new evidence or witnesses to light. The only thing they knew was that the woman had died by drowning approximately four weeks before she was found. There was no evidence of trauma or violence but there had been track marks on her body. Images of the woman's body flashed through her mind as she thought back. She remembered her waxy skin, her thin strands of light brown hair with dark roots. Her slightly crooked nose.

She shivered. 'Well, well. Deborah Jenkins. It's been a long time. She's still close by and she's alive,' said Jacob.

'That's a result I wasn't expecting,' said Gina. 'Bloody hell.'

'Who could the stranger on the phone be? The one requesting the DNA test?' O'Connor asked.

The wind howled and rain began to hit the window. Gina dragged her old cardigan from the back of the chair and pulled it over her shoulders. 'I'd bet all the money I have that he's the father. What on earth is going on? She vanishes for four years. She gives birth in secret a couple of days ago. Her baby turns up outside Cleevesford Library. A man calls anonymously.' The room was silenced as everyone fell deep into thought. 'We need to set up a task force and we need to do it now. Her life could be in danger. We need to find this man. If we find him, we find her. Make a start, O'Connor. I'll join you in a minute.'

'I'll get onto it right now,' O'Connor said as he left, closing the door behind him.

She sneezed once again. 'I think I'm going to need more than coffee when we speak to Deborah Jenkins' husband and mother about this,' Gina said.

Jacob nodded and rubbed his eyes. 'I love this job. You never know what's coming next.'

'You certainly don't. We need to refresh ourselves with the old case notes.'

'I'm going to drag up the history. I'll check back with you in a while.'

'Do that. I want every resource at our disposal used on Deborah Jenkins. I want her found. That case has haunted me for years.'

He nodded and left her office. Gina slumped in her chair and remembered the night she'd interviewed the husband in his home. Deborah's mother had been with him. She'd been looking after their children that day while he and Deborah had been at work. Deborah had worked late to make up time. Both Deborah's mother and husband were adamant that her disappearance was out of character. Their relationship was better than ever. They had two lovely children who he said had 'completed them'. She'd never seen a man so broken.

Unless bringing the baby back was a symbolic gesture, Deborah was close by. How come there had never been a sighting or a medical appointment? Her details had been passed on to all the local GP surgeries at the time and nothing had ever come back. Gina made a note on her pad to consider that Deborah had changed her identity. Had she received medical care during her pregnancy? Looking at the notes on the clumsy delivery, she suspected that Deborah hadn't been to see a doctor. They'd found the identity of the mother, but finding out her whereabouts was going to be the difficult task.

The man on the phone. What did he have to do with it all and why did he want the baby identified? They were definitely looking at a possible abduction. Gina ran a scenario in her head: it's a wet wintery night, at a time where most of the people working on the industrial estate have gone home. Deborah is walking alone in the dark, aiming to get to the bus stop. To get there she has to pass several units by walking on the pathways alongside the road. She is heading towards a tree-lined cut-through, where there are only a few street lamps to light the way. Just before she gets there she is approached. There is a struggle and she loses a shoe. He forces her into his vehicle and drives off. He's had her all this time.

An email popped up on her screen from Briggs.

This is going to be big. I want to know everything as and when it happens. Find Deborah Jenkins.

CHAPTER THIRTEEN

The rising sun, still low in the sky, glinted off the draining board as Luke finished wiping it. He threw the cloth beside the sink and walked over to the photo of him, Debbie and the kids. He traced her face with his index finger before placing the photo in the top drawer. Cathy was right, he had to move on, and the photos were a constant reminder of what had happened. He would get a few of the best photos of Debbie framed for the kids' bedrooms, but today was the start of the next chapter in his life. He grabbed his phone off the worktop and called Brooke, but she didn't answer. He looked at his watch. The kids would be out with Cathy for a while. Maybe he'd take a walk over to Brooke's and see if she wanted to go for a stroll over the fields. It was close enough that he could get home quickly if Cathy came back and called to see where he was.

He thought back to when they'd gone to the party, hand in hand, to pick their children up. There were no sneers, only people smiling kindly, as if they'd hoped for this outcome all along. And then there was the night before that, when they'd gone back to hers and had a movie night with the kids. If only Joe hadn't interrupted them. The feel of Brooke's soft skin lingered in his thoughts.

There was a knock at the door. Brooke. She always tapped twice in quick succession. His heart buzzed with excitement.

He grabbed the tea towel off the side, folded it up and then placed it neatly next to the cooker. He hadn't been expecting her to call by. Maybe she'd been thinking about him as much as he had her. He checked his reflection in the stainless-steel splash plate behind the cooker and jogged to the door.

'Brooke, come in,' he said as he leaned down and kissed her. 'I was just cleaning up. The kids had demolished the place.'

'I know how that feels. One minute everything's clean, the next there's rubbish everywhere,' she replied as she looked up at him. He closed the door. 'Joe's gone to Jake's for a couple of hours. Where are Max and Heidi?'

'With Cathy. Gone out for breakfast in town.' Luke felt his heart fluttering and his desire increasing as Brooke smiled and backed up against the wall.

'So, you're alone?'

'Yes.'

They stood in silence. Luke felt his muscles tensing up as he tried hard not to fidget. 'Shall I get you a drink?'

'Shh.' Brooke placed her finger over Luke's mouth. He felt her body heat penetrating through his clothing. She slipped off her coat and passed it to him. As he dropped the coat on the hook, he inhaled her fragrance, then turned and grabbed her face before kissing her hard. She tugged at his shirt and began to run her fingers up his back. Her touch felt electric, a feeling he hadn't experienced since first meeting Debbie. There had been a one-night stand about a year ago, after a night out in a bar, but he'd been drunk and he wasn't even sure if he'd managed anything. It would remain a mystery forever.

As they kissed harder, he grabbed her jumper and pulled it over her head. He steered her towards the living room, towards the settee. As he stepped across the rug he trod on something hard and yelled.

'What is it?'

Luke pulled away. 'Max and his bloody Lego.' As he bent down to pick up the plastic brick, he caught sight of another photo of Debbie, lying with baby Max lying on a towel in the garden, on a sunny day. He remembered that day as being perfect. His wife and son; he'd been so proud of her. What the hell was he doing?

Brooke began to caress him over his jeans, leaning in to kiss him. He began to kiss her back, but then abruptly stopped, pulling away. 'I can't do this,' he said. 'I'm sorry.'

She stepped back and slumped down on the settee, took a deep breath and looked away. He knew he'd hurt her.

'I know we probably need to take this slowly,' she replied as she snatched her jumper off the floor. He stroked her blonde hair, which now lay tangled over her face. She looked back at him and laughed. 'What are we like?' She began straightening her clothes up and pushing her hair back behind her ears. 'I suppose you're expecting the kids back any time?'

He remained silent and looked away.

'Is it something I did?'

'It's not you,' he said, sitting down beside her.

'I understand. I know what it's like to lose someone.' Brooke looked towards the photo on the hearth. 'I know I can never replace her. You can't ever replace him. We're not looking for replacements. You know something, though? We deserve to be happy. You deserve to be happy.' She kissed his cheek.

He leaned in and buried his head in her chest. It felt so right holding Brooke, but it felt deceitful that he'd desired her. 'Thanks for being so understanding. Shall we have that drink?'

'I'd love a cuppa,' she replied, a tear rolling down her cheek. 'Or maybe a brandy,' she said under her breath.

Luke walked out to the kitchen and stared at his reflection in the window. His hair was ruffled and his shirt was half undone. In the hallway, the coats had fallen off the hooks. He was sure he'd hung Brooke's coat up properly. He put the kettle on and opened the drawer containing the photo. 'Sorry, Deb,' he whispered as he grabbed the photo and placed it back on the shelf. The doorbell rang and Brooke answered the door.

'Daddy, we've had sausages, bacon and eggs and beans and what was that other thing we had, Nanny?'

'Whoa. You don't have to shout so loud, little man,' Luke replied.

'It was a hash brown,' said Cathy as she picked up the coats and placed them back on the hook.

'Max doesn't know what a hash brown is,' Heidi said.

'Shut up,' Max replied, slapping her on the arm.

'Right, little sprog. I'm going to get you. Run, sprog, because I'm coming for you,' Heidi shouted as she held out her arms and roared like a monster. Max turned and ran up the stairs, giggling and screaming.

Cathy passed Luke a couple of bags. 'There was a pre-Christmas sale on and I couldn't resist.' She pulled out two Christmas jumpers, one for Max and one for Heidi.

'They're beautiful,' Brooke said.

'So, what have you both been up to?'

Luke glanced at Brooke, noticing her wet eyes. 'Nothing. Just making tea. Do you want some?'

'I'm all tea'd out, I'm afraid. At my age, too much tea means too many trips to the loo and I still have to pop to the supermarket and pick up a few bits.'

'Thanks for taking them out this morning. They love going out with you.'

'I have a little secret. I love going out with them too. Anyway, I have to dash. I'll pop by for a cuppa another time. Enjoy the rest of your day.' She winked at Luke as she turned and walked towards the door. Luke smiled uncomfortably. Cathy paused and looked over at Brooke. 'Are you both okay?'

'We're fine,' Brooke replied, forcing a smile.

'Okay, I'll leave you both to it. Bye, kids,' she called out.

The children didn't respond. They were still running around upstairs, screaming and shouting. Cathy waved and left.

'There goes my tidy house. I'm sorry—'

'It's okay, really it is. I'm just being silly. She's lovely – Cathy, I mean. You're so lucky to have her,' Brooke said.

'I know I am. I'm so lucky to have a lot of people in my life. I really am sorry about earlier.'

'It's probably a good thing it didn't happen. Look at the timing. What would she be thinking if she'd walked in on something she couldn't unsee?' Brooke stared out of the window. He'd hurt her, he knew it. He had to right things. He couldn't lose her.

'She's already thinking it. That woman knows everything. The way she looked at me, my messy hair, and my shirt. She knew. She always knows.' Luke paused and stared out of the window, at the spot in the garden where Debbie was tending to Max in the photo. 'There's something I need to do.'

'What's that?'

Luke didn't answer. Instead, he walked to the living room and picked up the photo from the hearth. He could sense that Brooke was behind him, wondering what he'd meant, so he turned his back on her. Some things he needed to be alone for, and this was one of them.

'I'll finish making the tea then, shall I?' she asked.

'Please.'

As he heard her taking the mugs off the mug tree and setting them on the worktop, he looked at the photo of Debbie and Max. 'It's not that I don't love you, Deb. It's just… You understand, don't you?' he whispered. He held the photo to his heart and stared out of the window.

As he snapped out of his thoughts, he stared back at the man he now noticed in the distance. Sitting on a wall several houses down, with a dark hood covering his head and upper body, he sent a shiver down his spine. The scarf he wore covered his mouth, but his stare felt intrusive. The man stood and walked away. Luke watched as he reached the end of the street and looked back once before disappearing around the corner.

'Are you alright, Luke?' Brooke shook his arm.

'What?'

'I called you twice to say that the tea was made.'

'Sorry.'

Brooke reached out. 'Shall I put the photo back on the fireplace?'

'What? No. That's why I came in here. I'm going to put the photos away for now.'

She looked down, passed him a cup of tea and took the photo from his limp hand. She walked over to the fireplace and put the photo back where it belonged. 'The people we love from our past are part of our children's lives. She should stay. She's their mother.'

'I know, but I'm scared I'll never be able to move on,' he replied, as a tear ran down his cheek. 'Look at me. I have you, a beautiful woman who wants to—'

'Don't say any more. I'll not have your kids resenting me if all the photos go. The time will come when you're ready. I've been where you are. I've grieved, mourned, thrown things in temper, even felt like ending it all. It's a good job I had Joe, he's been my rock. The time will come when you can move on, and that photo will still be there. Your kids need that photo there. They need their mother in their life.'

'What have I ever done to deserve you?' He put his tea on the window ledge and squeezed Brooke. She held him back. He glanced over her head, out of the window. The man hadn't come back. He reached across and pulled the curtain slightly as an uneasy feeling washed through him.

CHAPTER FOURTEEN

'I did what you wanted. I think the police should figure out that Florence has someone to stay with, for now,' he said with a grin as he entered and sat on the end of her bed. She edged away from him, forcing her malnourished frame into the tiniest space possible.

There was hope. He'd done as she asked. She wanted to scream with joy, but that joy was soon quelled by doubt. Had she put her family in danger? Had she done the right thing? She wanted to punch the wall until her knuckles bled. Her chaotic thoughts threatened to expose themselves as she clenched her hand into a fist under the sheet.

He leaned into a bin bag and pulled out a brand-new quilt, a couple of pillows and some thick fleece blankets. 'It's about time you had something new. Let me take these dirty blankets away.' Debbie shivered as he pulled the soiled blankets off her and deposited them in the bin bag. 'Oh dear. It's been a bit of a blood bath here. I'd better clean you up.' He left the room, and she listened to the tap running as he filled a bowl.

The damp that she'd been lying in was getting cold now that she'd shuffled off it. The broken fan in the corner of the room led straight to the outdoors, allowing a little ray of light to shine through, especially now the trees were bare. She flinched as she moved further away from the dampness before taking a long look at what she'd been lying in. An array of lumps and blood stained the sheets underneath. She began to yank at them, pulling them from under her. As she twisted to grab the corner of the sheet that was under her bottom, she yelped in pain. She reached down and examined the hot stabbing pain that came from within and she knew she needed stitches. She closed her legs and began to pull at the sheet again, finally releasing it. Shuffling towards the edge of the bed, over the stain, she threw the clogged sheets into the bag. She needed to try and keep as clean as possible to reduce the chance of infection. He whistled as he reappeared with a bowl of water and an old, soiled flannel.

'Move closer,' he instructed. She shuffled, dragging the chain with her, until she was sitting on the edge of the bed with her feet on the floor. He kneeled in front of her, lifted up her nightdress and began to flannel down her stomach before moving on to her groin. She could kick him now, but what then? Run until the chain pulled her back? And then a beating, no food? He rinsed the flannel in the bowl and the water instantly turned a dirty brown. He reached back up and began to rub the top of her legs. 'A bit of stubborn dirt,' he said, scrubbing hard. He washed her legs, then her feet. 'There. You're all better now. Looking splendid.' He dragged the dirty nightdress over her head, revealing her thin, naked frame, then grabbed a new flannel nightdress from where he'd dropped it on the floor. He fed it over her head, lifting her hair through once she'd put her arms in.

'Thank you,' Debbie replied.

'I need you to stand against the wall while I make the bed.' She whimpered as he pulled her to a standing position and led her over to the wall. The chain had reached its limit. 'Wait there.' He began to put the new sheets on the bed, followed by the coverless quilt. He threw the fleece blankets over the top and patted them down, smoothing out the lumps in the stuffing. 'Lovely. See, I do care for you.'

Cold tears trailed down her cheeks as she fought the urge to break down. If she let her emotions out, he'd punish her. She wiped her tears away with the backs of her hands.

'Do you want to swill your hands before I remove the bowl?'

She stared at the dirty water and shook her head. Her fingernails were black and her hands were gritty, but she didn't want to plunge them into the filthy, bloody water. 'Can I please have a shower soon?' she asked.

'I've bloody well washed you, what more do you want?' he yelled, throwing the flannel to the floor.

'I'm sorry. I need to be more grateful,' Debbie said as she shuffled back to the bed. 'Please don't be upset with me. I didn't mean anything. I know you treat me well.'

'Do you love me?'

Debbie looked up at him. He walked towards her, sat on the edge of the bed and placed his hand under her chin. She nodded.

'I know you love me, but you must say it. You know I like to hear the words.'

Debbie swallowed the mucus that had built up in the back of her nasal passages. She needed him to leave so that she could cry.

'I love you,' she said as she began to weep.

'Why do you cry?' He paused. 'You wonder about me, don't you? I went there today, to Luke's house. There are things you need to know.'

Debbie felt her heart pounding as she hoped desperately for more information. If she asked, he'd know she was eager and that she loved Luke. He knew where Luke and her children lived, and she wasn't going to put them all in danger now. 'I don't love him, I love you. I just wonder, that's all.'

'He doesn't care. He has a new life, a new lady. I told you, he never loved you as much as I do. I did what you wanted though. The police have been given enough information.'

'Thank you,' she said as she slumped back.

'Don't worry, my love. We'll have her back one day.' He lay next to her on the bed and held her tight. Pain shot through her body as he squeezed her and kissed her tangled hair. 'You're the only person for me. If something happened to you, I'd never find another. That's what makes our love more special. I love you more than life. I'll never let you go.'

Debbie flinched as someone hammered on the door below. 'Son. Are you in your office?'

He jumped up off the bed. 'Don't murmur a word. If she hears, she'll go a little mad. She's sick, you know. If you upset her, I may have to end her and that would be your fault. Nothing can come between our love. Do you understand?'

Debbie stared at him. He grabbed her hair. Wrenching her head back, he kissed her hard on the lips. She almost gagged as his tongue rolled around hers. 'Do you understand?' She nodded as tears spilled from her eyes.

'Why are you crying? Stop it.'

Choking sobs spilled from her mouth, filling the quiet room. As he stood, he slapped her hard. 'I said stop it. Or do you want another one?'

As her silent tears fell, Debbie shook her head.

'Coming, Ma.'

'Can you go to the shops? We have no bread,' the old woman yelled. 'Is there someone else there? Who's there?'

He grabbed Debbie's chin and squeezed. 'Enough,' he said as he pushed her back and left.

His smell was all around her, in her hair, in her nightdress, on her tongue. Even the stench of his acrid breath still hung in the air.

'No one's here and you don't need groceries, Ma. I got everything we need the other day, remember?' He paused. 'Yes, you do remember. Come on, Ma, it's cold and you'll get ill. Let's get you back into the house.'

The main door slammed shut and she heard him lock it. Once again, she was alone with her thoughts, which had taken an even darker turn than usual. Luke had found someone else. She imagined her photos being taken down, Heidi and Max having a new mother, a new family, maybe. Luke was the devoted type. If he met the right woman, she knew he'd marry again, and he'd be the perfect husband. But he was her husband. She punched the wall and heard her knuckles crack. 'No,' she yelled as she scrunched her pillow tightly and sobbed into it. 'I want my babies,' she cried as she thought of Max and Heidi. She wanted to hold them and tell them how much she loved them.

She cried into the darkness. The darkness was still, the darkness was plain; the darkness gave her nothing back. It incubated an evil sickness with which she'd been infected for many rotten years – four winters. She closed her eyes and entered a better world. The one where she had a big homecoming, the one where she was rescued, the one where he slipped up and allowed her to escape. That world was much better and it was where she'd stay, for now.

CHAPTER FIFTEEN

Gina grabbed another tissue and sneezed into it. 'Right, Baby Jenkins.' She lifted the file that she'd retrieved from the archives earlier in the day. The work notes were all bunched up with an old elastic band. She removed the band and opened them up. All the original statements were there, as were the DNA results and photos of Deborah and her family. There was also a batch of witness statements, and a map of where the shoe was found, outlining the direction Deborah would've taken to head home.

They interviewed her husband, Luke, her neighbours and colleagues, parents from the school her children attended and her friends, but they'd added nothing to the case. Deborah had simply disappeared. No one was out of place and they'd failed to find a convincing motive. Deborah had a loving family and had been described as happy with her life by all who knew her.

One of the parents had spotted a person lurking around the school. Again, no description. The figure had been too far away and had been wearing a hooded top. Then there was Samuel Avery, the pub landlord. She felt her skin crawl as she read his name.

There was a tap on her door. She grabbed the paperwork and slid it back into a pile. 'Come in.'

'I noticed that you'd marked a file "Library Baby",' said Jacob. 'Is that what we've called the case? Anyway, we've set up the task group as you requested.'

'You, me, Wyre and O'Connor?' Gina asked.

'That's right. And PC Smith, if we need him.'

'Great. We need to get started. There's a man out there who needs to know that his wife is still alive. And not only that, but she's had a baby.'

Jacob looked down at his feet. 'Shall I go with Wyre? Only, you look like tripe.'

Gina felt a cold trail running from her nose. She grabbed a tissue, quickly wiping the mucus before it reached her top lip. 'You know how to make someone feel good about themselves.'

'I sure do. Full of charm, I am.'

'No.'

'You mean I'm not full of charm?'

Gina stared up at Jacob. 'I mean no to me not being there when you visit Luke Jenkins. I will be there. It's a case I was part of four years ago – it was my first case here – and it's still unresolved. If anyone's going to close it, I am, stinking cold or not. And in answer to your other question, you score zero on the charm-o-meter.'

'Say it as it is, why don't you? But I totally understand about you needing to tell Luke Jenkins. Shall I go and brief the team?'

'Tell them I'll be through in a moment. I'll handle it.'

'Will do. O'Connor's dropping in at the sandwich van on the way in. Do you want anything?'

She swallowed. Her throat was sand-papery and dry. She wasn't exactly looking forward to informing Mr Jenkins of the news either. Her stomach flipped at the thought. 'No, I'll pass this time.'

'It's not like you to pass on a greasy butty. Now I know you're sick.'

'Sick I am. Right, let's get back to the tasks in hand. I'm going to call Luke Jenkins and arrange a visit. Be ready to tag along, I want you with me for this one. This is now our prime investigation. Watch his reactions, watch every movement.'

He nodded. 'Will do,' he replied as he left her office, pulling the door behind him.

Gina opened up the file once again and began to read Deborah's medical information. The usual things were contained in it. She'd had two children, no major illnesses and no ongoing conditions. She focused on the information at the bottom of the page: Deborah had a contraceptive implant fitted the month before she disappeared. She typed the name of the implant into Google. Scrolling down all the links, she selected the NHS website and opened the page. Apparently, the implant would last three years before needing to be replaced. She sat back in her chair while staring at the screen. Deborah's implant had run out of its contraceptive properties, and that's why she'd ended up pregnant.

Head pounding at the thoughts that ran through her mind, she grabbed the box of painkillers from her top drawer and threw a couple of them into her mouth before swallowing them down with an inch of cold coffee. Her stomach fluttered, a combination of nerves and excitement. She pictured Deborah being held by someone. Maybe this person had rendered her pregnant once the implant had worn off, and almost four years to the date of her disappearance she'd given birth to a daughter. The timeline was falling into place. If she was being held against her will, they needed to find her quickly. Time was against them. She couldn't let Deborah go through this level of trauma again. Gina stared into her empty coffee mug and shuddered at the thought of what Deborah might be going through. It reminded her of her own past.

Before Hannah was born, she and Terry had seemed like any normal young couple, but soon they were living far away from her parents and she eventually lost touch with them. A few months later, her mother died of an aggressive form of cancer and her father drank himself to death, leaving her heartbroken. Terry only drove her back for their funerals. She'd never forgiven herself for not being there for either of them. She thought of her father, sitting in his favourite chair whilst he watched Birmingham City playing on the television. She could've left at any time, gone back home and comforted him, but Terry had her under his control.

After that, Terry's drinking and recreational drug use became more frequent. As she'd lain in bed weeping on the night of her father's funeral, she'd felt her tender breasts and thought of the life she was carrying inside her. She didn't want Terry to come home that night, but he had. Gina shivered as memories ran through her mind.

Was Deborah that scared all the time? Was she trapped? Gina took a deep breath as the room began to sway. The tablets needed to kick in, before her pounding head exploded. She had a team briefing to deliver. She placed her head in her hands and closed her eyes, but the woozy feeling continued. Breathe in and out, in and out.

'Ma'am,' Wyre said.

Gina flinched and forced a smile as she hid her trembling hands under her desk.

'I knocked twice. Are you okay?'

'I'm fine. Just this cold. I'm not letting it win though.' This case was already getting to her and she hadn't even started. Gina wiped her nose again. The frequent contact with dry tissue was starting to scrape the skin from her tender nose.

'I'm off out in a while to see Deborah Jenkins' husband. I'll be taking Jacob with me. Can you continue going through all the calls? Anything you come across that's relevant, let me know straight away. We're going to find Deborah.'

'Will do.' Wyre smiled.

'I'll be through for the briefing first, be just a moment,' Gina said, picking up the phone to dial Luke's number.

CHAPTER SIXTEEN

Jacob drove. Gina sat in silence as she looked out of the passenger window. He hopped the car over a road littered with speed bumps. 'Easy, Driscoll. I may lose my stomach,' she said.

'Yes. Wouldn't want puke all over my windscreen.' Jacob laughed as he hopped the car over another hump. 'How're things with you lately? You seem a bit distant. Is it a man thing?'

Gina turned to face him. She certainly wasn't going to be discussing the finer details of her tryst with Briggs. 'That would both be telling and none of your business. How about you?'

Jacob laughed as he indicated left. 'I normally get kicked out in the mornings. Breakfast is a never. Even a cup of coffee would indicate that seriousness was on the cards.' He paused and a big grin appeared on his face. 'I lie. I lived with a woman for several years, as you know. Beth. It didn't work out. I'm not sure where this thing with Abigail is going.' He slowed down as he reached the street running adjacent to Luke Jenkins' house. 'We're nearly there.'

'I feel like puking even more now.'

'Don't do this to yourself. We are here to deliver news and investigate. We can't control how people react. Anyway, guv, it's not like you to let things like this pull you down.' Jacob braked as he pulled up on the road beside the house.

Gina looked back at him and smiled. 'You're right. I feel for her, Jacob. What she's going through is big and traumatic, and we've got to tell her husband.' She began to bite her nail. 'This cold is playing on me. Let's get this over with.' Jacob released his seat belt and opened the door. A breeze whipped through the vehicle, fluffing up his fair hair. He patted it back down as he stood.

Gina stepped out into the icy, damp air and took a deep breath as they approached the front door. As she went to ring the bell, a short woman in her sixties answered. Gina recognised her from the investigation. 'Mrs Beddows,' Gina said as she nodded. The woman opened the door wide and stepped back.

'Please, come in. Luke is in the lounge. And call me Cathy,' she said as she closed the door behind them. 'It's just through that door.'

Gina could see that Cathy's eyes looked a little puffy. The woman pulled a crumpled tissue from her pocket and dabbed her nose. 'Can I get you both a drink?'

'Not for me, thank you,' Gina replied. Cathy nodded and ushered them into the lounge. 'Are your grandchildren here?'

The woman shook her head. 'They've gone to Brooke's house. She lives on the next road. They'll be back shortly. We thought it best.'

Luke stood. 'Please take a seat.' He sat back down on the settee and began twiddling his thumbs. 'Have you found her?'

'She's dead, isn't she?' Cathy cried, and she burst into tears.

'Mrs Beddows – Cathy – it's quite the opposite,' Gina replied. She licked her dry lips and swallowed.

'You mean you've found my wife? She's alive?'

'No. I wish I could say that. Let me explain.' Gina swallowed again and rubbed the back of her neck. 'We have reason to believe that your wife is still alive. Do you know about the abandoned baby, the one found outside Cleevesford Library?'

Luke hunched over and placed his head in his hands. 'I saw something on the local news.'

'We ran a DNA check on the baby. Your wife's DNA is on record from the time we had to eliminate her from a previous enquiry, and it turns out that her DNA is a match for the baby's.'

'You must be joking.' Luke stood and began pacing the living room. 'That can't be right.'

Mrs Beddows followed Luke around the lounge and grabbed his hand. 'Luke, please sit.' He shook her hand away, walked towards the window and stared out.

'What does that mean? What does it all mean? Did she leave us on purpose?'

Gina stood and walked towards Luke. 'I don't believe she left you that night. In fact, we're still treating Deborah's disappearance as highly suspicious and we're reinvestigating the case.'

Luke turned to face her. She noticed how his eyelids seemed to have a red rim around them and his skin had taken on a pale tone. He once again ran his hands through his hair before bursting into tears. 'She's been abducted, hasn't she?'

'We don't know that for sure—'

'She has. I know it. I always knew it. Some psychopathic creep has abducted her and is abusing her. You need to find her.' Luke's knees buckled. Cathy steadied him and led him back to the settee.

'What's happened to my baby?' Cathy asked, her voice cracking. Gina could see that she was trying to stay calm, but tears streamed down her cheeks.

'We are going to do everything we can to find your daughter. Whatever it takes, we are going to do it. I will be going over the whole investigation again and contacting everyone involved.' Gina felt her nose tickling again. She grabbed a tissue from her pocket and sneezed violently into it.

Jacob leaned forward in the chair and continued speaking. 'The investigation is now back open. You need to let us know if you hear or see anything suspicious. Anything at all. It could be something or it could be nothing, but we are determined to find her.'

The room went silent. Luke had his head buried in his hands. Cathy was holding a tissue out in front of him. 'I need her back,' he said, sobbing. His breathing quickened and he began to hyperventilate. As he gasped for air he started shaking.

Cathy held him tight and rocked back and forth with him in her arms. 'There, there. We'll find her.' Luke stood and held his arms up in the air before allowing them to fall back down. Still trembling, he jogged to the kitchen. Gina placed the wet tissue in her pocket and listened as Luke began to run a tap.

'I need my wife back. You gave up on her back then. You lot let her down!'

'We had no leads, Mr Jenkins, and we certainly never gave up. We're not giving up,' replied Gina, pacing between the hall and the lounge. She felt her face redden with the heat of the house. They had given up, he was right, but they'd reached dead ends all round. 'We're really sorry to have caused you so much stress, but you both needed to know what was going on.'

'Don't apologise. For the past couple of years, I'd resigned myself to thinking that my Deborah was dead, but you've given me hope and—' Cathy sobbed as she forced her words out. 'And I have another grandchild.'

'She's being well looked after,' Gina said.

'There's one thing I know for certain that Deborah would want, and it's for us to take care of her child. That's my daughter's baby, my grandchildren's sister. Can I see her? I need to see her.'

Gina watched as the woman continued to dab her eyes and nose. Luke was still sobbing in the background. The tap stopped running. 'Of course,' said Gina. 'I will arrange for you to see her. She's beautiful.'

The woman looked up and forced a smile. 'She has a beautiful mother.'

As Luke entered the lounge, there was a knock on the door. 'I can't deal with the kids right now.'

Cathy passed him, placing a hand on his shoulder. 'Why don't you go upstairs and sort yourself out. I'll deal with the kids.'

The knocking continued, faster and louder. 'Dad! Let me in, I need a wee,' Max shouted. Luke passed Cathy and ran up the stairs. She opened the door and Max darted in.

'Max has weed his pants!' Heidi shouted as she entered, throwing her bag on the floor. 'Max is a baby!'

'Shut up, you ugly hippo,' he called back as the toilet door slammed shut. Heidi began banging on the toilet door, shouting at Max.

'They've had a spot of lunch. Is Luke okay?' Brooke asked as she stepped into the hall, holding Joe's hand.

Cathy stepped forward and took her other hand. 'It's probably best if he calls you in a while, dear. He's had to go and have a lie down. Thank you so much for watching the kids.'

'Can I see him?'

'He's not in any fit state to talk,' Cathy replied.

Brooke frowned and stepped back out of the door. 'We'll just be going then,' she said, pulling Joe behind her.

'Wait,' said Cathy. 'He will call you in a while. There's been some news and he needs—' And Cathy burst into tears once more.

Brooke walked back and placed her arms around the woman. 'He can call me when he's ready. Is there anything I can do?'

Cathy shook her head and hugged Brooke.

'I'm here if any of you need me. Just call, okay?'

Gina, standing half in the hall, leaned back to watch out of the lounge window as Brooke closed the garden gate and walked down the road. 'I'll call you when we get back to the station,' she said to Cathy. 'Hopefully you'll be able to visit your granddaughter today.'

'Thank you.' Cathy wiped her eyes and blew her nose.

'Here's my card. You have my number. Again, if you see or hear anything, let me know. Even if it seems like it's nothing, it could be the key to cracking the case and finding Deborah.'

The woman nodded, thanking them again as she showed them out and closed the door.

'Well, that wasn't easy,' Gina said.

'No. I don't know how they're going to cope. Imagine finding out that not only is your daughter potentially being held by some psycho, but that you might have a grandchild fathered by that same psycho? I don't know how I'd feel.'

'Me neither. I feel for them. Back to the station now. I need to call children's services, see if I can arrange a visit for Mrs Beddows at the hospital. The fun never ends with this job—'

'But you wouldn't have it any other way,' Jacob continued.

'You know, I hate it when you finish my sentences. I might just puke on your dashboard to get my revenge. Do we have the name of the social worker in charge of the Baby Jenkins case?'

'Yes, Devina Gupta.'

Gina found Devina's number and waited for an answer. She stared out of the window as they travelled down the road with the speed bumps before leaving the estate and joining the main road through Cleevesford.

'Devina, hi, it's DI Harte. I need you meet me at the hospital in an hour… I know you're busy, we all are… Thank you, see you there.' Then Gina dialled the Jenkinses' home number. She had no idea if just Cathy would turn up or if Luke would manage to make it too. She did know it would be an emotional introduction.

CHAPTER SEVENTEEN

As they walked along the hospital corridors, Luke stopped and leaned against the window ledge, staring out into the courtyard below. 'I don't know if I can do this.'

Cathy stepped closer and placed her hand over his. 'You can. You have to. For Debbie.'

'Do you need a moment, Mr Jenkins?' DI Harte asked.

'No,' Cathy replied.

'Yes,' Luke said.

Cathy placed her arm around his shoulders. 'We have to do this, for Debbie. I know it's painful, really I do,' she said. Luke went to speak but stopped. He rubbed his eyes and continued walking along the corridor with Cathy until they reached the ward where Baby Jenkins lay. They stopped outside and Cathy peered through the tiny window in the door.

'You just have to press the buzzer,' said DI Harte.

Luke leaned across and pushed the red button. Cathy bit the skin on her bottom lip as they waited. The detective walked ahead as they were buzzed in. Luke couldn't work out what she was saying to the nurse, but within a moment they were pointed in the right direction.

As their footsteps echoed through the corridor, Luke kept thinking of the huge mess that everything was in. He hadn't called Brooke back. Hell, he didn't even know what he was going to say to her. *Well, you know my missing wife, the one presumed dead, the one I'd just about given up on? Well, she's just had a baby. Have I found her? No. Just her baby. The baby's not mine. They think she might have been taken and held captive all these years. We'll probably be looking after the baby, I think.*

Maybe he wouldn't say that. He didn't know if he really meant the things that were unfolding in his thoughts or if they were just a reaction to his increased stress levels. He was walking towards the room where his wife's baby lay. Another man's baby, but she was part of his wife and his wife was going through something, somewhere. What if she never came home? Could he rise to the challenge of bringing up this baby alone, in Debbie's absence? Would that be too much to ask? Would Cathy bring the baby up? His wife's mother gripped his hand as they reached the entrance to the room.

He paused at the door to the room, staring across at the little baby, dressed in a white all-in-one vest, sleeping in a tiny plastic crib. This was the baby he was possibly meant to take responsibility for. His legs felt weak and he began to tremble. What had Debbie been through? His lovely Debbie had been forced to— he couldn't say it, even in his mind. It felt like his heart was ripping apart, taking his breath away. 'I just want Debbie back. I need her.'

'We will get her back. We will,' Cathy said.

'You don't know that. None of us know that. I searched for her everywhere and found nothing, just like that lot. None of us know.' He almost broke down as he looked back at DI Harte. She looked down. They both knew there were no guarantees. His mind whizzed around and eventually stopped on an image that would haunt him. He imagined Debbie shackled in some dungeon, with a psycho raping and beating her. His lovely Debbie, the gentle mother, the beautiful young woman he'd married on that chilly October morning. His mind flashed back to the day they'd started senior school. She was the cutest girl in the class and he'd known then that they would one day be together. Then the chains came back, the image of a monster, a devil, stooping over her.

'Hello, I'm Devina Gupta, caseworker for Baby Jenkins. I'll be sitting with you and can answer any questions you might have.'

'Thank you,' Cathy whispered as she peered into the room, trying to catch a glimpse of the baby.

Devina led the way and sat on a chair in the corner of the room. Luke watched as the woman fought to drag a notepad out of her oversized handbag. She flicked her frizzy black hair out of her eyes and began making notes.

His eyes met Cathy's. He wanted to speak but he couldn't. The words were muddled in his head. How on earth would he get them out in a coherent way? 'Luke, would you prefer to wait outside?' He shook his head and followed Cathy's lead as she tiptoed towards the crib. She reached in and placed her finger on the baby's hand. The baby stirred and gripped her finger before letting out a half-hearted cry. 'I think she's hungry.' Cathy smiled at the baby and began to stroke her fine hair. 'She's beautiful. She's one of us, Luke. We have to take care of her. I know you're probably not ready for this, so when the time comes, she can stay with me, if you're not—'

'She has a brother and a sister. She's part of Debbie.' He broke down, sobbing until his face was completely wet and his nose was beginning to bubble. His heart had melted. This was Debbie's baby, a connection to the only woman he'd ever truly loved, and he wasn't about to let her down now. 'We'll look after her and love her, for Debbie.'

Cathy took his hand. 'I'm so proud of you, Luke. When she comes home, we'll all be waiting. One happy family. And she will come home.' Cathy turned to Devina. 'Can the baby come home too?'

'We have a lot to go through. I'd certainly support short supervised home visits to begin with, as this is a big thing for you both. We'd need to see you in your home and we have procedures to follow, but our aim is to always keep families together if we can.'

'Please make it happen. This little one needs me,' Cathy said, shaking as she wiped the corner of her eye.

A doctor entered and grabbed the chart from the end of the crib. 'Are you relatives?' he asked.

'Hello. Doctor Nowak, isn't it. We met the other day,' Gina said as she beckoned for the doctor to follow her outside the room. Devina followed, closing the door behind them. Luke peered out. He knew they were discussing their situation, their rights and the baby's needs. He gripped Cathy's hand and sat down. 'I'm not prepared to let Debbie down. I know we can do this. I don't know what we'll say to Max and Heidi, but we'll think of something.'

Cathy smiled. 'They'll be fine. We'll work something out.' She continued to rub Luke's back. 'We must think of a name. She can't be called Baby Jenkins forever. Did Debbie ever tell you about her doll, Isobel?'

'No. I don't think so,' he replied, wiping his eyes with his hand.

'When she was a little girl, we used to read her this story about a little girl called Isobel who had the most awful nightmares. Debbie used to get nightmares sometimes, which is why we got her the book. In the story, one night, after a battle with the monsters under her bed, Isobel realises that they were only nightmares and that she ultimately has the power over them, as they aren't real. Debbie's father was working away one time, and he brought her back a rag doll. She loved the doll and called her Isobel, after the girl in the story. She went everywhere with the doll, until she started senior school and grew up, that is.'

'And met me,' he said with a smile.

'And met you. My wonderful son-in-law and the best father in the world. When she first brought you home I made you each a fish finger sandwich. I knew then that you were the one for my daughter.' Cathy leaned over the crib and lifted the baby up. She hugged her gently, carefully cradling her head.

Luke noticed Devina looking at him through the window in the door, checking his responses. He stroked the baby's hair. 'I love the name Isobel. Isobel Jenkins sounds like it was always meant to be.'

'Are you ready to hold her?'

He reached out and took the tiny baby from Cathy. He was surprised at how light she was. He remembered Max and Heidi being quite chunky babies. Isobel was a dainty little flower. His arm shook as he laid her against his chest. Her warmth seeped through his T-shirt. The little one gurgled and brought her hands to her face before sucking on her knuckles. 'You were right, about her being hungry.' He kissed the top of her head and placed her back in Cathy's arms.

'We're all going to be just fine. I'm going to be with you on this, every step of the way. We can do this.' He smiled. Cathy was right. She was always right, and with her help he knew Isobel would be just fine. He thought back to sleepless nights, teething and nappies. What if Debbie never came home? Could he cope? His heart began to race. He closed his eyes and swallowed. One minute he was filled with optimism, the next with doubt. He opened his eyes and noticed Devina taking notes and glancing up at him, scrutinising his every move and reaction. Every part of him wanted to scream, to shout and punch the door, but he couldn't lose control. He had Cathy and Isobel to think of. He had to be the man Debbie needed.

CHAPTER EIGHTEEN

'We've finished setting up the incident room,' DC Paula Wyre said as Gina walked through the door.

'That's great, thank you.' Gina returned Wyre's smile. She reached for the crumpled tissue in her pocket and wiped the bottom of her scabby nose.

'Looks sore, guv.'

'It is, and it's getting worse with every wipe. I certainly wish this cold would do one.' She looked at Wyre. 'How on earth do you manage to look so... tidy? It's like we're always here, always busy, always into one case or another. I don't know how you do it. I feel like a tramp some days.'

'Err...' Wyre shrugged her shoulders and smiled at Gina.

'I'll catch you in a minute.'

'Thanks, guv.' Wyre headed towards the incident room.

Jacob entered from the corridor. 'Did it go well at the hospital?'

Gina removed her coat and hung it over her arm. 'As well as it could. I can't imagine what they're going through.' She followed him past several offices to the incident room. 'It's great to see you've all been so busy. Nice work.' She threw her coat over the back of a chair and proceeded to the board, on which all the information they'd collated so far was written or attached. In the centre was a photo of Deborah Jenkins.

The young, healthy woman smiled out at her. Details of her family life were outlined. The witnesses were listed under five headings: school contacts; colleagues; social life; family; and other. The list was huge. They'd contacted so many people after she'd first disappeared.

A map of Warwickshire and Worcestershire had been hung on the wall, to the left of the board. Cleevesford had been outlined in red. Her eyes trailed over the pins, starting at the point they'd found her shoe to the point they'd discovered Baby Jenkins. She grabbed another pin and placed it on Luke's house on the map. Photos of the school, her work and everywhere else she frequented were also pinned under their headings. She turned her attention to O'Connor, who was sitting in a chair facing away, wearing earphones. He had one hand on his keyboard and the other was scratching his head. He flinched as she tapped him on the shoulder.

He fumbled with his computer and attempted to remove the earphones that had got caught in his badly knotted tie. 'You're back. I was just going through the calls to see if I could find anything in them.'

'Anything standing out as useful?' Gina asked.

'No, not as yet. We've had a few new ones. I'm working through them at the moment. Wyre and I divided them up after we pinned all the info to the boards as you requested. Mrs O has made cupcakes, by the way. Help yourself. They're over by the coffee pot.'

'Thanks. Will do. I won't keep you any longer. Let me know straight away if anything that might be of use comes up,' Gina replied as she began to cough, only catching it in her hands at the last minute.

O'Connor held his hand over his mouth. 'Sorry, guv, I don't want to catch it, not with my bike ride coming up.'

'Don't blame you. Sorry.'

O'Connor smiled and placed his earphones back in. Gina walked over to the kitchenette and grabbed the coffee pot, pouring a cup of the strong dark liquid and taking a long swig, savouring its soothing properties as it trickled down her sore throat. A tickle caught her tonsils and she began to cough and splutter again. Great, the sneezing and headaches were subsiding, only to be replaced by a sore throat and an annoying cough.

'You okay?' Briggs handed Gina a handful of old crumpled tissues that he dragged from his pocket.

'I think I'd rather use my sleeve. I don't know where they've been,' she said as she handed them back to him.

'Your loss,' he replied, smiling as he grabbed a pink cupcake and took a bite.

'They're bad for your waistline.'

'I think I'm past caring,' he said as he patted his belly. 'I also think O'Connor's a bit offended, as I never eat any of his wife's baked goodies.' Just as he said it, O'Connor turned and spotted him eating a cupcake. Briggs held it up and smiled. 'I'm eating one,' he called out. O'Connor shrugged and pointed at his earphones.

'He's not listening.' Gina coughed again and cleared her throat, unsure of what to say next.

Briggs nodded as he chomped on a mouthful of cake. 'You know, they're pretty damn good.' He held the plate up.

'No, I think I'll pass.'

'Do you fancy a drink later? We could try the new wine bar in Stratford, sit and look out at the river, get away from things for a couple of hours. I hear the Christmas decorations are good this year on the High Street.'

Gina glanced around, checking to see if anyone had noticed them talking. 'Not here,' she murmured. 'Someone will hear us. Besides, I'm meant to be seeing my daughter tonight.'

'Exciting though, isn't it?' He moved closer. She could feel the warmth of his body. A succession of thoughts flashed through her mind: the night in question, her legs wrapped around his body, him moving back and forth above her just where she'd needed him, the wine, and the laughs. He knew exactly what she was thinking. Her face had become an open book.

'No, just no. I'll text you later,' she said, as a nervous laugh escaped her guarded expression.

'Anyway, it's not like you to miss out on eating junk,' Briggs said with a grin as he wiped the last of the crumbs from the side of his mouth and binned the cake case.

'Feeling poorly.' Gina pulled a sad face.

'Well, I could stand here all day and give you sympathy or I could go and do some work.'

'I don't need your sympathy. Look, I'll have a cake if it makes you feel better.' Gina grabbed a cake off the plate and took a large bite out of the top. As the buttercream mulched in her mouth and slipped down her throat she instantly regretted it. The sugary butter mixed with mucus was making her nauseous.

'Enjoy,' Briggs replied as he rubbed his hands together. 'You know, you look beautiful, even with a scabby nose.' The last word his, he turned and walked off.

Gina glanced around the room, hoping that no one had noticed the mixed expression on her face. Everyone was busy working; she needn't have worried. She placed the rest of the little cake in the bin and threw a few sheets of kitchen roll on top to hide the evidence. She wasn't sure if this thing with Briggs was worth pursuing, but there was something there that made her feel good. Was that enough?

She walked back to the board and stared at Deborah's photo. Images of Luke and Cathy ran through her mind. She had no idea how they were going to cope or how they'd even begin to tell the children. She shuddered. How do you tell young children that their missing mother has had a baby and that the baby has turned up abandoned outside their local library? She had to find Deborah. She was under no illusions that finding Deborah and placing her back with her family would throw up problems of its own, but it would be a start to rebuilding their family unit, however difficult.

'I think we have something,' O'Connor called. Gina slammed her coffee down on a desk and ran over, grinning as she almost coughed over O'Connor. This was just what she needed, a lead.

'What is it?' Gina asked.

'Music to my ears,' Briggs called out as he passed Gina and walked over to O'Connor.

CHAPTER NINETEEN

The incident room was bustling with bodies, all crowding around to hear what O'Connor had to say. Wyre removed her earphones and jogged across the room, pushing her way through everyone to get close to O'Connor. 'What have you got?' Gina asked. The room went almost silent as everyone hung on O'Connor's words.

O'Connor frowned as he twiddled the earphones that hung over his chest. 'Jill just sent me this one through. We have to go and interview the woman straight away, while she's remembering things. She lives at number seventeen Bell Terrace, on the road running behind the library. Her name's Mabel McDonald.'

Gina took out her notebook and pen and jotted the address down. She caught a glimpse of her watch. Hannah and Gracie would be at her house in two hours for their visit, and a lead had just come in. She could get this woman interviewed, get back to the station and compile the notes, then make it back home to meet them. She felt her stomach flutter. Who was she kidding? She pulled her phone out of her pocket and began to text Hannah. Her finger hovered above the send button. She couldn't do it. She deleted the text. She had to make it back to see them. There was no other option. If she disappointed her daughter one more time, she feared she may never get another chance. 'Tell us what you know,' she said to O'Connor.

'Right. Here's what we have. She saw a hooded person walk past her house between six thirty and eight on the night that Baby Jenkins was discovered. She states that she was looking out of the window for her cat, who had not been home all day. Apparently, this figure was cradling a bag in his arms. She's also partially deaf. Jill had trouble communicating with her during the call. That is all I have, unfortunately, but it's something.'

'It could very well be everything. We need to get onto this straight away. Jacob, you can come with me to interview her. Everyone else, stay at it. Keep going through everything until you come up with another lead.'

As they dashed across the car park to Jacob's car Gina checked her watch again. 'My daughter's meant to be coming to visit this evening. I could do with being back for her.'

'We can do our best. Let's hope this old dear's on form.'

She frowned as she got in the car and buckled up. Her granddaughter had been walking for weeks and she hadn't observed her taking a single step. 'Remind me, Jacob, why the hell do we do all this?'

'All what?' He disengaged the handbrake and began driving.

'This. Sacrifice a family life for this job.'

'If only this was just a job.' He laughed. 'I wish it were that simple.'

Gina grabbed a sweet from the glovebox, hoping it would soothe her scratchy throat. 'That's the problem. I wish I could just see it as a job, but it's my life. That sounds really sad, I know, but I need to feel like I'm putting wrongs right and making the world a better place.'

'That's why we do it. After all, what is the real meaning of life? In my opinion there is no meaning. Life as a concept is pretty crap. You're born, you reproduce, you spend your life trying to keep up with the neighbours and working yourself into an early grave. Cycle starts again.' Gina looked out of the window as Jacob drove down a long road in silence. 'I suppose I feel that you can choose to do some good while you're here. Though I do it mostly for O'Connor's wife's cupcakes. Boy, that woman has talent.'

'Let's celebrate O'Connor's wife's cupcakes and their role in creating our dedicated team,' Gina replied.

Jacob kept his eyes on the road as he turned into Bell Terrace. 'To cupcakes.'

He steered along the slightly curved road as Gina admired the trees lining the paths. Springtime would bring out their beautiful blossoms. As they neared Mrs McDonald's house, Gina shivered. The houses were all decorated – one had a pretend Santa climbing up the wall and another had an outdoor tree covered in fairy lights. Would Deborah know it was Christmas? Gina knew Deborah's heart would be savagely torn apart as she thought about her children waking up again without her on Christmas day.

She spotted number seventeen and saw an elderly woman standing at the window. 'Let's work on catching the bad guy,' Gina said, as she crunched the rest of the sweet in her mouth.

CHAPTER TWENTY

She grabbed a tissue from her pocket and blew her nose as the old lady fumbled with the locks on the door. After a moment, the door opened the length of the chain. 'Can I see your credentials?' Mrs McDonald croaked. Gina and Jacob pulled out their warrant cards and fed them through the gap. A shaky hand reached out and took them. 'Oh, so you're a DI, how wonderful,' she said as she handed the cards back and slid the chain off.

'That's right. DI Harte and DS Driscoll. We're just following up on your call to the station,' Gina replied.

The door opened and a hunchbacked woman wearing several layers of clothing invited them in. 'Come through to the sitting room,' she said as she led them through the musty hallway into an unlit room. The clouds outside made it seem almost dark in the lounge. 'Please sit.'

The old lady left the room as they sat on the two-seater cottage suite settee. Gina took out her notebook. 'I hope I can see what I'm writing,' she muttered. Jacob grinned, and they listened in silence as rain began to tap at the bay window. Gina stood and looked out. She had a clear view to the end of the road. A few doors down, there was a small path that cut through the houses and led to the library. 'That could be the route he took. There's no CCTV along the back of town.

At night, it would've been dark and half of the street lamps are out of use due to lack of maintenance. If he – I'll refer to the perp as a he – he did come here, I'd say he knows his way around. You don't just stumble upon this road.'

'Let's see what she has to say first. This person passing may not have had anything to do with Baby Jenkins.'

'Maybe not.' Gina walked back over to the suite and sat next to Jacob.

Mrs McDonald returned with a tea tray and a plate of biscuits. She shuffled right up to them and placed the tray on the coffee table. 'Please help yourself to tea. I would do it for you but I'd probably cover you with it. My hands aren't too steady.' Her hearing aid whistled and she fiddled with it for a moment. 'Damn thing. Do you know, however many times I get this thing adjusted, it's never comfortable?'

'Mrs McDonald, would it be okay to turn on your light while we talk?'

The old lady peered over her glasses. 'I don't have a main light. My son is meant to fix it but he's been busy. If you just reach behind you, you'll be able to turn on the lamp.' Gina reached around the back of the sofa and felt for a cable. Her hand waded through an entanglement of what felt like cobwebs until she reached the switch, and then she could finally see the room in all its peach and pastel glory. The décor had been the height of fashion during the early nineties.

'That's much better.'

'I know. It is getting wetter,' Mrs McDonald replied. Gina looked at Jacob; he smiled and looked away.

'This tea is lovely, thank you,' he said as he took a bite out of a garibaldi.

'Mrs McDonald,' said Gina loudly, 'you called us with information relating to the appeal. Can you tell us what you saw on the evening of Friday the first of December?'

The old lady took a biscuit and bit into it. A smattering of crumbs fell into her lap. 'I remember that night because it was the night of the storm. The water was running down the roads and the drains were bubbling over.' She stopped talking and took another bite of her biscuit. Gina flinched as a plump black cat leaped from the dresser behind them into her lap. 'It's okay. He won't hurt you. He just wants a bit of fuss, don't you, Junior?'

Gina stroked the cat, but it jumped down and scurried off towards the kitchen. Gina glanced at her watch. She needed to be back soon for Hannah.

'Go on.'

'Where was I?'

'The roads and drains were bubbling over,' Jacob said as he stared at his notebook.

The old lady leaned forward and made eye contact. 'I was looking out the window for Junior, as I wanted to go to bed. As I stated on the phone, I don't know what time this was exactly, but it was between six thirty and eight, that's the best I can remember.' She cleared her throat. Gina took the opportunity to cough away the tickle in her throat at the same time.

'Between six thirty and eight on Friday the first of December?'

'That's right. I was looking for Junior. I've already told you that, haven't I?'

'It's okay, Mrs McDonald. Just tell us everything in your own words as they come to you,' Gina said with a smile.

'I was so worried about Junior. The rain, it was pelting. He doesn't like the rain. I also felt bad as he'd piddled on the floor earlier that day. I was angry and threw him out in the rain. You're not going to report me to the animal welfare people, are you?'

'Of course not, Mrs McDonald. We're just here to establish what you saw on that evening. I can see that Junior is very well cared for,' Gina replied.

The old lady began to pick at her crepe-like cuticles. 'The lights were off in the house and I hadn't got the television on. I'd been reading a book about local historical murders that my son got me last Christmas and I'd scared myself a bit. Anyway, I decided to go up to bed and watch telly but I needed to get the cat in first. I do that, go to bed early. It's how I keep warm. I stared out the window, thinking, where is my Junior? Will he ever come back? That's when I saw the man. He had the gait of a man anyway. A straight waist under a hooded dark jacket. The type the kids wear all the time. I tried to look at his face as he passed but I couldn't see a thing. He had a scarf wrapped around his mouth and he was soaking wet. I remember thinking, why would anyone be out on a night like this without a raincoat or umbrella, or indeed, even wellingtons? He just seemed out of place. Does that make sense?'

Gina checked her watch again, and nodded. Jacob continued to scribble in his pad. The cat meowed and ran back into the room.

'I think he's hungry. Will this take long?' she asked.

'It shouldn't take too much longer,' said Gina. 'If you'd like to continue. You were saying that this person passed by outside and was wearing a hooded jacket?'

The woman leaned down and grabbed the cat. It yelped and wriggled. She gripped him and placed him on her lap.

He immediately jumped back down. 'That was it really. He passed and turned into the cut-through, just down the path. The one that leads to the library.'

'When you called, you mentioned that this person was carrying something,' Jacob said.

'Yes. He had some sort of sports bag. He wasn't carrying it like a sports bag though, over the shoulder or with arms linked under the handles. He was cradling the bag and talking as he scurried past.' The woman looked up at the ceiling and shook her head. 'Was he the one who left that baby to die in the rain?'

The smattering of raindrops had now turned into hailstones that tapped on the windowpanes. 'We don't know that. We're just collecting witness statements at the moment, so that we can try to establish the facts of what happened that night. He may well have been the person who left the baby, or he may well have been doing something else. We need to identify and find him, to eliminate him from our enquiries.' Gina stepped back towards the window. 'Was he walking on this side of the path, right outside your window, or was he on the other side of the road?'

'The other side, until he reached the cut through, that is. He then crossed and disappeared down it. I gave up on looking for Junior and went to bed then. I did feel bad but what could I do? He was scratching at the back door the next morning though so all was fine. Would you like some more tea?'

Gina looked at her watch and shook her head. 'It's very kind of you to offer, Mrs McDonald, but we have to get back to the station.' Jacob nodded in agreement.

'It's lovely that you could come. If you need to come back to talk about anything else, I'm always in except on Monday between nine and ten thirty. You're always welcome.' Mrs McDonald's hands trembled as she stood and went to lift the tea tray.

'Here, let me take this for you,' Gina said, reaching for the tray.

'Thank you, dear. I tell you what, getting old is the worst thing ever. Enjoy your youth.'

Gina walked through to the pale blue kitchen and set the tray down on the worktop. The tap dripped, the wallpaper above the sink was peeling and fungus was growing around the window frame. The cat ran through and coiled himself around her ankles. She looked at her watch. Hannah would arrive at her house in just under an hour. She had to get back to the station, get the report to Briggs and get home.

Jacob was being led towards the door by Mrs McDonald. 'You've been very helpful. Thank you so much. Here's my card if you remember anything else in the meantime. Just call that number and ask for me.'

Gina joined them at the door. 'Thank you, Mrs McDonald. Don't forget to put your chain back on when we've left.'

'I won't. You never know who's knocking about.'

'You certainly don't,' Gina replied as they stepped into the hailstones. The woman hunched over as she closed the door. They watched as she entered the living room and turned the lamp off.

'I hope I'm never that alone,' Gina said.

Jacob looked back at her as they raced from the porch to the car. 'It's sad, so sad. There are so many Mrs McDonalds though.'

Total darkness had descended upon the road. Only three lamps were working. She hoped that Mrs McDonald's account was an accurate one, that she wasn't just a lonely woman, making things up. If true, she'd given them a useful start, and the fact that the suspect had been cradling a bag suggested highly unusual behaviour – behaviour consistent with someone who was carrying a baby in a bag.

Gina nervously checked the time again. She knew Hannah would let herself in with the key she'd given her, but would she wait? If she didn't wait, what then? Gina wondered if she would end up like Mrs McDonald one day. It would be easy to think badly of Mrs McDonald's son after that conversation, but had she let him down? Had he given up on her the way Hannah might eventually give up on Gina? Maybe there's more to the story. Maybe, like Gina, Mrs McDonald harboured a dark secret, one she could never share with her son. If she told Hannah the truth, she might not believe her. She might never speak to her again. But keeping the secret was pushing Hannah away too. Gina flashed back to the night of Terry's death, taking a swift intake of air as she relived the moment he tumbled down the stairs as baby Hannah cried in her cot.

'Let's hope we never become Mrs McDonald,' Gina replied as she turned away and wiped an errant tear from her cheek.

Jacob smiled. 'I've took some good notes in there. When we get back to the station, you could get your car and go straight home. I'm happy to get the report done before I leave. Go see your daughter, get in the bath or something and come back tomorrow feeling better.'

Gina coughed into her hand and returned his smile. 'You've made my evening. I think I might just do that,' she said. She might just make it home for Hannah.

CHAPTER TWENTY-ONE

She pulled onto her drive, next to Hannah's red hatchback, and saw that her lounge was brightly lit. Hannah had let herself in and was in the kitchen. Her heart pounded as she grabbed another tissue and blew her nose. She should've cancelled on the grounds of having an infectious illness, but she knew Hannah wouldn't believe her and things would sour between them even more. The car's fluorescent clock stared back at her. She was only ten minutes late. She wondered if Hannah had arrived early. She had a knack for doing that, and her earliness always made Gina's rushed lateness seem worse than it was.

Gina walked down the drive and peered through the window. Ebony pranced across the window ledge, holding her tail high as she spotted her owner. From outside, Gina watched as Hannah made a cup of tea and Gracie shuffled along the floor in a lilac romper suit. The toddler spotted Gina and began cooing. She couldn't hear the words but she could see as Gracie shuffled closer to her. The toddler stood, took several steps and then fell. Hannah ran to grab Gracie and spotted Gina. She glanced at her watch and frowned. 'Sorry,' Gina mouthed. She walked over to the front door and let herself in. 'Sorry I'm late. I was held up in an interv—'

'Don't tell me, Mum, I don't want to know. I've been here twenty minutes, bored out my tree. You could've texted or something.' She grabbed the toddler and walked back into the kitchen. 'It's freezing in this house. Gracie is cold. I didn't know how to turn on the heating.' She placed the toddler and a couple of plastic toys on the rug.

Gina bent down and flicked on a switch at the side of the gas fire. 'There we go.' The red and orange flames flickered and the room suddenly had a cosier feel. Gina switched on the lamp and turned the main light off. 'It should warm up in a minute. How's my little Gracie?' She kneeled down and stroked her soft fair baby hair.

'She doesn't know who you are.' Hannah grabbed her tea and closed the door to the lounge before sitting down.

'That's not true, is it, chicken?' Gina asked as she picked Gracie up and hugged her.

'Nannananna,' she shouted.

Gina smiled and looked up at Hannah. 'Of course she knows who her nana is. Don't you, Gracie?'

The wind howled outside. Ebony jumped off the window ledge and began competing for Gina's attention. Gina held Hannah in one arm and stroked Ebony with her free hand. The cat soon tired of the fuss and wandered out towards the kitchen. Hannah slurped her tea and placed the cup on the coffee table. 'We need to talk about things.'

It had to be about Terry and the bloody memorial service. She could see the seriousness on Hannah's face as she leaned forward and linked her hands together. 'Okay,' Gina replied as she bit her bottom lip.

'I've managed to save most of the money for Dad's service. It doesn't seem a lot, but with Gracie and all, I have three hundred pounds. I can get everything in, including a little buffet at the pub after, for six hundred. Mum, please give me the rest. He wasn't just my father, he was your husband. Don't you care? He's been gone twenty years. He'd be fifty this week.' Hannah looked away.

Gina's stomach dropped. The flickering of the fire seemed distorted and she felt a chill tickling her neck. Yes, Terry had been Hannah's father, in a biological sense. But they were talking about the same Terry who would probably have killed Gina had he still been alive; the man who subjected her to levels of brutality and control that people only experience in captivity, in a war zone. The last thing she wanted to do was remember him and the birthday he was missing out on. She reached for her chest, aware of each and every one of her bones, and flinched.

'Are you even listening to me?'

Gracie grabbed a strand of hair that had fallen over Gina's face and tugged. She teased the hair from the little girl's hand and turned away. 'I'll give it to you, all of it. Six hundred pounds, is it?'

'Thank you. That would really help me at the moment. I'd like a decent remembrance for him. I've invited Nanny Hetty and Uncle Steven and the rest of the clan. They miss him, you know. I would've asked them for the money but Uncle Steven hasn't worked for years with his bad back and Hetty is on a pension. Both of them have nothing. You have a good job—'

'Look. I think the service is a good idea but I can't be there. I'm sorry, Hannah, but I can't.' Gina felt a tear begin to seep from the corner of her eye. She couldn't go through all that with his family again. She wanted to scream, to tell Hannah that Terry's funeral had been one of the oddest days of her life.

She remembered how drunk she'd allowed herself to get during the wake, slowly celebrating his end and drowning her guilt with gallons of wine. No one could explain her odd behaviour that day. It hadn't stopped bloody Uncle Steven speculating though. She remembered hearing him whispering to another one of his knuckle-dragging relatives. He'd been spreading rumours that she'd been having an affair, that's why his Terry had to keep a close eye on her. If only that were the truth.

'You must really hate him,' Hannah said, her face reddening.

'It's not that.' Her body tensed up. Only once had she considered telling anyone about what had happened, but she never wanted to tell her daughter – grown up or not. After Hannah was born, he'd become so much worse. The supermarket had been one of the only places she was allowed to enter alone. There, she'd seen a stand collecting money for the local women's refuge. As she passed the money collectors on the way out, she'd hesitated. A woman stopped her and started to talk about the refuge. Gina remembered staring blankly at the woman, then thrusting a pound coin into her hand before scurrying off. The woman chased her out of the shop and pressed a card into her hand. Before she reached Terry's car at the back of the car park, she let the card slip out of her hand. If he'd caught her with that—

'There you go again, in your own little world, ignoring me. You can be so unreasonable sometimes. You don't want this, but what about me? He was my father.'

'I'm giving you the money, aren't I? I'll transfer it now.' Gina pulled her phone from her pocket. In a matter of seconds, she'd sent six hundred pounds to her daughter. 'Done.'

Hannah's face was pink with anger as she grabbed her ponytail and pulled it tight in the bobble. She grabbed Gracie from Gina's arms and proceeded with putting their coats on. 'I don't know what your problem is. We're off. Maybe you can come and see us, when you have time. Oh wait. I'm busy for the next month or maybe two – or three. That should make it easier to schedule an hour in.' Gina stood and helped Hannah feed Gracie's arm into her sleeve. Hannah stepped away. 'We manage fine without you. Oh, my job's going well too and Greg's had a promotion. It's nice of you to ask.'

'I was going to. Why don't you stay? I've got some ice cream. We could talk or put some cartoons on—'

'Another time, when you're not in such a weird mood,' Hannah said.

'Me in a mood? I have my reasons for not wanting to do the things you demand of me, you know.'

Hannah stopped what she was doing and stood in silence, her stare boring into Gina's eyes. 'Tell me then.'

Gina opened her mouth to speak but no words escaped. She sneezed and pulled a crumpled tissue from her pocket. She swallowed, aggravating her sandpapery throat.

'In that case, goodnight. And by the way, thanks for not letting on that you had a cold. You've probably given it to us now. And your milk's off. Wouldn't be surprised if I'm sick tonight.' Hannah grabbed her changing bag and left, slamming the door behind her. Gina fell onto the settee and hugged a cushion. Ebony jumped up onto her lap. She hugged the cat and cried into her fur. But even the cat soon tired of her and jumped back down, scurrying into the kitchen and out of the cat flap.

She booted up her laptop and watched it whirring into action. An email pinged up. Jacob had uploaded the report. She read it, trying to absorb all the information, trying to put herself into Mrs McDonald's mindset, trying to see it as she'd described.

Why couldn't she tell Hannah? It would make her behaviour so much clearer. Shame still hung over her head like a heavy sack, threatening to cut off her oxygen supply. DI Gina Harte had once been a nobody, had once allowed a man to treat her that way. All the yes, Terrys, no, Terrys, whatever you want Terrys. *It's okay that you've broken my ribs, Terry, because you love me. It was my fault.* She looked away. If she began to cry, her nose would be even stuffier than it already was. As she felt her ribs again, she thought of Debbie, out there somewhere – where? She grabbed her little laptop mouse and threw it at the fireplace. She knew what she'd gone through was nothing compared to Deborah's ordeal. She couldn't fail Debbie again. She'd failed four years ago. No more. She leaned across the floor and picked the mouse back up and placed it next to her laptop.

She walked through to the kitchen and grabbed the half bottle of red that was next to the sour milk in the fridge and began swigging from the bottle. Her phone beeped. Briggs had messaged.

'Wine bar?'

She needed to talk about anything, to anyone. Her stomach flipped as she called him back. He answered after a couple of rings. 'Gina.'

'I don't want to be alone tonight,' she replied, wiping her tear-stained face.

'Shall I bring the wine to you then?'

She could play his game too. She ended the call, knowing full well he'd turn up. What the hell was she doing? What were they doing? He was her DCI. She was lonely – no, she was slowly dying inside, being eaten up by the secrets that were invading her new life, secrets she'd tried to bury. She'd bury them tonight, at least, and worry about the consequences another day. She swigged the rest of the wine and stared at the window, waiting for Briggs to pull up, like some desperate schoolgirl hoping her date didn't let her down. Needy little Gina. Terry had summed her up well.

CHAPTER TWENTY-TWO

Monday, 4 December 2017

He closed his eyes and gave up fighting the overwhelming urge to sleep. If he had another nightmare then so be it. Luke took a deep breath and welcomed the images that came to him.

As he drifted off into deeper slumber, Debbie was soon lying next to him in bed. He rubbed his eyes to get a clearer view then he stared at her in awe as she slept soundly. Her soft hair tangled in his fingers and her lily-scented moisturiser delighted his nostrils.

In his dream, the light from the moon outlined the shape of her face. Isobel began to coo in the next room. Slowly he turned and rolled out of bed.

He left the room and entered total darkness. Isobel's cooing turned into screaming before hitting a piercing shriek. As he entered her room, he saw a beast. The huge shadow with red eyes bore deep into his mind. But it disappeared, gone in a flash. His heart pounded as he gazed at the crib. The crib was empty and hadn't even been slept in. The bawling continued to sound through his head. 'Isobel,' he called.

'Daddy,' said Max in a distorted voice. Luke ran and ran, from one room to the next, searching. His heart beat like it was going to explode from his chest.

'Debbie,' he called. 'Max.'

'Daddy,' the voice called back as it disappeared. Isobel shrieked louder. He ran faster. How had his house turned into a maze of dark concrete walls that all led to nowhere? Every turn he took led to another walled corridor. He ran until he reached his bedroom.

'Luke?' Debbie called. He ran and turned into his bedroom. The beast was upon her, suffocating her with his large body. Isobel was trying to feed from her breast, being crushed between the beast and his darling Debbie. The creature turned to him, fiery eyes glowing in the dark and rancid saliva dripping from its mouth, contaminating every part of Debbie. He watched as the beast enveloped his wife and they both disappeared, taking the suckling Isobel with them.

The latch on the back gate clicked back into place. Luke jolted up in bed, covered in sweat, his eyes wide open. His heartbeat was so erratic, he thought he might vomit. He turned on the lamp as he fought to get his breath back. Debbie wasn't next to him, she never was. He listened in the dark as someone walked across his garden slabs before stopping outside the back door. The handle rattled.

He leaped out of bed and ran to the window. He stared out and saw a dark figure trying to open the door. His heart continued to pound as he ran down the stairs and crept across the kitchen floor, trying to remain out of the intruder's sight. The figure was now on the other side of the windowpane. Luke wanted to turn on the light but he knew his eyes would be slow to adjust. He had to see who this person was. Maybe it had something to do with Debbie.

He remembered the man sitting on the wall the other day, watching him and Brooke from afar. Had that been a coincidence? Too many odd things were happening now. He slid open the kitchen drawer and snatched a bread knife. He'd never used a weapon before and had no idea what to do if it came to it, but he clenched it in front of his chest.

The intruder gave up on the window and walked back to the kitchen door. Luke watched as the hooded figure stepped back and grabbed the plant pot that sat by the side of the door. As the man leaned back to smash the pot into the window, Luke pressed his face against it and held up the knife. The figure dropped the pot with a loud crash and darted out of the garden before Luke managed to get a proper look at him.

Luke ran into the living room, knocking into the Christmas tree as he swerved towards the window. He watched as the intruder ran off into the darkness. He looked at the illuminated clock on the DVD player; it was just gone three in the morning.

He ran up the stairs into Heidi's bedroom. She lay there open-mouthed, sleeping soundly. Holding his chest and exhaling, he crept into Max's room and watched as Max stirred then went back to sleep.

He darted back into his bedroom. A few minutes before the intruder had disturbed him, he'd believed that Debbie was next to him. He'd touched her, smelled her, felt his heart burst with love as he'd stroked her hair. But he'd gone to bed alone and he had woken up alone, as he had done for years now. The dream had felt so real. He felt his eyes begin to tear up. He rolled over onto Debbie's side of the bed and hugged her pillow. 'I miss you, Debbie,' he whispered as he let his tears fall, slamming his fist into the pillow.

'Daddy?' Max walked into Luke's bedroom with one eye open, clutching a small blanket.

'Hello, little man. What are you doing up?' Luke wiped his tears away and forced a smile.

'I heard a funny noise. Were you running around the house?'

'Yes. It was nothing. I just had a bad dream.' Luke knew he had to call the police about the attempted break-in. 'Do you want to get into my bed for a bit?' He lifted his son's tired body onto the bed and placed him gently under the covers. He leaned across him and turned off the lamp before kissing him on the head.

'Love you, Daddy,' Max whispered. 'Where's Mummy's picture?'

Luke pulled open his bedside drawer and placed the photo back on the table. 'I just moved it when I was cleaning,' he said as he stared at Debbie's photo.

He'd tried so hard to find her, back then. All the searching and all the following of her friends and colleagues had yielded him with zero information. It had however yielded him with many a hangover. As the seasons had passed following her disappearance, the reward posters he'd left on all the local lampposts had become weathered, eventually falling off and flying away in the wind, along with her memory. Life went on. The news channels and papers stopped reporting about her and the children eventually found a new normality.

The world was moving on, but how could he ever do the same?

'Do you think Mummy's ever coming home?'

A tear fell down Luke's face. 'Of course she is.'

'I'm going to dream of Mummy. I like dreams of Mummy,' his son said as he snuggled into the quilt and closed his eyes.

Luke slid out of Debbie's side of the bed and crept downstairs. As he passed the lounge, he noticed that several Christmas baubles and a Christmas snowflake chain that the children had made out of coloured paper lay on the floor. He bent down, picked them up and hung them back on the tree. He went into the kitchen. The DI's card was on the side, exactly where he'd left it. He ran his fingers through his sweaty hair and called the number.

CHAPTER TWENTY-THREE

Briggs stirred as Gina grabbed a jumper and a pair of black trousers from her wardrobe. 'What time is it?'

'Early. Duty calls. Attempted break-in at the Jenkinses' household.' She grabbed his crumpled shirt off the floor and threw it towards his face.

He opened one eye and reached for his phone. 'Three-thirty?' He turned around and hugged the bent-up corner of his pillow. Ebony jumped on the bed and began pressing her paws into his back. 'Okay, I'm getting up,' he said as he gently shoved the cat off the bed.

As Gina zipped up her trousers, he reached over and started putting his shirt on. She almost heaved from the taste of sour wine that hung at the back of her throat. She dashed to the bathroom, splashed some water on her face and quickly brushed her teeth. Briggs followed, doing his trousers up as he stood beside her in the bathroom. 'Can I use your toothbrush?' he asked.

'No way. Use your finger.' He shook his head and swapped places with her and began washing. Sprinting down the stairs with Briggs close behind, she grabbed her car keys and coat before dashing out of the door. 'I'll see you back at the station as soon as I've checked out what's happening.'

Briggs leaned in to kiss her as he passed, heading for his own car, but she turned to avoid him. 'I'm sorry. This doesn't feel right.' Getting close to him was the last thing on her mind. Terry had been enough to put her off relationships for life, and then there was the question of how their fling would affect their working relationship.

'Have I upset you?' He stood beside his car, flattening his messy hair.

He hadn't done anything wrong. They'd had a good night. She'd had another glass of wine; he'd had a couple. He'd set her desire alight but she definitely wasn't in the market for a relationship, particularly not with her superior. Sex was one thing, but she'd let him sleep over. She should've asked him to leave afterwards. She looked back at him, wondering how to respond. There was something about him that definitely turned her on.

'Georgina?' He was awaiting her answer.

'Stop calling me Georgina,' she said, allowing a smile to escape. 'We have work to do... Chris.'

'You know, I can't work you out.'

'What's that supposed to mean?' She stood, holding her keys, awaiting his answer.

He smiled back, got in his car and drove off. Now she'd have to go all night and possibly all day wondering what he'd meant. What was so complicated to work out? He was a DCI, her DCI, and she worked directly under him. She could hear the gossip in her mind, going around the station. She started up her engine and turned the headlamps on. It was going to be another long day.

CHAPTER TWENTY-FOUR

Although the report was of a break-in, with all the strange occurrences happening with Luke Jenkins and his missing wife, she felt she had to be at the scene to interview him, to be first in finding out if there could be a connection between tonight's incident and Deborah being missing. As she drove through the damp night, she thought about Briggs and their fling. One positive was that he'd never resent her job if anything more came of the relationship. It was doubtful that Hannah would ever come around and understand what it meant to her. Maybe her daughter resented the fact that Gina needed more than family. Maybe they had become so distant due to Gina's lack of disclosure about past traumas. Or maybe Hannah's opinion of her was correct. Maybe she was a selfish cow who was always late and puts her family second. Maybes, lots of maybes.

She pulled up outside the Jenkins residence and spotted PC Smith's car. The living room light was on. Luke opened the door wearing his dressing gown, T-shirt and pyjama bottoms.

Heidi stood at the top of the stairs in a Disney princess nightie. 'Dad, what's happening?'

'Go back to bed, sweetie, or you'll wake Max. I'll come up in a minute.' Luke smiled warmly at his daughter.

The girl rubbed her eyes. 'Can I sleep in your bed?'

'Yes, sweetie. Max is already there so please don't disturb him. And turn the landing light off.' The light went off as Heidi left. 'Kids,' Luke said as he massaged his temples. Gina followed Luke through to the kitchen, where Smith was taking a few notes. 'This is where he tried to get in.' A knife lay on the worktop. 'I was scared so I grabbed it. I didn't know what else to do. Can I get you a coffee?'

'That would be lovely, thank you,' Gina replied. She'd not had a drink since the night before and a coffee would certainly perk her up. Although she'd brushed her teeth, the distant taste of wine still assaulted the back of her throat, making her nauseous. She coughed into her hand. Luke turned away and began filling the kettle.

'So, what have we got?' she asked Smith.

'Nice to see you, ma'am.' He paused. 'Do you think this has something to do with Deborah Jenkins?' he whispered as Luke's back was turned. The kettle boiled away.

'I don't know, but we certainly can't rule it out.'

Luke poured the coffee and handed it to her. 'Are you okay while I check on the kids?'

Gina nodded as he left the room. She listened as he walked up the stairs. 'Have you called forensics? I want the gate checked, the garden, the handles – every part of it.'

'They're on their way. I've managed to take an account of what happened.'

'Can you give me an overview?'

Smith flicked back a couple of pages in his pocketbook and began squinting at his writing. 'My mum says I should've been a doctor,' he said. Gina had heard that one before. 'Right, at approximately 3 a.m. he was awoken by the sound of the latch being slid on his gate. It is apparently a little stiff and screeches as it's slid across.' Smith slid an imaginary lock before continuing. 'It was at this point he looked out of the window and came downstairs. He said he left the light off so that he'd be able to see what was happening in the garden.'

'Sensible,' Gina replied.

Smith turned the page in his notebook. 'It was then he saw someone trying to open the kitchen window before heading to the back door. He was standing there.' He pointed to the kitchen door. 'He saw a person he described as male, wearing dark attire which included a hooded top. He couldn't make out hair or eye colour. He said he thought the man seemed slightly taller than himself so I'm guessing five ten, eleven maybe. There's also a small step down into the garden, so we have to take that into account also. It was at this point Luke grabbed a knife out of the top drawer. Oh, and the man was wearing gloves.'

Smith walked over to the door. 'The perp approached the back door and tried to get in. After failing, as the door was locked, Mr Jenkins stated that the man then grabbed the plant pot that was positioned to the left of the door and was about to hurl it through the window. Mr Jenkins then came into view and held the knife up and stood close to the window. The perp scarpered out of the back gate. Mr Jenkins ran to the lounge and noticed him running across the road and down the street, towards the entrance to the close.'

'That's great. Thanks. I'll have a quick word with him in a minute. When you have the report typed up, can you email me straight away?'

'Will do, ma'am,' he said, scribbling in his notepad.

Gina coughed again and her nose began to run. She grabbed a piece of kitchen roll from the side and caught her sneeze.

'You still sporting that cold, ma'am?'

'Certainly am. I think it's easing a little though now.'

Then came the sound of Luke walking back down the stairs. He entered and poured a coffee. 'Can I get either of you anymore?' They both shook their heads.

'Can we just have a chat?' said Gina. 'I've just been updated by PC Smith, so I have the initial report. We've got a crime scene investigator on their way also.'

'Yes. Please come through.' Luke led her to the lounge. The Christmas tree looked a little off balance. 'I nearly knocked the damn thing over when I was trying to catch sight of him running off.'

The lounge was strewn with toy trucks and colouring books. Most of them had been pushed into a neat pile but some remained scattered on the floor. Gina stepped over a box of felt tips and sat on the settee. Pen and notebook in hand, she began. 'You say you got a look at the man?'

'Yes. I saw him, but I seem to barely be able to recall a thing. It was dark and although my eyes were accustomed to it, I remember feeling shaken, sick to my stomach. In fact, I could throw up now if I thought too hard about it. My hands were trembling and I remember hoping to scare him off with the knife. I couldn't look him in the eye. I just wanted him to go away.' Gina watched as Luke clutched the coffee cup with both hands and began to, very slightly, rock back and forth. 'My children were upstairs asleep. I was scared for them. I just wanted him to go. I held the knife up at the window and he went. I wish I could remember more.'

'I understand. It's not easy, I know that much. Especially being in your position, with a strange man trying to get into your home in the night, with your children upstairs.'

Luke stared into his lap. 'I can't cope with all of this. I don't know what I'm going to do,' he said, and burst into tears. His hands began to tremble and his coffee lapped over the edge of the cup. Gina took it from him and placed in on the hearth, catching a glimpse of the photo of Deborah.

'Something strange happened the other day,' he said. 'I thought nothing of it until tonight. It probably has nothing to do with what happened, but it might also have everything to do with it. I'm rambling, I have no idea, but I think it's the same man.' He picked up his coffee again and took a long swig.

'What happened, Mr Jenkins?'

The man wiped his eyes and walked towards the bay window. 'Yesterday morning, about eleven, I was standing here, looking out of the window, and there was a man sitting on the wall, over there. That's number fifteen.' He pointed. As Gina walked over, she made a note of the house number. 'He was just staring at me. It only lasted a few seconds and then he walked off. He was wearing a dark hoodie. The hood was up. I can't recall anything about his features. He was a fair way off, as you can see.'

'You're doing really well,' said Gina, quickly taking notes.

'I can't believe so much has happened since then.' He sat on the window ledge and began to cry. 'I was here with Brooke, a friend. We've become close and I don't know what to do. What does a person do in this situation? My missing, presumed dead wife has been gone for four years. Only now do I allow myself to move on. I meet someone I really like and just as we're getting close, my missing wife's baby turns up – without my wife. The woman I'm involved with has no idea. I have to tell her. Very soon, I have to explain to my kids that they have a new sister. What do I do?'

Gina stared at the wall. She wished she could wave a magic wand and make things better for the people she came across who were suffering, but she couldn't. The world wasn't a good place. It wasn't all roses, cake, parties and nice things. It was a dark place, a place that she'd yet to fathom. Luke sat there, rubbing his eyes, broken. 'I'm so sorry for everything that has happened to you. You can rest assured that I'm doing all I can. Is there anywhere else you can stay for a while?'

Luke sniffed. 'I think I'll send the kids to my mother-in-law's tonight. I don't feel it's safe for them here and it'll give me time to think.'

'That's probably wise,' Gina replied. In a normal case of attempted burglary, she'd have thought it unnecessary, but they both knew this was different. She watched as a van pulled up. The crime scene investigator had arrived.

'I'd best let them in,' Luke said as he walked to the door. Gina went back into the kitchen. She made a mental note to arrange for Luke to attend the station to give a DNA sample as soon as possible. His involvement wasn't likely, but they still had to officially eliminate him.

'I'm finished here, ma'am,' said Smith. 'Good thing is, no one has been in the garden since the incident so let's hope our unwelcome visitor has left something behind.'

'I'm not holding my breath. He was wearing gloves and a hooded top, and it's drizzly and blowing a gale out there. You never know though. Can you stop by at number fifteen across the road in a while and ask if they saw a man sitting on their wall yesterday morning? It was around eleven. This man matches the clothing description that has been given to us tonight.'

'Will do.' Smith placed his notebook in his pocket.

'I'm going to head back to the station for an hour then I'm going home for a shower.

Gina yawned and walked towards the door. As she stepped out into the cold, she nodded at Dr Freeman as he hobbled along the path. 'You look tired, Keith.' A strand of his combed-over hair flapped in the wind.

'My back's been playing up, been keeping me up all night. I'd just dozed off and the phone went.'

'I'm sorry to hear that. Anyway, we've spoken to Mr Jenkins. The perp tried to get in through the back door after gaining entry through the back gate and no one has been in the garden since. The perp was wearing gloves and a hoodie so I'm not expecting much, but you never know. Can you call me when you're finished here?'

He nodded back as he passed her with his toolbox. 'Will do.'

'Thanks,' she called as she reached her car.

CHAPTER TWENTY-FIVE

She heard a dog barking in the distance. He was back. She went to turn but flinched. The pain from her tear burned and throbbed. She hoped he'd stay at the house with his mother but she heard his footsteps approaching. The key turned in the lock and he entered. She listened as he stomped up the stairs.

'He was looking, he had a knife, that bastard had a knife and he'd have used it,' he yelled as he slammed his hand into the door she lay behind. She remained as still as she could. She had to look like she was sleeping, that way he might just talk to himself for a couple of minutes then leave.

He unlocked the door and a shaft of light entered her cell. The oil lamp flickered and lit up the room, casting elongated, moving shadows over the walls. The last shape looked just like a rabbit. She'd played puppet shadows with both of her children. She closed her eyes and tried to think back to better times. If she thought hard enough and looked like she was asleep, he might go. She swallowed. He stopped still. Had he heard her? 'What to do, what to do,' he whispered, beginning to pace, taking the lamp with him. Through closed lids she could see the light flickering. *The shapes, concentrate on the shapes*, she thought.

The first shape was a circle, what could it be? The circle disappeared off into the distance before being replaced with another circle. The sun, she was looking at the sun. Heidi would've agreed. Max didn't like doing shadow puppets, preferring colouring or generally making a mess.

He stopped pacing; she kept her eyes closed. All she could see was red through her eyelids. He was close. She felt the warmth of the lamp on her back. She needed to swallow and gasp for breath but she forced herself to breathe in and out, in and out. She couldn't show him that she was awake.

He took a few steps back. She heard him place the lamp down on the worktop outside her room. She exhaled and opened her eyes, then watched as his shadow almost filled the wall. She held her breath and closed her eyes again.

'I don't know what to do. What do I do?'

She ignored him and remained still.

He pulled back the quilt. She shivered as a cold draft went up her back. His cold hand rubbed her neck. She remained still. The pain in her groin and lower stomach was making her feel like heaving. He sat beside her and began stroking her back with both hands before lying next to her. He dragged the blankets over his body, spooning her. His warm breath made her shiver. A tear rolled down her cheek. *Not now*, she thought, *please not now*.

Tears flooded her face and her nose began to fill. She couldn't stop the sniffling that came with it. 'Boo.' She flinched and sobbed. 'I knew you were awake.'

'Please, I'm tired and not feeling well.'

'What harm do you think I'm going to bring? For heaven's sake,' he yelled, abruptly getting out of the bed. 'I need to talk. I need some love and comfort. I'm always looking after you, but where are you when I need you?'

She turned and sat up. 'I'm sorry.' She wiped her tears away. At least he'd moved away from her. 'What do you need to talk about?'

'I went to the house.' Debbie shivered. 'I just wanted to know if Florence was there, by God I'll kill him if she ever is. He's not having my Florence. That bastard threatened me with a knife.'

Debbie imagined Luke being disturbed in the middle of the night. Were her children scared? Luke had seen him off. She wanted to smile but she held back. She imagined Luke there with a knife, standing in front of him. She then imagined Luke pressing the knife into his flesh and twisting it until the life drained from his body, but that's not what had happened. Her kidnapper was standing in front of her, looking shaken but well. He removed his black hooded top and dropped it on the floor outside her room. Sweat trickled down his face and his hair was stuck to his forehead.

'Was she there? The baby?' Debbie almost regretted asking. He could answer or he could question her motives for asking. He stared at her before walking over and sitting on the bed.

'I couldn't hear her crying. Maybe she's still at the hospital. I can't go there again.' He paused. 'That man can't have my Florence. I swear—' He punched the bed and roared.

Debbie closed her eyes and tried not to weep. She had no idea where her little one would end up, but there was a possibility it would be with Luke. The thought of him going to her house, scaring her children and attacking her husband was too much. Once again, tears flooded her face. 'Luke won't have her. I promise. My mother will have her. She's not his baby, she's our baby. Can we please leave Luke alone now and get on with our lives, our plans?'

He stroked her hair and wiped away her tears before leaning down and kissing her on the head. 'I will do anything you want, but I'll snap his neck before he ever gets his hands on my child, my Florence.' He lay on the bed and put his arm around her. 'I'd do anything for you.' He kissed her again.

Anything? She wanted to be unchained, she wanted to be set free, she wanted to go home and she wanted to be out of pain. She whimpered as she turned away and faced the wall. He rested next to her.

'I've never felt like this about anyone before. Love is a funny thing, makes a person happy. Happiness is everything, isn't it?' he whispered in her ear.

She moved her hand to her lower stomach and tried to squeeze the pain away, but it made it worse. She bit her bottom lip in a poor attempt to force her sobs back.

'Are you happy?'

Debbie swallowed the mucus in her throat. 'I'm happy,' she replied.

'Do you love me?'

'I love you.'

'How much do you love me?'

'I love you a lot.'

He sat up and inhaled. 'But I need to hear how much. If you don't tell me, how will I know?'

'I love you more than the earth, the skies and the planets,' she replied. That was his preferred response, the one that had helped her in the past.

'Good.' He lay back down. 'I need to be reassured. Things are hard at the moment, with the baby and all. It's hard for you, too, but you have no idea how bad it is for me. You only have yourself to think about all day. I have Mother and she's getting worse.'

'I'm sorry about your mother. Maybe I can help you look after her?' She hoped that he'd take her up on the offer, but he hadn't ever taken her up on any of her offers to date.

'No, you're a princess and you shouldn't have to work hard. I will do everything and look after you too. It's my job, my destiny, my one passion in life.'

'But I'd like to help.'

'I said no.' He reached over and squeezed her throat then let go. As she coughed and wheezed, he sucked air in through his teeth and clenched his fist.

'I'm sorry,' said Debbie. 'I'm sorry.'

'Okay,' he replied. 'Don't ask again.'

She faced into the pillow with him lying behind her. She moved her ankle and heard the chain rattle on the floor. There was no way out. She'd tried to talk herself out in every way possible, she'd tried to run and she'd tried violence. Nothing she'd tried had worked out. Deep down, she knew there was no escape. But she also knew that by day he had a job and a normal life where he interacted with people who knew her. They had no idea what lay behind the mask he wore every day. Her only dream was that he'd one day take off that mask and reveal his true self to just one person who would help her.

He squeezed her from behind and kissed her neck. 'I have to tend to Mother now. The old dear always seems to be searching for bread as soon as the sun comes up. I haven't got long until I have to make the breakfast. Honey with your toast?' She nodded. Refusal wasn't an option. She let out a long breath as he loosened his embrace. He left, locking the door behind him, and she listened until his footsteps disappeared. The dog barked as he reached the house.

Darkness and solitude were her greatest fears and enemies, but at times like this, they were also her friends. She was now alone to dream.

She thought back to when she'd held her little one after giving birth. It had been only three days ago, but the image of her baby's perfect little face was beginning to fade. The only thing that had any substance in her mind was the birthmark on her leg. Her baby's memory had been reduced to a birthmark.

She cried as she tried to recall Isobel's exact features. The images weren't coming to her. Was that it? Was that the end? Her stomach clenched as she turned and sat up. The burning heat had spread from her perineum to surrounding areas. She smelled her hands. A sweaty, oily scent assaulted her nostrils. She wiped them in her tears, then on the bottom of the quilt. She wanted to be clean, she wanted to rid his smell from her body and she wanted to go home.

But where was home? Luke had replaced her. She had no home; she had nothing. She needed her mother. She stared into the darkness. 'I miss you, Mum.'

CHAPTER TWENTY-SIX

Luke yawned as he prepared the kids' lunches. He chopped Max's cheese sandwiches into squares and Heidi's strawberry jam sandwiches into triangles, and placed them in their respective lunch boxes. He'd decided against packing the children up and sending them to Cathy's after the attempted break-in. One look at his two children sleeping soundly in his bed had changed his mind.

He glanced at the time. Brooke would arrive in less than ten minutes. His heart quickened and his mouth was dry. He ran the tap and poured a glass of water. He'd texted her the previous evening to tell her to still come around in the morning so that they could walk together as they usually did, but he'd made it clear they needed to talk. He'd given her no clue as to what was happening in his life. The last she'd remember was their near sexual encounter and him being frosty with her since. He wished his life were simpler. He took a swig of water.

The door knocked. He opened it to see Cathy on the step. 'Max left his PE kit at mine. I knew he needed it for today. I've washed it.' She smiled. Luke moved to one side and let her in. She reached over and hugged him.

'I don't know how I'm going to get through today. Brooke is due soon.' He felt a tear squeeze out of the corner of his eye as she stroked his hair and pulled away.

'You have to be honest with her, Luke. Let her know what's happening. You'll get through this. We'll do this together.'

'I know I do, and I will. Can you walk the kids to school? Joe too?' He couldn't face the school run today. He knew that Cathy was also going through a lot, but he couldn't go to the school and he didn't want to mention the intruder and upset her further.

She nodded. 'Of course I will. When I've walked them, I'll come back and we'll have a chat and a cuppa. I suppose we need to start thinking about things.'

'You mean the baby?' he asked as he walked back into the kitchen.

'Yes, I called up the social worker, Devina, to arrange a home visit, as we discussed. I thought maybe here would be a good place to start.'

Luke stared blankly out of the window.

Max stomped down the stairs. 'Dad, I can't find my PE kit.'

'It's okay. Nanny has it here. Just go and brush your teeth. And tell your sister to hurry up. You have five minutes then I need you guys downstairs and ready to go.'

Cathy held her head. 'Anyway, we'll talk about the baby and other things. We're close to finding out what happened to Debbie, I'm sure of it, but I'm scared. What if some monster has her in his home, trapped? It keeps going through my mind. She's still my baby, Luke.' She tried to hold back her tears.

Luke placed his arm around her. 'And I still love her. I want her back more than anything.' Silence fell upon the pair as they stared out of the kitchen window. There was a slight frost on the back lawn. He couldn't keep the news of the intruder from her any longer. 'I didn't call you, but we had an attempted break-in last night.'

Cathy pulled back and blew her nose. 'What? You should've called me.'

'There's nothing you could've done. I was going to bring the kids round to yours in the night but they were tired and I didn't want to alarm them.'

'I know, but I could've been here, for you and the kids,' she replied.

'It's okay. I called the police. Forensics came. He didn't get in anyway. I think I scared him with the kitchen knife.' Luke filled the kettle and switched it on. 'So I have a lot to sort out today.'

'Are the kids okay?'

'They aren't really aware of what happened. They were disturbed by the police being in the house but they were easily placated when I let them have my bed, hence why I'm so tired this morning. Sleeping in Max's car bed for the last couple of hours wasn't the best move.' He yawned and spooned a couple of heaps of coffee into a mug. 'Quick cuppa?'

Cathy looked at her watch. 'No, I'll have to leave in a couple of minutes. I'll have it when I get back.'

'Daddy, Heidi won't let me in the bathroom to brush my teeth!' Max yelled from the top of the stairs.

Luke took a sip of the hot coffee. 'Every morning, same story,' he said with a smile as he walked into the hall. 'Heidi? Out of the bathroom now and get downstairs.'

'But Dad,' was the muffled reply.

'Don't "but Dad" me. Downstairs now.'

There was a knock at the door and he opened it to see Brooke, looking at him nervously. She tucked her hair behind her ears. He noticed the bags under her eyes and the lack of make-up.

Joe ran into the house and up the stairs, shouting for Max.

'I'm so sorry I haven't called. Do you mind if Cathy walks Joe to school with Max and Heidi this morning? I need to talk to you.' She shook her head and stepped into the hall.

'Morning, dear,' Cathy called.

'Morning, Cathy,' she called back. Brooke hesitated in the hallway. He could tell she didn't know where to stand or what to do. She began to bite her nails.

'Do you want to sit for a few minutes?'

She nodded and went into the lounge.

The phone rang, and Cathy answered it in the kitchen. 'Hello?' She paused. 'What?' She paused again. 'Maybe so, but this is just ridiculous.' She looked down the hallway at Luke. 'I'll tell him.' She placed the handset down.

'What is it?'

'The police. They want you to give them a DNA sample this morning. Asked if you could pop in as soon as possible.'

'What the hell for?'

'It's just for elimination purposes, they said.' She passed him his coffee from the worktop.

'I bet they think I've done something to Debbie. Maybe they think I have her in the shed or something. Maybe they think I'm making all this up.'

He heard a thunderous stampede coming down the stairs. 'We're ready!' shouted Max. The three children stood in the doorway of the kitchen.

'What's wrong, Dad?' Heidi asked.

'Nothing, sweetheart. I'll see you after school.'

'Come on then, you lot. Let's get going,' Cathy shouted. They ran to the door, laughing and shouting as they left the house. 'See you in a bit,' said Cathy, following them out.

Luke leaned against the countertop. They wanted him to go to the station and do a DNA test. It was just to eliminate him, he knew that, but he couldn't help but feel like a suspect. He'd been questioned previously about the night Debbie disappeared, but he had an alibi. He'd been walking a client around a house several miles from where Debbie had vanished. So why were they putting him through this? Perhaps they thought he was in on her disappearance with someone else. His hands began to tremble the more he thought about all that was happening.

'Luke? I don't know what's going on, but—' Brooke crept through the door, startling him. He dropped the cup, spilling coffee all over the floor. 'Oh God. What is it? Is it me?'

He shook his head. 'No.'

'The other day, I thought the time was right, but I've been thinking. Maybe you're not ready to—'

'It's not just that,' he said, as he began to shake and then burst into tears. She hurried over and hugged him.

'What is it? I'm sure it can't be that bad.'

'I don't know whether it's bad or good, Brooke, I really don't,' he wailed as he stepped back onto the broken cup, cutting his heel. 'Bloody hell. Can things get any more complicated?' he said as he grabbed a tea towel. He stumbled back onto a kitchen chair and began to wipe the blood from his foot. 'I can't dress up what's happened.'

'Then don't,' she replied as she sat beside him.

'You know the abandoned baby that they found? Did you read about it or hear anything?'

She nodded. 'The one at the library?'

'Yes. It's Debbie's. The police have confirmed it. She's alive and she's just given birth. I don't know where that leaves us. I don't know where that leaves me, and just to top it all off, the police investigating have called me in for a DNA test this morning.'

He watched as she looked away. Her lip quivered as she wiped a tear from her cheek. There was nothing he could do to quell her pain. He'd felt something with Brooke, a genuine connection.

'Where does that leave us?' she asked. 'I mean, I know you weren't ready, but I thought we had something.'

He sobbed and rubbed his foot. 'I'm sorry. I'm just so confused.'

She leaned down and picked up the pieces of cup that were strewn on the floor. She grabbed the kitchen roll and began mopping up. 'We've been friends for a long time now, haven't we?' He nodded. 'I'm here for you. I'll help you with the kids. If they want to come to mine to stay or for tea, like always, they're still welcome. If you want to talk, that's also fine.' Brooke looked to one side and wiped her eyes on her sleeve. 'What I'm trying to say, damn it, is that I don't want to lose your friendship. Nothing really happened and I... I really like you.'

'I'm sorry.' He stood and hugged her. He had no idea what the future held, or if Debbie was going to be found, but he did know he needed time to digest all that was happening. 'I have to go and get ready for this DNA test now,' he said as he hobbled across the floor, hoping that she'd leave him to think. He'd get the DNA test done, the quicker the better, then they could start looking for real suspects – like the intruder in the hoodie, the man who'd been watching him.

'Shall I come with you?'

'No. I want to be alone.'

Brooke's cheeks were soaked with tears. 'Well, you know where I am.' She snatched her bag off the table and left. He smacked the door with the flat of his hand and continued to hobble towards the stairs, wondering where his life was going.

CHAPTER TWENTY-SEVEN

Gina crossed the car park and thought about the night before. Briggs was good company when he wanted to be. They'd laughed, chatted about the case, then they'd enjoyed each other's bodies until they were spent. She inhaled the fresh smell of coconut conditioner coming from her hair. She certainly felt more human after popping home for a shower and a piece of toast. As she grabbed the door, Jacob stepped out, almost knocking her over.

'In a hurry?' she asked.

'Thank you so much for my lovely cold,' he said, sneezing a load of mucus into his hand. 'Feeling well? You look well. In fact, you look better that you have done in days.'

'I'm on top of the world,' she replied with a smile. Jacob stuck his tongue out. 'Bleugh, thanks for infecting me.'

Gina passed him a tissue and laughed at his sullen face, contorted intentionally into a grimace. 'You know, Driscoll, you could win a gurning competition with that face.'

Briggs, who had just pulled into the car park, stepped out of his car. 'Morning, sir,' Jacob croaked as he wiped his red nose.

'Sir,' Gina muttered as she looked away.

He grabbed his briefcase from the passenger seat and stomped towards the pair. He glared at Jacob's runny nose. 'Not you too.'

'Afraid so, sir.'

Briggs took three large steps back from Jacob. 'See this distance. I want you to stay at least this far away from me all day. Do you hear?'

'Yes, sir,' Jacob replied.

Gina almost wanted to laugh. He hadn't kept her at a distance, even though she was nursing the same cold.

'He can be a tosser sometimes,' Jacob said.

'What? Because he doesn't want your cold?'

'I didn't want your cold either, but shit happens.' A couple of raindrops landed on Jacob's face. 'I'll see you in there. I'm just going to grab some painkillers from my glovebox.' Driscoll ran towards his car.

'Morning,' the desk sergeant, Nick, called as she entered the office. She smiled and checked her watch. It was almost nine. Luke would arrive at the station for the swab she'd ordered in about half an hour. She had just enough time to catch up. First, though, she needed approval to take the swab from Luke. Briggs was monitoring every cost that passed through the station. She raced to her office and booted her computer up. As soon as it came on, she printed out the paperwork pertaining to the sample. She passed the incident room, and saw that Jacob had updated the board with details of the attempted break-in from the notes that she'd uploaded. She knocked on Briggs's door.

'Come in,' he called.

'Are you okay? You look a little tired, if you don't mind me saying.'

'I got woken up abruptly in the night.' She smiled at him, and he looked at his computer. 'Right, why are you here?

Have you solved the case? Got me some good news to report to the powers above?'

She shook her head and held out the paperwork. 'I wish. As you know, we need to eliminate Luke Jenkins. We've asked him to come in for a DNA swab. He's due in a few minutes.'

'And you want me to sign off?'

'Yes.'

He took the paperwork and scanned over it before signing the bottom of the page. 'I don't think for one minute this will come up with anything, but I suppose we have to be seen to be doing things right. I've read the notes on the attempted break-in last night. We need to get to the bottom of this as soon as.'

'Mr Jenkins also mentioned that he'd seen someone watching him, sitting on the wall at the entrance to the close. Too much of a coincidence?'

'Definitely.' Briggs began to chew the end of his pen.

'Timings of Deborah's baby being found and all this happening?'

'Definitely too much of a coincidence.' He threw his pen on his desk. 'I enjoyed last night.'

She smiled, grabbed the form and closed the door. As she headed towards the interview room, she grabbed a swab pack and a pair of blue medical gloves. She got on well with Briggs, but a relationship in the conventional sense wasn't going to happen. Though she didn't even know if that's what he wanted.

Her thoughts leaped back to Terry and the night he had been pronounced dead in their home. The night she had been liberated, finally able to live the life she wanted. People still extended their sympathy when they'd heard that she was a widow, but she'd never wanted it, never asked for it and was certain that she didn't deserve even an ounce of it. She took a deep breath and tried to shove Terry from her mind. Free from abuse, but never free from his memory.

She approached the interview room. Wyre was standing outside. Her black suit was beautifully tailored and her posture was perfect. Gina barely had time to shower and eat properly. *The woman mustn't sleep*, Gina thought. 'Here to assist?'

Wyre nodded and held up a swab pack, smiling when she saw that Gina held one too. 'Great minds and all that, ma'am.'

The desk sergeant called her over. 'Mr Jenkins has arrived.'

'Thanks, Nick,' she replied, as she waved Luke over. 'Thanks for coming. Sorry to spring this on you.' The tired-looking man hobbled beside her. 'Are you okay? I don't suppose you got much sleep after last night.' She noticed that his suit looked a little creased and he hadn't shaven.

He rubbed his eyes. 'I trod on a broken cup.'

'Sounds painful.'

'Look. Why am I here? It's obvious that the baby isn't mine.' He sighed as they reached the entrance to the interview room.

Wyre held the door open. 'Please take a seat, Mr Jenkins. As you know, we have procedures to follow and this will be totally painless.'

He scraped the chair across the floor, sat and folded his arms. 'I'm meant to be at work. What am I meant to tell my employer?'

'Shall I contact them for you?' Wyre asked. 'I can tell them that your house was broken into last night and you're here giving a statement.'

'Thanks, but I'll be fine. This just seems ridiculous, a bit over the top, that's all.'

'Mr Jenkins, we have to do this as a process of elimination. May I just remind you that you are not under arrest and you are here voluntarily? What you are doing is helping with your wife's case, so thank you so much for coming. This will only take a moment and won't cause you any discomfort at all.'

He unfolded his arms and sat up straight. 'I know. I guess I'm just feeling a bit uptight. It's not every day that a man whose wife has been missing for years ends up being the mother of an abandoned baby. It's not every day some weirdo stares through your window and it's not every day you come face to face with an intruder in the middle of the night. I'm sorry, but nothing in life has ever served to prepare me for this. I just want you to do your job and find my wife.'

'I understand,' said Gina. 'I can't imagine being where you are, Mr Jenkins. Really, I can't. But we're doing this for Mrs Jenkins, for Deborah.'

'I know. I'm sorry.'

'You have nothing to apologise for. Right, let's get this done.'

Wyre slipped the blue gloves on and ripped the packet open. 'Can you open your mouth, please, Mr Jenkins?' He leaned back and did as she requested. She rubbed the swab against the inside of Luke's cheek before removing it and dropping the head from the stick into the sealed tube. She did the same with a second swab then placed them into an evidence bag. She sealed the envelope, removed her gloves and completed the details on the front of the bag as well as those on the form.

'Thank you, Mr Jenkins. All done,' Wyre said as Gina leaned over and countersigned the envelope. 'I'll just go and drop this off. Do you need me for anything else?'

Gina shook her head and smiled as Wyre left.

Luke began biting the skin on his lip. 'What happens now?'

'You can go to work and we'll be in touch. Obviously, if you see, remember or hear anything, you have my number. We've set up an incident room for the case. We're working flat out as hard as we can on finding your wife.'

'Thank you, and I do appreciate what you're all doing.' Luke flinched as he stood. 'Bloody foot. Literally, bloody foot.' He let out a short burst of laughter then bit his lip again. 'I suppose I'll be off then.' As he reached the door, he paused. 'Please do everything you can. I mean everything. My children would love nothing more than to have their mother back. I would love nothing more than to have my wife back.'

'I promise you I'll do everything I can,' she replied as she followed him out. Nick was putting up some new posters aiming to deter people from being tempted to drink and drive over the festive period. 'Bye, Mr Jenkins. I'll keep you updated.' He didn't turn around. He hobbled towards the car park and vanished out of view.

Gina walked to the window and watched as he stepped into his car and drove off. It was only morning, but she'd have sworn that it was about four in the afternoon. It was as if daylight had barely broken for days. She watched as a few heavy raindrops plopped into the large puddle gathered in the pothole in their car park.

'Mince pie?' Nick asked.

'Working here is making me fat,' she replied as she took one.

'Nonsense. They're good for you. They've got fruit in them – one of your five a day.' He put another poster up, highlighting the number to call for reports of female genital mutilation. Gina took a bite of the pie and left him to it.

She wandered through reception and back to her office. She picked up the file of the investigation four years ago. A photo of the woman found in the river dropped onto her desk. She stared at the waxy face with the crooked nose then looked away. She and Driscoll would start by re-interviewing the staff at the Angel Arms in Cleevesford. Maybe, just maybe, someone might be able to add to her notes. She read over the dog-eared pages and spotted some names she recognised. She had originally interviewed the four members of staff that were there at the time. She remembered smarmy Samuel Avery and the other members of staff: Jeff Wall, Ally Perrins and Charlene Lynch.

She picked up the phone and pressed Wyre's extension. 'Can you and O'Connor track down Deborah Jenkins' friends who played pool with her at the pub? Also, give Lynne Hastings at Avant Conservatories Limited a heads-up. Let them know we'll be coming in tomorrow to discuss Deborah Jenkins and we're likely to be there a while. Ask if we can use their boardroom.' Wyre acknowledged her request and ended the call.

She finished off the rest of the mince pie and flung the case in the bin. It tasted of Christmas. All the decorations were up in the town but she didn't feel very Christmassy yet. Mince pies were a start, but so were the drink drivers and antisocial behaviour offenders, and the general traffic through the station. Welcome to the festive season.

She placed all the case notes back in the file and grabbed her coat. The ticking of the clock in her office pierced her thoughts. They'd get down to the pub at twelve, bang on opening time. If Deborah's abductor was someone they'd already spoken to, she was determined they wouldn't fool them this time.

CHAPTER TWENTY-EIGHT

They pulled up outside the drab village pub. The paintwork was crumbling and smashed glass had been swept against the wall. Gina stepped out and headed towards the main door, stepping over a pile of vomit as she entered. 'Nice way to great the customers,' she said.

Jacob dry-heaved and covered his mouth. He stopped for a moment and closed his eyes. 'I feel like total tripe,' he said as he followed her, avoiding looking down. He began to cough and pulled a tissue from his pocket.

'You'll be fine in a couple of days. Mint?' she asked as she held out a packet of Polos, hoping that sucking on a sweet would lubricate his throat and ease his nausea.

He reached over and took one. 'Thanks.'

A woman Gina recognised was wiping the bar down. 'Charlene. You remember me?'

The woman put down the cloth and wiped her damp hands on her jeans. She removed her hair band and stretched her dark greasy hair into a tighter ponytail. 'I remember. Inspector...'

'Harte.'

'That's it. You were investigating that woman who went missing. The one who used to come in here. Deborah. What you here for this time?'

'Same case. We've actually had a lead and we wanted to go over the statements that were given at the time. We will need to chat to yourself, Mr Avery, Mr Wall and Miss Perrins.'

'Ally left. Ally Perrins. She and Jane had a baby two years ago. Some sort of donor thing but it all worked out in the end. As far as I know she's a stay-at-home mum, but we don't keep in touch. She could be anywhere and doing anything by now.' The woman pulled out a cigarette and placed it behind her ear.

'Are Mr Avery and Mr Wall in?'

'Samuel's upstairs, doing the books, he said, and Jeff's in the cellar attending to the barrels.' The woman placed the cigarette in her mouth. 'I really need a ciggy. Do you want to talk to me first or shall I call one of the others?'

As Gina went to answer, Samuel Avery entered the bar and placed his grimy hands on the back of Charlene's neck. 'Got a smoke for your favourite landlord?' he asked. Charlene smirked and passed him a cigarette. He looked up at the two detectives. 'You're a bit early for a drink. We're not open for another ten minutes. You can see we're still cleaning.'

'I can tell, nearly stepped in the puke on your doorstep,' Jacob replied.

'I haven't got to that yet,' Charlene replied. 'Do you want to go to the beer garden out the back instead?'

Jacob nodded.

'You lot. I remember you', Samuel said as his eyes met Gina's. 'You were here when Deborah disappeared.'

Samuel Avery was exactly as Gina remembered. If there was ever a case for workplace sexual harassment, he was it. She remembered how, back then, she'd spotted him ogling Ally's bottom as she bent down to grab a tonic water from the fridge; how he always brushed against Charlene and Ally, even though Ally would never have been interested in him. She remembered that some of the customers said he got a bit hands-on when he'd had a few. He had a record of provoking husbands after he'd tried it on with their wives. It looked like Charlene didn't mind though. She seemed to embrace his touch and reciprocate his advances. He placed his arm around her shoulder and she smiled. He still wore long shirts and skinny jeans, and his fifty-six years were showing more than the average man of that age. The smoking and drinking had aged him quickly in the few short years she'd known him. She watched as he twirled the cigarette between his bony fingers with his pale, liver-spotted hand.

'The garden sounds good. We'll have a smoke and a chat there,' Charlene said.

Samuel grabbed Charlene's cigarettes from her pocket and held them out. 'Smoke?'

Jacob and Gina shook their heads. 'We'd like to talk to Charlene first – alone,' Jacob said.

'I see. I suppose I'll stay here then and wait my turn,' he said as he grabbed a paper and sat on a stool at the bar.

Gina followed Charlene to the garden, which was an extension of the car park. Empty glasses, bottles and overfilled ashtrays covered the benches on the dirty patio. The cellar flap opened and a gaunt man popped his head up. He rubbed his hands together as he climbed to the top of the steps. He flinched and rubbed his neck, nodding at the three of them as he leaned down to lift a barrel. 'Jeff,' Gina called. 'Jeff Wall.'

He nodded and smiled with an open mouth. Gina noticed that he had a chipped front tooth.

'You do remember me, don't you?'

The man shook his head as he balanced the barrel on his shoulder.

'DI Harte. The detective investigating the Deborah Jenkins case a few years ago. Don't go anywhere, we're speaking to everyone.'

The man ran his fingers through his hair and smiled. 'Sure thing. I've just got to get the empties out ready for collection,' he replied as he continued into the pub.

Gina turned back to Charlene. 'Right, down to business. Just to recap your statement, you stated back then that Deborah Jenkins was a regular on Wednesday nights. She was a member of the women's pool team and had been for two years.' Jacob took out his notebook and marked it with the date. He blew his nose and wiped his eyes. Charlene leaned away from him, took her cigarette from behind her ear and lit it. She drew in the nicotine and blew the smoke out slowly. Jacob coughed. Gina watched as the lines on the side of Charlene's mouth became more prominent as she sucked on the cigarette.

'That's right. From what I can remember, she wasn't very good at it, but she was friends with Lottie. Now that's a woman who is shit-hot with a cue. The girls all still have a remembrance once a year for Debbie.'

'Can you tell me about the last time you saw her again?'

'Now you're expecting a lot. It was ages ago.'

'Try your best.'

'From what I can recall, it was the week before she went missing. The team plays on Wednesdays so it had to be that day. We'd lost at home to the Spinster and Black Cat. The atmosphere, from what I remember, was a bit sombre, as they were bottom of the league and then, after that game, we were. That's the only time we've been bottom of the league. We should've beat them.'

'Did you play?' Jacob asked.

'No, I don't do sport. When I say we, I mean us at the Angel. I still wanted them to win. Anyway, the Spinster lot all went on their merry way with an unexpected victory to their name and we sat there drinking for a couple of hours. I remember drinking tequila shots after my shift that night and was sick as a dog in the night – never again. Deborah always got a taxi home with Lottie—'

'By Lottie, do you mean Charlotte?'

'Yeah, Charlotte Livingston. She did live a few doors down from Debbie but I know she moved to the outskirts of the village. Her hubby got a promotion, they got a bigger house with apple trees and a gated drive. Alright for some. My husband did one seventeen years ago when my youngest was born. He's a little git now, like his father.' Charlene took another drag of her cigarette.

'Can we get back to that night in question please, Charlene?' Gina asked.

'Well, we'd all had a few, to commiserate, you know. Samuel gave 'em all a drink on the house and joined them for the last couple while we went through the strategy of play, trying to dissect where it all went wrong. I've told you all this before.' The woman finished her cigarette, dropped it to the floor and stood on it. Gina couldn't understand why she did that, as she was ultimately the one who had to clean it up.

'You said in your statement that Deborah slapped Samuel on the arm.'

'Yes. I couldn't hear what was being said but she did slap him on the arm. I think it was playful. I call him spaghetti hands, they're always winding their way around some woman. She was having none of it though. Debbie was a good girl, not one for a fling. Lottie, on the other hand, was an outrageous flirt. Never went home with 'em though. We thought Samuel was getting a bit too big for his boots with her and was probably going to have to face another angry husband. But it wasn't as if he was going to pounce on any of 'em, and they always came back.'

Jacob nodded at Gina. 'You've been most helpful, Charlene. Is your address still the same?'

'Yes, still in that dump.' Charlene looked at her watch. 'Bloody hell. Is it that time already? I've got to ring my lazy-ass son to get him out of bed for work. If I don't call him, he won't get up and I ain't giving him any money to waste on weed.' The woman paused and stared at Gina. 'I didn't mean weed. I meant—'

Gina shook her head. 'Thank you, Charlene.'

'You will let me know if you find her. She was a nice girl, always friendly. Such a shame for her husband and babies.'

Gina nodded. 'Will do.' The woman scurried off to the end of the garden with her phone pressed to her ear and began yelling at her teenage son.

Jacob stared at his notes as he rubbed his throbbing head. Gina noticed how glassy his eyes looked. 'Why are you such a martyr?' he said. 'You come into work on death's door, and because you do that, it means I have to as well.'

'Stop whining, Driscoll. You're standing, aren't you?' Gina replied with a grin. Jacob coughed and smiled as he followed her back into the pub.

Jeff Wall had picked up the cleaning where Charlene had left off. Samuel entered through the front door with an empty bucket. 'The threshold is all back to full freshness, ready for your departure.'

'Looking forward to us leaving already, Mr Avery?' Gina asked.

'I never said that. I'm always happy for lovely young ladies to stay, including yourself, Detective. Not so much your sidekick though. He'll scare my customers off with his germy image. Jeff, pour me a brandy.' The man obediently grabbed a bottle off the mirrored shelf and poured a large measure into the glass. Samuel took a seat at the table beside the fireplace and they joined him.

Gina looked at Jacob. Jacob shook his head and rolled his eyes. 'Mr Avery. On the last night that Deborah Jenkins attended this pub, the night of the pool match against the Spinster, which you lost, you were seen to be having some sort of disagreement with Mrs Jenkins. In your statement, you said that you asked her if she wanted another drink on the house, and she accused you of trying to get her drunk and got a little upset.'

'That's exactly how it happened. I'll make no bones about it. I thought she was something special. She was the quiet one, silent but alluring. I'm an old man who was trying my luck. She turned me down and took offence, what more can I say?'

Gina thought back to the file. On the night of Debbie's disappearance, Avery had been in the airport, waiting to board a flight. She'd checked the validity of this information and he had indeed checked in. Had he been involved though? Did he get someone else to assist with his dirty work? If so, who?

'Do you know if she was having problems with anyone here?'

'She got on with everyone – except me, after I propositioned her. She came in once a week, had a couple of drinks while playing pool. Laughed with her friends. There were no dramas that I can think of. I really do wish I knew something. She was a nice person. I'd like nothing more than for her to be found and come here every Wednesday and play pool with her friends.'

'Where were you at approximately 7 p.m. on the night of Friday the first of December? Last Friday.'

'I was staying with my sister in the big smoke.' He grabbed a small pen from his top pocket and wrote a number on a beer mat. 'Here's her number. You ain't pinning anything on me.' A grin spread across his face.

'And this morning at 3 a.m?'

'I was in bed.'

'Alone?'

'Yes. What's all this about?'

Gina watched as Jacob made a couple of notes, summarising what Mr Avery had said.

'Thank you, Mr Avery,' Jacob said as he pulled out a tissue and sneezed. Avery stood and walked to the bar.

'Follow up on this when you get back,' said Gina. 'I want his alibi checked out.' Jacob took the beer mat from her and slotted it into his notebook.

Looking up, Gina saw Jeff Wall leaving the pub's cellar.

'We need a word, Mr Wall?' Jacob called.

The man nodded and joined them at the table. Charlene appeared with a bag overflowing with empty beer bottles and then began emptying the internal bins into another bag.

'We have in your notes that you were here, working on that last Wednesday before Deborah's disappearance. You were also here working on the night of her disappearance. Is it right that you were managing the place in Samuel's absence?'

'Yes. It's hard to remember. How long ago was it now?'

'Four years. In your statement you mentioned reordering stock.'

'Yes, I can just about remember now. I had to do the ordering that night. I was in the office from late afternoon until about eight thirty—'

'On the night she disappeared or the Wednesday before?' Jacob asked.

The man looked up at Jacob and paused. 'It was a long time ago. It was the night she disappeared. Samuel had already left for the airport. When I finished the paperwork, I came down and worked the bar as I always do when he's away.'

Gina remembered them examining the car park CCTV of the night Deborah had disappeared. Jeff's old Rover had been parked up until eleven that night.

'Do you remember what happened the night of the pool match against the Spinster? You told us at the time that Deborah had seemed a little offish with Mr Avery.'

The man tapped his knees with his hands. 'That's right. I don't remember much more. She was sitting with the other five. Lottie, Juliet, Zoe, Barbara and Steph. They still make up the core of the team. We have others come and go, but they stay in the team. I'm sure I said this at the time, when you asked me before.'

'I know, we're just going over things. You've been very helpful,' Gina said as she stood.

Jeff nodded. 'She was a lovely young lady, I hope you find her.' He walked over to the fire with a bag of kindling sticks, a newspaper and a lighter.

'And where were you last Friday evening, around seven?' Gina asked.

'Where?'

'Yes. Where were you? Simple question.'

'I was managing the place while Sam was away, like I always do. I worked between the bar, the cellar and the office. I changed a barrel at one point and I put in an order for some more lager. Check if you want. Why do you want to know where I was?'

Avery brushed past and grinned.

'Just following up on another investigation. Thank you. We'll check into that.' Gina made a note to check that Wall was shown as working on the staff rota and that he had indeed made an order for lager. She also made another note. Could Avery be an accomplice in Deborah's disappearance?

'Can I go now? I've got to sort the cellar out.'

'Yes, we'll be in touch if we need to speak further.' Gina watched as Jacob finished making notes and closed his notebook.

Albert walked through the door and headed to the bar. 'Have you found that baby's parents yet?' he asked as soon as he saw Gina.

Gina looked at him for a minute, struggling to recall where she'd seen him before. Then she remembered speaking to him when he found the Jenkins baby. Gina smiled, but she couldn't say that they had. If the press were to get hold of the rest of the story, it would most likely be sensationalised and all sorts of assumptions would be made. If Deborah was in any sort of danger and being held, letting the press loose with the story might put her in more danger. She needed Deborah to be kept safe. She needed the investigation to stay under wraps.

'Not yet. The baby is looking well thanks to you though, Mr Thomas. It's lucky you were walking past and stopped. Who knows what might have happened had you not been there. You should give this man one on the house for what he did, Mr Avery.'

Samuel Avery stared up at her and dropped his shoulders before nodding at Charlene to offer Albert a drink.

'What will you be having, love?' she asked.

'An extra-large Scotch,' he replied. 'Thanks, officer.'

'Don't mention it.' Gina replied, turning her attention to Avery. 'Can you get me your staff rota for last Friday night? Oh, and I'll send someone to verify the orders that were made that night. I assume we have your full cooperation.' Avery stared at her then stomped out of the room. A moment later, he shoved a scuffed piece of paper into her hand.

'Take it with you. Always happy to help the pigs. I mean, the police.'

'Thank you Mr Avery.'

She passed him without looking back and they left the building, noting that he hadn't put up any form of resistance. As they headed for the car, Gina glanced at the rota and searched for the evening in question. Charlene was on bar and Jeff was down as being on a shift from four in the afternoon to close. They got in the car and headed back to the station, ready to compare findings. Gina looked down at her phone, which had been on silent. There were no messages from Hannah.

She called the station and O'Connor answered. 'Could you organise the collection of a copy of an order made for lager at the Angel Arms last Friday? You can speak to Samuel Avery. I want a copy filed under the Baby Jenkins case. Verify the time the order was made.' O'Connor acknowledged her request and she ended the call. As Jacob drove, she tapped in the number on the beer mat and waited for an answer. Time to start working on verifying Avery's whereabouts. There was something about him she just didn't trust.

CHAPTER TWENTY-NINE

Gina kicked off her shoes and switched her laptop on. Briggs had told her to leave a bit earlier as she'd been doing so much overtime. But they both knew she was bringing her work home, as was Jacob. And she was sure Briggs had spent all day looking at the station's finances, worrying about overspending. With all that was going on, there wasn't time to sit around, watch soaps and take long candlelit baths. Every time she settled down to bathe, the phone would go.

She looked out the window into the rural darkness. Living on the outskirts of Stratford-upon-Avon had given her the peace she'd never had as a Birmingham city dweller. As her struggling laptop finally powered up, she pulled the files out of her bag and placed them on the floor. She sat next to them with her legs spread out and opened her email, but she'd received no new messages since she'd left the station. She'd confirmed that Avery had been in London at his sister's on Friday, and O'Connor had come back to her with a copy of the lager order, which had been made at five forty that evening. Her mind came back to Avery. The thought of him near any woman made her skin crawl, but he'd covered himself well on two occasions. She'd considered that he could be working with someone else, but who?

An email pinged up on her screen. It was a sponsorship request for O'Connor's bike ride that coming weekend. She doubted whether O'Connor would live through a fifteen-mile bike ride. He'd laughed in her face when she'd suggested that he should train for it. She clicked on the link, which explained that any money raised would go to the local hospital. She tapped in her details and sent him twenty pounds.

A call lit up her phone and it vibrated across the coffee table. She grabbed it, hoping that it was Hannah calling back, but it was Jacob. 'Hello.'

She waited a moment while he coughed down the phone. 'Sorry about that. Right, I managed to catch up with Wyre and O'Connor just after you left.'

'Great. Did they come up with anything? I got the news back about the lager order. What else is there?'

'They're making out their reports right now, so they should be available to view in an hour or two. But I have spoken to them and I can give you a summary.'

Gina took some photos out of the folder and laid them out in front of her. Smarmy Samuel stared back at her. 'Great. Go ahead.'

She winced as she listened to Jacob coughing loudly before continuing. 'Deborah's pool team friends Barbara Pace, Steph Steel and Juliet Derby had nothing really to add since last time. As we know, they all have alibis for the night she disappeared, and no motive. Zoe Ellis is working away for the next week but her husband seemed to think she'd have nothing to add. Wyre and O'Connor asked for her to call the station when she got back. Charlotte Livingston was in. She told them that Samuel Avery had been bothering Deborah for sex and that had been going on for weeks. Deborah had rejected him several times but he had been a sleaze about it. When asked why she didn't mention this back then, all she said was that he was in the airport at the time, so it couldn't have been him.'

'Interesting. I've been wondering if he's working with someone else. There's something about him. It's a possibility.'

'I suppose. Get this though. Charlotte also said that Samuel had tried to grope Deborah outside the toilets two weeks before her disappearance. By groping, I mean he grabbed her in the groin area and tried to kiss her, pushing her against the wall. She got upset about it in the taxi on the way home. She even said she wasn't sure if she wanted to play for the team anymore. She said Deborah didn't want to report the incident. She didn't want her husband to find out and she wanted to forget it. Obviously, we only have Charlotte's word for this, but given Samuel's previous, I'm inclined to believe her. Anyway, that's all. Abigail's coming over to nurse me in half an hour so I'm going to love you and leave you.'

'Great. Tomorrow we'll head to Deborah's workplace, see if anything new has come to light. I've checked with O'Connor and he's confirmed that we can use their boardroom and both Gabby and Callum will be in, so we'll be able to speak to them. I've read the files to date. Have a look over them so that you're up to date too and then get a good night's sleep. It's going to be a long one tomorrow.'

'When is it not?' he replied as he blew his nose.

Another call came through on Gina's phone. 'Have a good one. Got to go, bye.' She saw Hannah's name flash up and accepted the call. 'Hello.'

'Mum, I'm sorry I went off on one the other night. I thought I'd let you know that everything is sorted for Saturday.

It would be nice if you could come along, I need you there. I'll text you the details.'

Gina opened her mouth to speak and then changed her mind. A ceremony was the last thing she could deal with. 'I might be working—'

'Whatever. I'm giving you the chance to do the right thing here. It won't look good if you don't turn up.'

She swallowed. She'd have to face his mum, Hetty, and his awful brother, Steven, and the rest of his close family. She'd have to paste on her mourning face all over again for the man who had raped and beat her. 'Hannah, you know I love you and Gracie with all my heart—'

'Do I?'

'You're being silly now.'

'Me being silly? It's not like I'm asking you to jump out of a plane without a parachute. I'm asking you to attend a small ceremony to remember my father, a man you loved, who you now seem hell-bent on forgetting. I'm not saying any more on this. Turn up, Mum. Just come along for the half an hour it will take. You don't have to stay for tea and cakes or even make the effort to talk to anyone. I just need you to be there for me.' In the background, Gracie began to cry and a cat yelped. 'Gracie. Leave the cat alone. I've got to go. Think about it, half an hour, Saturday. That's all.' Hannah hung up.

Gina felt a prickling sensation wash over her skin as she flashed back to when she was pregnant with Hannah. She remembered trembling as Terry unlocked the door in the middle of the night. She'd heard him struggling to get his key in the lock. It had taken several attempts. As he reached the top of the stairs, he called out to her. 'Gina, baby, I need help with my zipper.' She'd pretended to be asleep as a tear escaped from the corner of her eye. 'When I say I need help, I mean get up and help. Bitch.' He'd dragged her from the bed by her hair. 'Oh, you're going to get it now,' he yelled as he undid his own zip. She never tried to resist him, resisting always led to more pain. Gina swallowed the tears back.

Was Debbie going through the same thing? Nausea swept through her body and the palpitations caused her to gasp for breath. She placed her fingers on her wrist; her pulse was high. Was she having a heart attack? She gasped for breath again as the room began to sway. Calm down, she thought. Breathe in and out. In and out. She'd been in control of her anxiety for so long now, but this case was bringing it all back.

An email alert pinged on her laptop. She rubbed her eyes and shook her head. Her breathing was slowly returning to its normal pace and the room had stopped swaying.

It was Wyre's interview notes. She opened the file and scanned the information. It contained pretty much what Jacob had said. She looked at Charlotte's interview notes, where she mentioned the assault outside the toilets. Wyre had also made a note that she thought something may have gone on between Charlotte and Samuel at some point, as Charlotte had paused and smiled when they spoke of him being a ladies' man. Gina began thinking. Maybe Charlotte had said what she had out of jealousy, wanting Samuel to get into trouble for moving his affections to Deborah. Samuel had never had an actual report of sexual assault lodged against him; he was always in trouble for fighting with jealous husbands.

She headed to the kitchen and grabbed an out-of-date pack of sliced cheese and shoved a piece in her mouth. What was she missing with Avery?

She thought back to her conversation with Hannah and felt a lump forming in her throat. Having to face Terry's family again was the worst thing she could think of. She tried to swallow but she couldn't, almost choking on the cheese. As she gasped for air, light-headedness took over and she grabbed a chair for support.

She shook her head. 'I can't go,' she said, sobbing. A ceremony with his family would be too much. Hannah thought Terry was the perfect father, taken from her too soon. She didn't know that the smallest thing would set him off and that her mother could never make him happy. 'I couldn't make him happy,' she yelled as she gripped the top of the chair. She hated herself for saying that out loud. It made it so real. Spoken like the abused person that she had been. The image of Terry lying at the bottom of the stairs, broken and bleeding, flashed through her thoughts. Tears dripped onto the kitchen table as exhaustion kicked in.

She fell to the kitchen floor, only the light of the fridge revealing her tears as she broke down and stared into the dark. *What are you going through, Debbie?*

CHAPTER THIRTY

Tuesday, 5 December 2017

Hailstones beat against the window as Gina swigged the rest of the cold coffee. She'd arrived at the station for a six thirty briefing, and the last hour had gone strangely. Thoughts of the case and her chat with Hannah had kept her awake most of the night, and had been whirring through her mind all morning. Her thoughts were filled by memories of her dark past, the abuse, the case. Saturday, Terry, Briggs, Hannah, Avery, Baby Jenkins and Luke, poor Luke. Deborah, where was Deborah? She'd stared at the case files for the past hour, after chasing the lab for results. She once again ran through the details of the reports from O'Connor and Wyre. There was a knock on her office door. 'Come in,' she called.

Wyre entered with a smile on her face and placed a printout of an email on her desk. 'Check this out. Forensic results on the towel Baby Jenkins was wrapped in.'

Gina lifted the page and smiled back. 'Let's hope it gives us a clue to this mystery.' After a moment of glancing back and forth at the pages, Gina looked up. 'Traces of red diesel and dog hair, specifically a black dog.' Gina placed the paperwork back on her desk. 'Call another briefing now. I'll be through in a couple of minutes.'

Wyre nodded and left. Gina swigged the dregs of her coffee and headed straight towards the incident room. As she reached the main hub, Jacob arrived, removing his coat and scarf while heading towards the kitchenette. 'No time for coffee at the moment,' Gina said. He pulled a tissue from his pocket and held it to his mouth as he continually retched and coughed mucus into it.

'Sorry about that. Even Abigail deserted me after about half an hour last night. Have we had a breakthrough?'

'We have a lead,' she replied. Gina noticed a crusty redness around Jacob's eyes.

'What is it?' he asked as he dropped his coat on a chair.

'I'm about to brief everyone now.'

He hurried beside her, blowing his nose as he walked. They entered the incident room. Everyone's eyes were on Gina.

'We've just had the forensics report back on the baby's blanket. Traces of red diesel and black dog hair were found amongst the fibres. As we are bordering the Warwickshire countryside, I suggest that, to begin with, we make a list of farms and country businesses within a ten-mile radius. O'Connor, I'm going to task you with the research. I want the name and address of every business that is operating in this area. Everywhere you go, everyone you interview, look out for a black dog. This could be the key to finding Deborah Jenkins. Wyre, check with all the local vets. We're looking for owners of black dogs. I know there will be stacks of them but we may be able to cross-reference later on.'

'Have we had the DNA results back on Mr Jenkins as yet?' asked O'Connor.

'No. I'll keep you updated. I'm sure it is just an elimination test though. Right, as you were. Let me know of any developments as soon as they come through. Jacob and I will be speaking to Deborah's colleagues today. In turn, we'll keep you updated at all times. Thank you.'

O'Connor swivelled in his chair to face his computer screen. Wyre was adding the new information to the incident board and everyone else spoke quietly, sharing thoughts and notes.

Jacob followed Gina towards the kitchenette. 'Time to grab a quick coffee before we head out,' she said. 'Are you okay?'

'It's much worse when I first get up. Give me an hour and I'll be back to my usual good-looking self. I'll go and have a good blow of my nose before we leave, shift some of this snot,' he said with a smile. His unshaven face and wonky tie said it all. He'd had about as much sleep as she'd had.

'I was looking over the workplace interviews this morning,' she said. 'I remember the director quite well, Lynne Hastings. I gave her a call this morning. All but one member of staff is still working there and they're all in today. Oliver Stain died six months after Deborah disappeared. His mother had picked him up on the night of Deborah's disappearance and he'd gone with her to the pub to have a family celebration. He was never a suspect.'

'What are you thinking now?' Jacob asked.

'There was a colleague, Callum Nelson, that we briefly considered, but nothing ever came of it. Not after initial investigations. But I need to go over this again. We've missed a trick somewhere.'

Jacob poured two coffees out and passed one to Gina. She leaned against the worktop and sipped the drink. 'There is still the possibility that it was a stranger,' he said.

'There is that. I can't think of anyone we've interviewed who lives or works on a farm. We haven't come across anyone with a black dog either. Maybe it is a stranger, but why Deborah? What were they doing driving up the road where she worked, when all the units were closed, opportunistically looking for a woman to enslave for years to come? I don't buy that it was that random.' Gina stared at the coffee in her cup.

'But we keep coming back with nothing when it comes to her friends and family,' said Jacob. 'My mind keeps going back to that smarmy Avery knowing something.'

'We have him on CCTV checking in at Birmingham airport. He never left the airport and subsequently had a holiday in Spain with a collection of tacky Facebook updates to prove it. I know what you mean though: he has a face that you'd just like to punch. If only this case were that simple. It's like we're dealing with a ghost. Someone who is right under our noses, but we just can't see them. Again, could the kidnapper have an accomplice?'

Jacob wiped his nose on the back of his hand. 'It's a possibility. I think I need to go to the bogs and sort out my sinuses before we head off.' Gina nodded and took another slow sip of her coffee.

CHAPTER THIRTY-ONE

Luke grabbed the baby carrier from the back of the social worker's car. 'This is just like Max's,' he said as he walked up the path with Cathy, the social worker following behind. 'I bet you can't believe Max ever fit into a seat this tiny.'

'I know, the little chunky bruiser.' Cathy smiled as she opened the front door, holding it open for Luke. 'I know this all seems strange,' she said as he stepped past her, 'but we can do it, together.'

The baby let out a small whimper as she slept. 'I know we can. I hope Isobel's going to be an easy one, like Max was. I don't know if we could handle another Heidi.' Luke glanced at Devina, who was taking notes.

'Please ignore me,' she said.

'Little tinker, she was. She's still high maintenance now, bossing Max around,' Cathy said as they walked into the kitchen. 'I remember when I went on that weekend break with Debbie and Heidi, when she was a toddler and you were on that course. She'd mastered opening the front door within the hour. We turned our backs for two minutes while taking the cases up the stairs, and she went into the yard and started chasing the chickens all over the place. The owner came out and gave us a right ticking off.' Cathy turned away and began to sniffle. Tears rolled down her face. 'I just want her back. She was more than a daughter; she was my best friend.'

Devina thoughtfully stepped out of the room, giving them a moment, as Cathy broke down in Luke's arms. He held her tightly, beginning to tear up himself. 'They're going to find her, I know it. They have to.' As he comforted Cathy, he stared at the photo of his family. Debbie stared back. Her warm smile only fuelled his sobs.

Isobel wailed. 'I think she needs feeding,' Cathy said as she leaned back and wiped her eyes on her sleeve. She walked over to the worktop and poured the ready-made formula into a bottle that they'd bought earlier that day, popping it in the microwave. 'It's been a while since either of us have had to do this. Shall I feed her?'

Luke nodded. He walked over to the shrieking baby, unclipped the chair straps and picked her up. He held the bundle to his chest and felt a warmth radiating from within the quilted baby suit. The microwave pinged. Cathy took the bottle out and tested its contents on her wrist. 'It needs a few seconds to cool slightly.' She grabbed a bowl, filled it with cold water and inserted the bottle. 'Are you okay while I pop to the loo and clean my face up?' she asked.

'Course I am. I have done this before, you know,' he said with a smile. Isobel settled as he rocked her back and forth. He smelled the baby's head and felt her soft cheek on his nose. He was holding Debbie's baby. He swallowed the lump in his throat as he fought back more tears. Isobel wasn't his baby and he had no idea what was going on.

He placed the baby back in the car seat and stared out at the garden. Nothing in life had prepared him for this moment.

Isobel began to yell again. He grabbed the bottle out of the bowl and tested the temperature. It was just right. He wasn't as out of touch as he'd thought. He scooped her up, laying her head on his bicep, and placed the plastic teat against her searching lips. She latched on and began to gulp the milk. They didn't share the same blood, but he knew at that moment he would be the best father in the world.

Devina reappeared. 'As we said earlier, I'm just here to supervise the visit. It's important that you and Cathy have this time to bond with baby Isobel. If there's anything you need to know, don't hesitate in asking.'

'Thank you.'

Devina smiled. She pulled a tablet from her purse and began tapping on it as she left the room.

'She's so adorable,' Cathy said, sweeping back in and putting the kettle on. 'Tea?'

'I would love a cup,' Luke replied. The little one opened her eyes, and for a moment, Luke thought he saw a smile. He knew babies of such a young age didn't smile and that it was probably just wind, but he smiled back. He wanted her to see her daddy, the one who would be there for her no matter what. The one who was waiting for his wife to come home so that they could be a family.

Cathy placed the cup of hot tea on the side. 'She likes you.'

'I like her too. I'd like her to stay.' He held Isobel in silence for a few minutes, and Cathy watched him feed her. 'Do you want to have a go?' he asked.

She nodded and sat at the kitchen table. Luke passed Isobel over.

'How's Brooke taking all this?'

'As good as anyone can. We spoke yesterday. I told her about the baby and Debbie. My life has been turned upside down, I can't deny that, but for the first time since Debbie went missing, I feel as though I have hope. I want her home. I want her here with me, you and the children.' I keep picturing us all being here for Christmas, happy, a family again.'

'When they find her, Luke, it may not be that easy. God knows what she's been through. But she has a good family. The best.' The baby turned her face away from the bottle and began to wail. 'Wind, maybe?'

Luke smiled and nodded. He grabbed a tea towel off the side and threw it over Cathy's shoulder.

'What I think I'm trying to say is, we can't expect too much too soon,' Cathy said as the baby cried into her ear.

Luke began fiddling with the buckle on the car seat. 'I know. It's weird, isn't it? We're talking like she's coming home. We still don't know where she is. All the police seem to have done is taken my DNA and that's it.' He paused and looked down. 'What if we never find her?'

Isobel burped and stopped crying. Cathy kept bouncing her gently. 'I'll never lose hope. All this is happening for a reason. I don't believe in all that luck stuff, but I feel it, Luke. I know something good is going to happen. We have this beautiful little girl and I know our Debbie will put up the fight of her life to be reunited with her.'

Luke looked away. He knew Cathy was right. Debbie wouldn't give up on her children, in any circumstances. Wherever she was, he knew she was thinking about home. She would be thinking about her little ones.

'I know that too, Cathy. Thank you so much for just being you.' He stood and placed his arm around his mother-in-law, inhaling the milky scent of Isobel. He needed Debbie. Isobel needed her. They all needed her. The thought of doing this without her filled him with dread. His heart raced and he gasped for air. What if she was dead?

Devina walked in, just as the kettle switched itself off. 'I'll make the drinks,' she said as she observed the family taking a moment. Luke took a few deep breaths, finally managing to control himself. He hoped his overwhelmed state wouldn't go against them having Isobel released into their care.

CHAPTER THIRTY-TWO

He wiped the crumbs from around her face. To her non-surprise, it had been honey on toast again. He placed the tissue on the floor and walked over towards the slop bucket. He lifted it and left the room. She listened as he walked to the other side of the barn, poured the contents down the loo and pulled the old chain. She dragged the blanket towards her chin, covering the patch on her nightie where her breasts had leaked. The sour smell filled her nostrils.

In the background, she heard the television. The Christmas Coca Cola advert came on. It was almost Christmas, again. Another Christmas would pass without seeing her children. Her eyes began to well up as she remembered past Christmases. She remembered the excitement Luke and she shared when they placed the presents under the tree in the middle of the night, their happiness when they saw their children's surprised expressions. She wondered if they'd be writing their letters to Father Christmas. Then the television was switched off and the sound of Christmas disappeared.

'Right. Shower time,' he said, dropping the bucket back at the foot of her bed. 'You need to get clean.' She continued to look beyond him, knowing it was time to remove her nightie so that he could watch her shower. Her legs trembled as she stood. He looked down at the sheets. 'You've dirtied them.

How could you? I only gave you new bedding the other day,' he said, as he rubbed his head and began to pace. She glanced back and noticed the blood-soaked sheet that she'd been lying on. 'For heaven's sake. You dirty bitch.' He stared into her eyes and held his clenched fist in front of her face.

'I'm sorry.' She began to weep and tremble. 'It's because I had our baby. It's normal, really it is,' she said, pleading with him. He opened his fist and moved his hand from in front of her face.

'You should've said something. You've just been lying there in filth, all this time. This is not the Debbie I know,' he muttered as he continued pacing. She stepped back as he turned towards her. 'I understand. I know what you're going through and I'm trying to support you wholeheartedly.' He leaned in towards her. She closed her eyes as he kissed her on the cheek. 'But it can never happen again.' He drew back and slapped her across the face. She wanted to flinch, she wanted to yell, she wanted to cry – but there was no point.

'I'm sorry. It's all my fault. I'll say something next time. I promise,' she said, holding back the sobs that were sticking in her throat. She placed her hand over her cheek and tried to soothe the burning pain. He broke his stare and hurried towards the chain ring. He unlocked it and linked it to a carabiner that was looped around his belt.

'Leave your dirty clothes there,' he said as he gripped the padlock.

She pulled her nightie over her head and dropped it to the floor, revealing everything.

'You need to cut down. Your belly is still swollen,' he said as he prodded at her stomach. She flinched and let out a small groan.

She remembered when she'd given birth to Max. It had taken her the best part of ten months to even fit into her larger pre-Max clothes. She'd been so disappointed that she hadn't been able to lose that last half a stone, almost to the point of obsession. She'd have done anything to be rid of it, anything. She remembered the photo that Luke had taken of them and their two little ones, soon after giving birth to their son. She'd given him a hard time when he'd framed it and put it on display in their family home. Now she knew why Luke had wanted that photo. He loved her and he hadn't cared about her chubby arms and tummy. That photo represented the love he had for her and their family. She remembered how disappointed he'd been when she said she thought the photo was hideous and that he should get rid of it because she looked like a whale. He'd refused, of course, reassuring her that he loved all of her, even the chubby bits.

She looked down at her postpartum belly. She still looked slightly pregnant, but things were different from when she'd given birth to Heidi and Max. Now, her belly was swollen but her legs were like sticks. Every action took effort. Using her arms in any way that put strain on them made them feel like they would snap. Back then she'd been dissatisfied with her weight, but now she'd do anything to be back at home, worrying about how she was going to shift her measly half a stone. Dark pigment ran in a line from her belly button to her groin, which would surely fade away soon, along with the post-birth swelling and any memories of her little girl.

He began to walk, dragging her chain as he did so. She followed until they reached the small shower room. She stared at the old toilet with its cistern up high on the wall. She remembered visiting one of her mother's old relatives as a child; she'd had a similar toilet in a lean-to room, off the kitchen. He turned the shower on and it trickled. The last time she'd had a shower, it had taken her several hours to get warm again.

'In you go. Squeaky clean, you'll be.' He smiled and gave her a nudge. She stepped in and shivered as the icy water hit her body. She rubbed the soap over her goose-bumped skin and allowed the water to soak her hair. As on previous occasions, she'd use the soap to wash her hair too. Brownish-red water gathered in the tray below, reminding her that she was still bleeding. She turned and saw that he was watching her. 'Don't forget the underarms,' he said, staring at her breasts. She hugged herself and he looked away. Under the scummy water, she noticed that her hair was blocking the plughole. She remembered losing a fair bit of hair in the past after giving birth. Perfectly normal, her midwife had said to her. She stared at the hair tangled in her wet fingers. Since when had she started going grey?

Through chattering teeth, she gasped for air. 'I need to get out now,' she said as she stepped aside.

'Turn off the shower,' he said.

She did as she was told. He went to grab a towel off the rail. The door below banged and the dog barked. 'Shut up, Rosie,' he yelled. The door banged again. She watched nervously as he ran his fingers through his hair, looking agitated.

'We've run out of bread,' a frail voice shouted.

He unlocked the chain and transferred it to the towel rail, securing it with the padlock. 'I'll be back in a minute. She's fragile, so don't scare her. I'll never forgive you if you scare Mother.' She looked away as he left the room. Shaking, she began to pull at the rail. It was embedded into some old damp plasterboard, which moved a little more with each tug.

'Rosie, get out,' he shouted from the bottom of the steps. A gust of cold air bellowed upwards into the tiny bathroom. The dog ignored him and ran up to her. It began to bark. She pulled at the rail again. One of the screws loosened. He burst in and grabbed the dog, directing it out of the room. 'Bad girl, Rosie. Get out,' he said as he kicked the tiny black spaniel up the rear. The little dog yelped and ran back down the stairs.

'I'm going to the shop,' the old woman yelled.

'Mother, no. Wait.' Her heart pounded as she stood in front of him, naked and shivering. She noticed a small pile of plaster dust on the floor, beneath where she'd been tugging at the rail.

'Come on, Rosie, we can go to the shop together,' the old woman called to the yelping dog.

'Hang on!' he shouted, running back down the stairs.

This was her chance. She yanked the towel rail and watched as a chink of plaster came away. Nearly there. When she yanked again, one side of the rail dropped. She pulled the whole thing away from the wall and grabbed the loose chain. Downstairs, she could hear him arguing with his mother while trying to round up the dog. The dog barked and yelped. She grabbed the towel and wrapped it around her shivering body. He'd be back any moment. She needed to take him by surprise and get out. She needed something to attack him with. She slid around on the floor until she managed to dry her feet on a small mat.

Running to the kitchenette, she grabbed the old metal kettle. With trembling hands, she opened a couple of drawers. Maybe there was a knife or fork. The drawers were empty.

She heard the door slam shut. He was coming back. The dog and the old lady had gone. It was just him and her. She waited at the top of the steps, her back to the wall. As he neared she held the kettle high. He stopped halfway up, not making a sound. She held her breath. The kettle quivered in her weak arms. She shuffled away from the wall, scared she would tap it. He took another step and stopped. The water falling from her hair threatened to expose her whereabouts. *Drip, drip, drip.*

'Come out, Debbie,' he called.

Her heart hammered as the sobs burst out from her chest. The chain rattled as she ran from behind the door straight into him on the stairs. She whacked him with the kettle. They both tumbled in a heap down the steps, landing on the oily floor below. She pushed up on her hands and grabbed at the towel around her chest. As he went to stand, she kicked him in the stomach and pushed him hard. She screamed as she scurried past him and darted towards the door. 'Help!' she called, knowing that the old woman couldn't be too far away. She'd surprised him with her attack. All she had were moments in which to get away. 'Help!' she cried again, as she reached for the main door.

CHAPTER THIRTY-THREE

Gina stepped out of the car, closely followed by Jacob. As the cold air hit his throat, he began to cough. She passed him a pack of lozenges. 'Thanks,' he said, as they reached the door and Gina pressed the buzzer. The grey industrial unit stood at the top end of the estate. It was surrounded by leafless trees that were crowned by the heavy grey winter sky.

A crow squawked as it landed on a branch. 'They're taking their time to answer,' Gina said as she checked her watch and rubbed her cold arms. As she pressed the buzzer again a woman opened the door. 'DI Harte,' Gina said, holding up her identification. 'We called earlier.'

'Please come in. I'm Lynne Hastings, we spoke on the phone.'

Gina had originally interviewed Lynne when Debbie had disappeared. The woman was now hobbling along and looking frailer than expected, considering she was only in her mid-forties.

'You'll have to excuse me; osteoporosis is a destructive condition. Some days good, some days not so good. Today, not so good – but less about my problems. You've come about Debbie, is that correct?'

'Yes.' The two detectives followed the woman past the workshop, up some metal stairs and along a mezzanine. The main office of Avant Conservatories was in front of them. Lynne opened the door to the left and led them into a small boardroom. The tired furniture filled the middle of the room. A picture of one of the conservatories they made had been left at a wonky angle. Gina felt her fingers twitching as her desire to realign the picture built up. Jacob pulled a tissue out of his pocket and blew his nose.

'I'm glad. Debbie's disappearance has haunted us all. We talk about her often.' The woman grabbed a walking stick that was leaning against the wall and used it as she headed to the door. 'Can I get you a drink?'

Jacob shook his head. 'Coffee, please,' Gina replied.

'How do you want to do this? Shall I gather up the staff you previously interviewed and bring them all in or do you want them in turn?' Lynne asked.

Gina opened her file. 'I'd like to speak to a couple of them separately. Are they all still here?'

Lynne pulled open the door to the main office and the corridor and boardroom were momentarily filled with the hum of ringing phones and people talking. 'Ah, Gabby, can you please get DI Harte a coffee?' Gina remembered speaking to Gabby before. Deborah had worked with her in the office, handling the administration.

'Will do,' the woman replied as she walked away.

Lynne hobbled back towards them and sat at the head of the conference table. Gina and Jacob took out their notebooks and pens.

'We are currently going over statements made in relation to the disappearance of Deborah Jenkins on the twentieth of December 2013. The last people to see her were her work colleagues.' Gina glanced at her notes. 'She'd been working late, making up time as she'd watched her children's school play earlier that day—'

'We told her she didn't need to make the time up,' Lynne said. Gina remained silent, listening for what was to come next. 'I've lived with this for a long time. If only I'd been more insistent that she went home, but Debbie was headstrong. She always paid her dues, as she described it. She wasn't one for having something for nothing, which is why she insisted on making up the time. We left her on her own. Not one of us wanted to stay that night. If I could change things, I'd stay, maybe even drive her home. I can't believe—'

'Mrs Hastings, it's not your fault. Can you remember anything else about that day, any small thing?' Gina asked.

Lynne stared at the table before shaking her head. 'From what I remember, it was just a typical day. Production was going at its regular pace for the time of year. There were no absences. I think we told you all that at the time. No one looked out of place or troubled. I've wracked my brain since, trying to make sense of it. Keeping an eye on things in case anything or anyone seems out of place, but nothing stands out at all.' Lynne began rubbing her wrist as she looked up.

'Thank you, Mrs Hastings. Can we just ask about your current staff? Has anyone left since?'

The woman glanced aside and looked back as she recalled the information. 'Oliver Stain in production sadly passed away six months after Debbie's disappearance. Leukaemia.'

'I'm sorry to hear that,' Gina said.

'It was a sad time for all of us here. What with Debbie too. In production, we still have Callum Nelson and Lukas Bosko.

As you can appreciate, many have come and gone, but I think the rest were eliminated from your enquiries at the time.'

Gina glanced at her notes. The rest of the production team had alibis for the evening in question. One had stopped at a petrol station, a group of four had gone to the pub together straight after work and the others had arrived home on time, long before Deborah had left. The time of her leaving had been confirmed by the setting of the company security alarm and the CCTV that showed her walking away, across the car park and down the path. Lukas had been picked up by his girlfriend and she'd provided his alibi. He'd been home by five thirty and had been Skyping his mother in Poland at the time Deborah left work. She'd placed a question mark next to Callum's name. 'Can we speak to Callum Nelson first?'

'Of course.' Lynne lifted the receiver on the phone and pressed a single number. She requested that they send Callum up. 'He's on his way.'

'Could we ask you to leave while we speak to Mr Nelson?' Jacob asked.

'Is he in trouble?' Lynne asked as she stood.

'We just need to speak to him,' Jacob said, giving her a reassuring smile. The woman seemed more at ease and returned his smile as she left the room.

Jacob grabbed another tissue out of his pocket and proceeded to hack up phlegm. He pulled out a lozenge from his pocket and popped it into his mouth. 'Nice one Gov. I wish you'd be more like O'Connor and share some cake instead of your diseased bacteria.' Gina smirked as Gabby entered with a coffee. She worked in accounts administration; Gina had interviewed her the first time around.

'I'll just pop it here,' Gabby said as she placed the chipped and stained mug in front of Gina and hurried out of the room.

'I think I'm about to be infused with more dodgy bacteria from this cup,' she said as she reluctantly took a sip. 'Good coffee though.'

The door knocked again. Callum entered and sat opposite the two detectives. 'I never did anything, you can't still be trying to pin this on me,' he said as he stared at Jacob.

'We were never trying to pin anything on you, Mr Nelson, just trying to get to the truth of what happened to your colleague and friend Deborah Jenkins,' Jacob replied as he sucked on the sweet. The scent of cherry menthol filled the air.

'Sorry. Most people who know me know I'd never harm anyone. I mean, I can't even run a spider down the plughole.' He rubbed his stubbly chin and looked away.

Gina leaned forward. 'Mr Nelson, can you please go over what happened on the day of Deborah's disappearance? I know we have your statement, and it was a long time ago, but I want you to think back. Did anything stand out to you? Please tell us again about when you left.'

The man leaned back in the chair and ran his fingers through his greasy hair. 'I've already told you everything. Do you think I can remember like it was yesterday? It was years ago. You have my statement.'

'Please try, Mr Nelson,' Gina said.

The man looked up at her and dropped his shoulders. 'It was a really miserable night, that much I remember. I got soaked. Debbie was working away in the main office when I left. I poked my head through the door and said bye. I left and that was it.'

'You say you left on foot,' Jacob said.

'I always walk home. I don't live too far away. Takes fifteen minutes. In the summer I cycle. You haven't pulled me in here to check out my damn travel habits, have you?'

'Calm down, Mr Nelson,' Gina said. 'We are doing this for your colleague, Deborah. Anything you can tell us may help.'

'Have you found something? Please tell me you're going to find her?'

Gina looked at the man. His finger-tapping, the show of anger and the look of despair in his every feature all led her to believe that Callum had a thing for Deborah. It was an angle she was going to press.

'Did you and Mrs Jenkins have a personal relationship?'

'No. I already told you that at the time.'

'I know what you told me at the time. Look at me.'

Callum lifted his head and looked over, his gaze darting from hers to Jacob's.

'Did you and Deborah Jenkins have a personal relationship of any kind?'

'No, I mean, it's nothing.'

'Let me decide that.' Jacob sat poised to write as the man began to speak.

'Bloody hell. You lot just won't leave me alone. I haven't done anything wrong. Look, I know she was a lot older than me but I had a thing for her. It was just a crush, that was all. She knew, but it was light-hearted. I didn't say anything because I knew you'd think it was me. She was married and I didn't try to make a play for her. I just liked her, that's all. Look, I'm married now,' he said as he pointed to his wedding ring. 'I love my wife and I don't want this brought up. Besides, not a thing happened, nothing, zilch. I left her that night. I walked down the path outside the building, in the dark. You saw me leave on the CCTV footage. That was the last I ever saw or heard of Deborah.'

Gina scribbled a few notes in her pad. 'Did you see anyone when you left?'

'A couple of cars passed, as I told you at the time. There was a van but I can't really remember the type. It was a small van – white, I think – but it passed quickly. I don't remember any more and I'm not even sure about the van. There was no one on foot, just me. It was raining, I had my hood up and I couldn't even hear much. I practically jogged home.'

'You never mentioned a van back then.'

'I forgot. Vans come up and down every day around here. I didn't think it was important.'

'What's important is for me to decide, Mr Nelson. It may have been just a van, but it was just a van on the night that mother-of-two Deborah Jenkins disappeared. You withheld information that may have helped the case.'

'I didn't know and I can't really remember. Maybe I didn't see a van. I don't know anymore. Can I go now?' Callum ran his fingers through his hair again.

'Have you ever been in the Angel Arms in Cleevesford?'

'No. Well, only once. I got pissed there when I turned eighteen. Puked beside the bar. I was too embarrassed to ever go back. Why do you want to know?'

'Do you know the landlord or any of the staff?'

The man stared at them. 'No.'

'Do you have a dog?'

'A dog? No.'

'Thank you, Mr Nelson. I'll get someone at the station to contact you to make an official statement later. We need to update our information relating to your relationship with Mrs Jenkins and the van. That will be all. You can go for now.' Callum stood and slammed the door as he left.

'I think we touched a nerve there,' Jacob said. 'Do you think he knows more?'

'He has no alibi, but we came up with nothing at the time after searching his flat and checking his phone records. Not a thing. The only thing we have is that Callum, twenty-two at the time, had a bit of a crush on Deborah. I'll get Wyre to give him a grilling though. If he does know more, we'll press it out of him and get him on tape.'

'Why didn't he mention his crush back then?' Jacob asked.

'That's a question to consider.' Gina ringed Callum's name on her pad. She also noted down the words 'small white van'.

Jacob turned a page in his notepad. 'Do we really need to speak to Toby Grove, Clive Henderson or Vernon McGuire?'

'No. I'll instruct Wyre and O'Connor to call them in just to make sure we've covered all angles. They can speak to them after dealing with Nelson. We looked into their whereabouts thoroughly four years ago. They were all in the pub with the other workshop staff. But we need to know if any of them know Avery. And I suppose we should talk to Gabby Dent; she was Debbie's closest friend at work. We may be able to delve a little deeper, see what she knows about this so-called crush that Callum Nelson had on our missing person.'

Lynne knocked and entered. 'Are you finished here?' she asked.

'Almost. Can we just speak to Ms Dent and we'll be off?'

'I'll send her through.'

A moment passed and there was a tap on the door. 'Come in,' Gina called. The tall, dark-haired woman sat in the seat that Callum had left sticking out. Her hunched posture told Gina that she wasn't confident in wearing her height.

'Have you got any news? Is that why you're here?'

Gina flipped to a fresh page in her notebook. Jacob crunched down on a lozenge, breaking the silence. 'Due to new evidence, we're just going over statements to see if we can shed any new light on the case.'

'I'm glad you haven't given up on her. I've always said I think she's still alive. Everyone here says she's probably dead, killed by some psycho, but I don't know. You guys have never found a body.'

'You were good friends with Deborah. Did she tell you of anything in confidence that may have bothered her?'

'What like?'

'Relationships, good and bad, maybe,' Gina replied.

'She told me lots of things. We spoke every lunch break. We spoke between jobs and we occasionally spoke on the phone after work.'

'Did she ever mention Callum Nelson?'

'I know she thought it was funny and sweet that Callum had a crush on her. I suppose that was one of the personal things she told me. It was obvious to us all though. He looked at her with puppy dog eyes and took more than his fair share of turns to make the coffee, but he meant no harm. I know you guys ransacked his flat at the time but he hasn't got it in him. He's a sweet boy, he really is and he was devastated when Debbie disappeared.'

Gina made a note. It would be easy to investigate Callum again and look deeper into his affairs, but he wasn't coming to the forefront of her mind as the person that could've snatched Deborah. The old case notes flashed through her mind. Maybe Nelson had lured her to his home, but why was her shoe left in the road, not far from where she worked? Would Deborah walk a further ten minutes in the rain, wearing only one shoe, to go to Callum's flat? Callum had no transport, and she was sure Deborah had been taken in a motor vehicle. Could Avery have sourced a van for Nelson to use? She noted that question on her pad.

'Was there anything else on her mind?' Jacob asked.

'I did tell you guys at the time. That bloody Avery bloke at the pub she played pool at, he attacked her. I've never seen her so jumpy at work. She was worried that Luke wouldn't believe her and that Samuel would spin what had happened and say that Debbie was sleeping with him and coming on to him. Vile man, he was. I wouldn't be surprised if that tosser had something to do with all this. He sexually assaulted her, you know.'

Despite being at the airport, Samuel Avery certainly was cropping up everywhere in this case. Gina realised she'd been so tense at the mention of Avery's name, she'd made a hole in the paper with her pen.

'Was the visit really worth it?' Jacob asked.

'We need to get back and find out where we are with all this. I didn't expect to dredge up much that would be of any use, but that damn Samuel Avery keeps cropping up like a dose of herpes,' she said as they both got back in the car. Hailstones began to fall, bouncing off the roof and bonnet of the car. A message came through on her phone. It was Wyre, telling her that Luke Jenkins' DNA results were back.

She opened the email, read it and gave her a call. 'We're just leaving Deborah's workplace,' she said. 'Can you call Callum Nelson in and interview him again? We've just confirmed he had a crush on our Deborah Jenkins. He also thinks he recalls seeing a white van on the night of her disappearance. While you're at it, call in Toby Grove, Clive Henderson, Lukas Bosko and Vernon McGuire. I just want you to go over their stories. I didn't want to disrupt the company any further during working hours… Thanks. See you in a short while.'

Jacob shivered. 'I feel dog rough.' Gina put the car into first and drove out of the car park.

CHAPTER THIRTY-FOUR

Jacob went ahead into the station. Gina checked her phone as she sat in the warmth of the car. She had a text from Briggs.

Dinner later?

She didn't reply. It would be hard for her to ever trust again. Terry's memory flashed through her mind. She could hear the control in his sentences that she'd once mistaken for love. No way was she ever being scared little Gina again. She knew that Briggs wasn't Terry, but then again, she thought she knew Terry – until it was too late.

Gina grabbed her folder off the back seat of the car and ran to the station door. As she opened her office door, she peeled her soaking coat off. Someone had left a hot coffee on her desk. She smiled and sat in front of her computer.

She looked over the DNA test results. Luke Jenkins was definitely not Baby Jenkins' father. She'd known all along, but this could now be placed on file. Another email told her that there was no forensic evidence left at the scene following the attempted break-in at Luke's house. That didn't come as a surprise either. She picked up the coffee and headed towards the incident room. Wyre was sitting in front of a computer screen, alone in the room. Jacob soon followed.

'Hope the coffee was welcomed,' he said as he took a seat next to Wyre.

'Thanks. It most certainly was,' said Gina. 'No O'Connor today?'

'He booked the day off, but he's coming in to help me with the interviews later. At your request, I've organised for them to come in after work. Nelson wasn't best pleased,' Wyre replied. 'Unfortunately, we're a bit understaffed today. I think this weather is making people take all their holidays. Who wouldn't want a duvet day today?'

'Can I have a duvet day?' Jacob asked as he wiped his nose.

PC Smith walked in and took a seat next to Wyre.

Gina grinned and took a sip of coffee. 'Duvet days aside, I have an update. We've got the results back on Luke Jenkins. He is definitely not the baby's father, which we all knew, I suppose.'

Wyre walked over to the board and noted the results next to Luke's name. 'This is all so weird. I feel so sorry for them. I don't know how they're coping.'

'I know,' said Gina. 'It must be hell for them. I'm going to pop by to speak to Luke in person in a while.'

Jacob sipped his drink. 'Do you want me to come with you?'

'No. I think you really should go home early and get some rest, maybe a hot bath and an early night. That poor family don't need your germs as well. You were right when you said you looked dog rough. Maybe Abigail will come over and give you a bed bath or something.'

Wyre sniggered and nearly spat her coffee out.

'I don't need telling twice,' he croaked as he did his coat up and headed to the door. 'If you need me, just call. I'll have my phone on and I'll be working from home.'

Gina listened to Jacob's heavy footsteps echoing through the corridor as he headed to his desk before leaving for home. 'Any more news on the case?' she asked Wyre.

Wyre looked at her computer and scrolled down her report. 'Nothing new, I'm afraid. I can't believe that no one has seen her in all these years but she's alive and well somewhere. Even the calls have dried up on the baby appeal.'

'Thank you. Is Briggs still in? I suppose I should update him before I head off.'

'He left about half an hour ago. You just missed him.'

'Any news from the vets?'

'Only that there are dogs with black fur registered everywhere. We're compiling a list at the moment of all the owners in the area and cross-referencing them against local farm owners. As you say, it may be useful later on.'

'Thanks. Right, I have some paperwork to catch up on. When I've done that, I'm going to head to Luke Jenkins' house. Let me know straight away how it goes with Callum Nelson and the others. I don't think there's much to garner from Toby, Clive, Lukas and Vernon, but Callum… I'm annoyed he didn't mention the van or his crush on Deborah. I know we checked him and his whereabouts at the time, but I want the details he missed out of his original statement on file. I'll type up my notes from this morning and forward them to you before you speak to him. Smith, are you okay to be there when they arrive, to assist Wyre and O'Connor? Call me straight away if you find any connections to any of them with the Angel Arms or Avery.'

Smith nodded.

'And one last thing. I know we're all stressed and we could do with more people assisting, so thank you for everything.

Thank you for the extra hours and all the hard work. When we find Deborah, it will have all been worth it. Maybe we'll all deserve a duvet day then.'

Wyre smiled and continued typing on the computer. As Gina left the room, PC Smith followed her out. She heard him instructing the PCs to continue with the door-to-doors on Luke's street and surrounding areas.

She went back to her office, slumped into her chair and pulled out her notes from earlier that day. Callum Nelson and Samuel Avery. Deborah wasn't short of unwanted attention. How had she handled that attention? She'd been upset about Avery but obviously hadn't been too bothered by Nelson's crush. Was there anyone else? Another admirer? Someone less obvious? Or maybe it wasn't an admirer. Maybe she was looking for connections that weren't there. She opened a clean file and began typing up her notes, ready to send to Wyre before the interviews.

'Where are you, Deborah?' Gina thought.

CHAPTER THIRTY-FIVE

Gina pulled up outside Luke's house and gazed through the bay window. The boy, Max, was playing with a plastic dinosaur and making it attack the voile. The girl passed him, snatched the dinosaur away then held it behind her back. She ran off and the boy disappeared after her.

She gazed up the road at the wall where Luke had reported seeing the stranger watching him and Brooke. He'd been loitering there, scoping the house out and planning his entry, which had thankfully been ruined because of Luke's quick reactions.

Was the watcher the intruder? Was the watcher something to do with Deborah's disappearance? Would the watcher be back? If so, when? Gina shivered.

The murky sky had darkened as she'd been driving. Rain began to trickle down the windscreen. She looked back at Luke's house and watched as Cathy pulled the curtains closed. The woman stopped and stared at Gina, then waved. Gina held her hand up and stepped out of the car. Time to tell Luke what he and everyone else already knew.

Cathy had already opened the door before Gina reached it. Gina smiled and wiped her feet. 'Go through. Luke's in the kitchen with the baby.'

Gina continued along the hallway, stepping over a pencil case and book bag.

The girl yelled and the children ran down the stairs. Max pushed Gina out of the way with the plastic dinosaur as Heidi almost got hold of his jumper. 'Daddy, she's after my dinosaur. She keeps saying my dinosaur is stupid and that I'm stupid. She was going to put him in the loo.' The baby began to wail. 'Sorry, Daddy.'

Gina entered the kitchen and smiled. Luke grabbed the dinosaur with his free hand and placed it on the table. 'Go upstairs, kids, and can you not fight for just a few minutes?' He bobbed up and down while pacing, trying to calm the baby down.

'But I want my dinosaur. It's mine,' Max yelled as his face reddened. A tear fell down the boy's face. Luke sighed and passed him the dinosaur.

'Just take it. Heidi, it's his toy. Leave it alone and play with your own toys. For God's sake.' The baby continued bawling into his ear.

'Daddy. Is this lady here about the baby?' Heidi asked, waiting in the doorway, suddenly shy.

'Stop asking so many questions and just take your brother upstairs while we talk.' The little girl stared at her father, then back at Gina. 'Please, Heidi. We'll talk in a bit.'

'Is Mummy coming home?'

'Heidi, please?'

Cathy entered. 'Go on up you two. Nanny will be up in a minute and we'll play a game, I promise.'

'Okay, Nanny. Come on, Max,' Heidi said, beckoning the boy over. The children left the room and walked upstairs. The baby was only wailing intermittently now. The children's footsteps stopped.

'All the way up! I can hear you both,' Cathy called. The footsteps continued until they reached one of the bedrooms and slammed a door behind them.

'What can we do for you, Inspector? Have you found the creep who tried to break into our house the other night? Or, even better, have you found my wife?'

Gina looked down. 'I'm sorry, Mr Jenkins. We have no news on either, I'm afraid. We've had officers on foot contacting everyone who lives locally to try and flush out more witnesses.'

'I know. I saw them walking up and down earlier.'

There were tubs of baby milk, used bottles, nappy bags and all manner of things strewn over the worktops and table. It was obvious that the family had been busy caring for their unexpected addition. 'Have you got everything you need?' Gina asked.

'Apart from my sanity and my wife. I suppose I have everything else.'

'Do you have any news for us?' Cathy asked.

'Only that Luke's DNA results came back. I thought I'd just pop by in person and confirm what you already knew. Your DNA doesn't match that of the baby.' Luke stood in silence. 'I know you weren't happy when you came to the station, but we were just following procedure. We have to rule the obvious out sometimes, just so that we can move on.'

Luke passed the grouchy baby over to Cathy and gave his stiff arm a shake. He placed his hand on his forehead and stared out of the kitchen window. The wind howled and there was a bang. The little trampoline had toppled over. 'Everything's falling apart, just like my life at the minute,' he said. 'I'm sorry about the way I was at the station.'

'I understand. You were right, but we have to do what we have to do. And what I really want to do is find Deborah. I still need you both to keep a look out all the time, tell me straight away if anything seems strange, anyone seems out of place or anything happens, however small. If you so much as have a phone call you can't account for, I want to know.'

Luke stepped closer to Cathy and placed his arm around the woman. 'Are we in any danger?'

Gina wanted to reassure them, tell them everything was okay and that they were all safe, but after the intruder the other night, she couldn't be sure. 'We're doing everything we can, and if I feel at any point you are in any danger, I will let you know immediately.'

'And that's meant to make us feel safe? Debbie is out there somewhere, missing her baby. Her children live here and they want her home too, and they know something's wrong. I don't care about myself, but I care about them. I need to know if my children are safe because I don't feel safe,' he said as he broke away and walked over to the kitchen window. 'I was this close to someone trying to break into our home. This close.' He turned and held his finger and thumb apart by a fraction. 'This close,' he said as he broke down. Cathy placed the now sleeping baby into the carrier and walked over to Luke. She placed her arm around him and patted his back as she embraced him.

'I'm sorry, officer. Unless there's anything else you have to tell us, it might be better if you leave us be,' Cathy said.

'Give me a call if you hear anything.' Cathy nodded and Gina walked away. As she reached the hall, she looked up and saw Max and Heidi sitting on the top step. Heidi was covering

Max's ears as she held him close to her. 'It's okay, Max,' she said, as she cried. The children could see the anguish Luke was going through. How would he ever to be able to explain what was happening to them?

She left the house, closed the door and hit the side of the wall. She flexed her fingers and noticed that she'd scraped a little bit of skin from the side of her hand. Maybe she could've handled everything better. When she'd arrived, they seemed to be coping. She'd thought turning up in person would be better than calling, but she couldn't have been more wrong, and his children had heard everything.

Devina ran up the path, holding her bag above her head as the rain fell. 'DI Harte, is everything okay?' she asked.

'Yes, just updating Luke. We took his DNA to eliminate him from our enquiries.'

'And?'

'He's eliminated. How are they getting on?'

'They're doing remarkably well, given the circumstances. It would be a tough one for anybody. They haven't properly explained things to the children as yet though.'

'How come you weren't with them when I arrived?' Gina asked.

Devina's smile disappeared. 'They've been doing really well, from what I've observed. They're an amazing, loving family, and I'd love nothing more than to eventually place little Isobel in their full-time care. I just popped to the car to make a few confidential calls. I didn't want them hearing. Are you questioning something, DI Harte?'

'No. I just wondered where you were when I arrived. I'm sorry. Things have just been strained. They're all a little upset, and they could do with your support. Unfortunately the children overheard me updating Luke and Cathy. They now know about Deborah.'

'Oh no. Poor kids. I'd best get back in there,' said Devina. 'Keep me updated, inspector.'

CHAPTER THIRTY-SIX

The main entrance was bustling with suspects who were being checked in. She recognised the short, stout woman who was swearing loudly at the front of the queue as being from the estate nearby. She was one of their regular shoplifters. An officer passed with a staggering male in his late forties and escorted him towards the cells. The shoplifter knocked the mini Christmas tree off the desk as she turned to watch the drunken male. It was clearly December.

Gina shoved past the desk, picking up the tree as she passed, and nodded at Nick, who was calmly dealing with the swearing woman. She headed along the corridor, past the main office, then past her own, until she reached the incident room. Wyre was speaking to someone on the phone while doodling. Gina leaned over. Amongst her scrawl were several doodles of cubes. Wyre ended the call and turned to face Gina. 'I found something. It may be something, it may be nothing.' Wyre grinned as she swivelled back towards her computer screen.

O'Connor yawned and walked towards the kitchenette. 'Sorry to call you in on your day off,' Gina said.

'No worries, boss. I will confess to being asleep on the sofa when the call was received. Anyway, we did the interviews like you asked. I'm just going to grab another coffee. Do you want one?'

'No, I'm good, thanks.'

Gina leaned in and watched Wyre open the early case notes on the screen.

'Do you remember Adele Sutter? You interviewed her when Deborah Jenkins first disappeared.'

Gina frowned and then looked back. 'Parent. Knew Deborah from the school run. She had a girl the same age. I looked over the notes a couple of days ago. Was that her calling in?'

'No. That was Briggs. He said to have all reports typed up and on the system ASAP.' Wyre placed her chewed-up pen on the desk.

'What happened with this Adele Sutter then?'

Wyre scrolled down the interview notes. 'A man wearing a hoodie was seen at the school a handful of times as far back as September, when the new term started. I know you tried to locate this person but the attempts were to no avail. He never turned up again.'

'Maybe he had no reason to turn up again after Deborah's disappearance,' said Gina. 'That's what we thought at the time anyway. We had appeals to locate him, but nothing came of it.' Gina looked at the incident board. A hooded figure outside the Jenkinses' home, spying on them from afar. A hooded figure tried to break into Mr Jenkins' house. Could it really be the same person that had been hanging around back then, at the school? The chances were slim and it really wasn't much to go on. 'Don't a lot of people wear hoodies this time of the year?' Gina stood in silence as she stared at the board. 'It might be a long shot, but we should run this scenario again. Maybe she was being stalked. Maybe this person knew of Deborah's work patterns. Maybe he waited for her to finish and relished the fact that she left late, alone, in the stormy darkness. Maybe this particular hooded figure took her and still has her.'

Gina walked over to the incident board and wrote the words 'small white van' and a question mark under Nelson's name. 'We went back to her workplace earlier and Nelson mentioned that he thought a white van passed him when he left that evening. This is something he didn't think to tell us the first time round. Maybe our hooded person has a van? We have traces of red diesel on the baby's blanket, so a van would tie in there. O'Connor is looking into local farms, and we have to consider this a likely scenario. We barely have a thread to go on, but it sounds plausible. Maybe this hooded figure is the baby's father? Maybe he's seething with jealousy, thinking that Luke might end up with the baby. But why did he abandon the baby, if that's the case?' Gina began pacing the room. 'Unless the other night wasn't an attempted break-in…'

Gina turned back to the incident board, wrote 'hooded figure' and circled it. Underneath she referenced Adele Sutter, Luke Jenkins' attempted break-in and the man watching from the wall. She also drew an arrow with a question mark above it, leading from the hooded figure to the baby's father. 'We should warn Luke to keep all his doors locked and to contact us at any time should he need to. Will you call him? He has my number. Tell him to use it, no matter what the time.'

'Will do, ma'am,' Wyre replied as she picked up the phone.

'How did the interviews go?'

'As well as expected. Bosko only just left as you arrived back. O'Connor and I will get the reports typed up as soon as. I'll let you know when they're there to read. In a nutshell, there's nothing new to add. Nelson just confirmed what he said about the van, only this time, he claimed he was certain he saw a van. He said that after we searched his flat back then, he remembered about the van. He thought we'd hassle him more if he said something, accuse him of hiding things and wrongfully charge him or something. As you'll see from the notes, I think he was just scared of being fitted up. The others had nothing much to report. Their stories haven't changed and I'm satisfied at how they come across. Also, no connection between Avery and any of Deborah's work colleagues.'

Gina wandered back to her own office. She couldn't face hearing anything from the Jenkins household that evening after the way she'd left them. She pulled her phone out of her pocket but there were no new messages. She opened Briggs's text, and before she knew it, she'd replied. She looked at her watch and grabbed her laptop so that she could continue working from home later. Her phone beeped. A rush of blood travelled through her head as she read the message.

See you at mine in a while.

CHAPTER THIRTY-SEVEN

The dark, snaking roads led to a bridge over the carriageway then onto Briggs's road. The car bumped over the potholes until it finally settled on the flat. Gina steered tightly into the only available parking space and got out of the car. There were only a couple of lights on in the row of small terraced houses, and only a few street lamps lit the way. Her heart began to flutter again. What was she doing? What was it about Briggs?

She followed the thin footpath towards his house. She'd only ever popped by once before, to drop some reports off to him on her way home. She remembered his home seeming warm and cosy. He'd had a wood burner on the go and he'd made her a warm milky coffee.

His dog barked as she approached the gate. She followed the small path down the side of the house, feeling along the wall as the lamplight disappeared. She grabbed her phone from her pocket and used it to light the way. As she turned into the back garden, a security light came on. Worms glistened on the path below. Her stomach turned as she carefully stepped over them. She'd hated worms ever since one of the boys at school had thrown one at her.

The dog continued barking and began scrabbling against the back door. 'Jessie, it's okay, girl. It's just Gina,' Briggs said.

Jessie dashed past Gina and sniffed the grass, where she stooped instantly, relieving herself. 'I hope you like egg and chips. It's about the extent of my culinary talents,' Briggs said. The old Labrador pushed its way back into the house and shook its wet coat all over the kitchen.

'I love egg and chips,' Gina replied. Holding a spatula in one hand, Briggs moved to the side so that she could enter. His kitchen smelled of hot oil, a smell she wasn't overly keen on. She watched as he continued pouring the chips in the fryer. She hadn't often seen him in casual wear, but his jeans fitted his tall, stocky body well. He turned, almost bumping into her and stopped. It was then she knew. There was nothing of Terry in Briggs. Okay, he was hard and a bit rough around the edges, but she wanted him. There was no denying the fact.

'Can I get you a drin—'

She placed her finger over his mouth, removed it, then kissed him hard. She needed something, someone, some close human contact. He kissed her back. She dragged his jumper over his head and dropped it to the floor. She unbuttoned her shirt and let it fall on top of his jumper. He placed his warm hands behind her back and unclipped her bra, before leading her to the rug in the lounge.

'I want you now,' she whispered, as he nuzzled her ears and lay next to her. Within seconds their bodies were entangled on the floor. Gina reached over and flicked the lamp off. The moon shone through the curtains, lighting up their almost naked bodies. Briggs stroked and kissed her. As he reached her breasts, she undid his fly and straddled him. He was ready; she was ready. With one trouser leg off and his jeans half on, she took all that he had to offer. She felt his breathing increase in speed as his open mouth found hers. He kissed her hard as they found their end.

'You said you liked danger,' she said as she leaned to the side.

'I like your version of danger. Good job you turned the lights off,' he said as he sat up. 'My neighbour is just walking his dog.'

She laughed – and then the fire alarm went off. 'Bloody chip pan,' he yelled as he leaped up, almost tripping over his jeans as he darted to the kitchen. 'Do you like pizza?' He threw her shirt at her.

Gina leaned back into the sofa cushions. 'So, we have a hooded figure, a black dog, red diesel. Let's run a few thoughts. What would Deborah be experiencing? Maybe she's on farmland, or in a house? In a room, a cellar? Would there be an outhouse or a shed of some description? A caravan, maybe? Does he live alone? He must do. How could anyone else stand by while someone's being held captive? How many people live on farms alone? Or are they in cahoots? Could there be two of them? Could the other one be Avery?' Gina ran through the list of possibilities as Briggs listened.

'Maybe this person lives with someone,' he said. 'Maybe he doesn't let her or him into his own private space. Maybe they're scared of him, and they don't understand or know? Does he have a family? How does all this tie in with Deborah's life pre-disappearance?' They were coming up with questions and no answers, no evidence, nothing pointing to any one person. Briggs leaned over her and grabbed another slice of pizza from the coffee table. 'Wine?'

'Not for me. I've got to drive home,' she replied. He topped up his half-full glass and took a bite of pizza.

She thought back to Avery's sickly smile. There was still something about the pub she couldn't fathom, something that kept bringing her back to Avery. The relationships amongst the staff weren't sitting well with her. She'd found Charlene happily working with Avery as if all was normal in their workplace. Had he sexually assaulted Deborah?

'You've been married before, haven't you?' Briggs asked.

'Yes. And you?'

'Yes. Divorced. We were far too young when we met. She remarried an office worker. He's home at five thirty every night.'

'We were too young as well. I was so stupid back then,' Gina said, and paused. 'Back then, Terry was working in a tyre garage just down the road from the college. Every day, he'd smile as I passed. Eventually I agreed to a date, only a walk. I should've known that the relationship wasn't going to go well from that point. He was late, really late, and I waited for ages, like a muppet. When he eventually arrived, he was so sweet that I forgave him instantly. Stupid.'

'We've all been made a fool of,' Briggs replied as he took a gulp of his wine.

But Terry had been bad from the start, and Gina had chosen to ignore the signs because she craved something from him: love, attention, self-esteem maybe.

She checked her phone for messages. There was still nothing from Hannah. She opened up Facebook to see if Hannah had posted any updates. For a change, there was nothing angry, just a couple of photos of Gracie sitting in her highchair with a yoghurt beard. Her finger hovered over the like button, but she didn't press it.

'Am I boring you?'

'No, sorry. Family troubles. My daughter's not talking to me at the moment.' As she made to put her phone down, it began to ring. 'Jacob?'

'I just thought I'd see if there was anything new to report,' he said.

'Wyre and O'Connor are still typing up the reports from earlier. They should be available to view soon. I'm heading home in a minute. I'll type up all my notes too, then I'll email you. How're you feeling?' Gina asked. Jessie began to bark as the wind howled.

'Sick, tired, headachy, full of it. Have you got a dog now?'

'No. It's just the neighbour's dog.' Briggs went red as he held in a snigger. 'I was talking to Wyre earlier, and we have a few thoughts. I'll fill you in as soon as I get back. I won't be long. Got to go.' She ended the call and slumped back into the sofa as Briggs burst into fits of laughter.

'That was close,' she said. 'What the hell are we doing?'

'We're doing what most mature, healthy adults do,' he replied.

'I'd best go.'

'Why don't you stay? You've got your laptop in the car, haven't you? And I have an unopened toothbrush in the cupboard.'

'Always prepared?'

'No. Mine is getting scraggy.'

'I'll pass. I have to feed my cat.'

'Okay.' He stood and walked with her towards the door. She grabbed her coat and kissed him on the cheek. 'Maybe another time,' he said.

'Maybe. I'll leave you to deal with your chip pan. Good-night, Chris.'

She looked at the time on her phone as she headed towards her car. It was almost nine. The past couple of hours had flown by. She needed to get home, type up her notes and message Jacob before it got any later.

CHAPTER THIRTY-EIGHT

Wednesday, 6 December 2017

Gina swigged her coffee as she talked Jacob through the points she and Wyre had discussed the previous day. He scrolled down the report, nodding as he read Adele Sutter's statement. He grabbed a tissue and blew his nose before throwing it on top of the pile that was rapidly filling up the waste paper bin beneath his desk. It had been a long week for them all. Most of them were putting in extra hours without pay. They were all hungry for a result. With budget reductions, everything was taking longer than it should. Lab results were taking longer to come back; research was being done by individuals rather than teams. It was hard to know how long they could all go on working under such high pressure before the department cracked.

Gina smiled as she thought back to the previous night. After she'd left Briggs, she'd spent what was left of her evening typing up notes in her cold kitchen. She'd eventually rolled into bed at about one in the morning, only to be back at the station for seven. Her whole night had been filled with one weird dream after another, with intermittent waking followed by constantly fidgeting in bed.

Wyre threw down her pen and smiled as she turned to face them both. The room went quiet as the other officers waited for her to speak. 'We've had a call, ma'am. An Alice Lenton from number twelve Brookfield Avenue, the road that starts on the corner of Luke Jenkins' road. She picked up the letter Smith dropped through her letter box yesterday while doing the rounds. She was at her daughter's all day and only found it this morning. She said something about it being tangled up in her net curtain. Anyway, she claims she saw someone loitering at about two thirty in the morning on the same night that someone tried to break into the Jenkinses' house.'

Slamming her cup down onto Jacob's desk, Gina smiled. 'We needed something and this is it. Come on, Jacob. Let's go and pay this Alice a visit.' Jacob stood with little energy, dragging his coat from the back of the chair. 'O'Connor, when we get back, I want all details on rural businesses in the area fully collated and on my desk. We can't delay any longer.'

'I'll have it all ready and waiting,' he said. 'Oh, and guv?' Gina turned as she zipped up her coat. 'Thanks for the money.'

Gina looked at him. 'Sorry?'

'My bike ride, this weekend. You sponsored me.'

'Oh yes. No worries. I just hope you survive it with all the training you're putting in.' She laughed and grabbed a digestive biscuit off his desk.

'You'll see. I'll show you all when I not only smash it, but come first,' O'Connor replied as he shoved a whole biscuit in his mouth. Gina laughed as she and Jacob left the incident room.

CHAPTER THIRTY-NINE

Jacob sucked on a lozenge as Alice Lenton passed Gina a mug of tea. 'Thank you, Mrs Lenton, that's very kind of you,' Gina said as she took the cup from the trembling lady. Mrs Lenton's bony hands reached for her own cup before she sat in what looked like an orthopaedic chair. It sat higher than the sofa they were sitting on, making the petite old woman look tall. 'As you know, we need to talk to you about the morning of the fourth of December.'

'Of course, Detective. I don't know if I can add much to what you know, but as I did indeed see something, I thought it only right and dutiful to call in.' She put her tea down and straightened her collar, tucking a strand of long white hair behind her ear and sitting up straight with a smile.

Family photos and Christmas cards adorned the immaculate bookshelf behind her chair. Gina noticed a photo of a woman in her twenties standing with Mrs Lenton. She was holding a baby. 'That's a lovely photo of you and your family,' Gina said as she pointed.

'Taken last year. My third great-grandchild, a little boy. I am so blessed to have such a wonderful family,' she replied. Gina smiled and opened her notes. She could see Jacob out of the corner of her eye trying to suppress a cough. He cleared his throat and reached for the glass of water in front of him.

'You certainly are. They're beautiful. Anyway, back to that morning. Tell me what you saw.'

'As I said on the phone, I often wake up in the night. I have sleeping pills but I try not to take them all the time as they really knock me out and, as you know, they're addictive. I treat myself to one a couple of times a week, but that night, I hadn't taken any. I'd watched a bit of telly in my chair, like I am now, and I'd fallen asleep. I awoke about two. The room was cold as the heating is on a timer, and all I had to keep me warm was a throw over my knees.'

'What happened when you woke up?' Gina asked.

Mrs Lenton twiddled her thumbs and stared at the window. 'I was tired but knew I wouldn't sleep once I went to bed, so I went into the kitchen and took one of my tablets. They act quite fast so I knew I'd have to get myself up the stairs and ready for bed as soon as possible. That's what I did. I turned the light off on the landing and felt my way along the walls to my bedroom. I remember my bedroom curtains being open. I can't rest with them open, even after one of my tablets. We all have our going-to-bed routines, don't we?'

'We certainly do, Mrs Lenton,' Gina replied.

'You can call me Alice. Mrs Lenton sounds too formal, like I'm a head teacher or something. I worked in a delicatessen that we used to own. Me and William, when he was alive. I'd serve; he'd present the goods and do the paperwork. We were a good team,' Alice said as she smiled.

Gina cleared her throat and glanced at Jacob. 'Alice it is. Can you tell me what you saw when you reached your bedroom?'

Alice pulled a small piece of fluff from her thick tights and looked up. 'I was getting a little sleepy at this point, so

I leaned on the windowsill. I was about to close the curtains when I saw a man leaning against the lamppost just outside my house. He didn't look drunk or ill, he was just loitering. At this point I was a little suspicious so I watched him, hoping that he would soon go away from my house. Being on my own, you can appreciate that I'm terrified at the thought of being burgled, especially when I'm at home. I have a good security system but people are clever, especially the young when it comes to technology. I suppose you know all this in your profession, don't you, Detectives?'

'We certainly do,' Jacob croaked.

'So, he was leaning against the lamppost,' Gina said, trying to bring the wavering conversation back on track.

'He was. It was odd. He wasn't wearing a coat and it was cold. He just had on one of those zip-up hooded tops. The hood was up. I remember it was a dark colour, maybe black or navy, definitely not a warm tone like brown. I could tell that much in the lamplight. I remember him turning to look up at the houses, my house. He looked right into my bedroom. I don't think he saw me, as the light was off and I was standing behind the curtain, but he did make my heart skip a beat. By this time my tablets were making me woozy.'

Rain began to tap on the window. Gina took a swig of her tea. It was just as she remembered her mother making: sweet with full-fat milk. 'Did you see his face?' she asked.

Alice pulled an embroidered handkerchief from her sleeve and wiped her nose. 'He had a scarf covering his mouth and nose. I didn't catch his eyes but he scared me. Something about the time it took him to stare up at our houses, like he was checking for signs of life before committing a crime. But then he walked away, down the street in that direction.' She pointed towards the Jenkinses' house. 'I was so tired by then, I almost pulled my curtains off the hook as I drew them. I stumbled to my bed and woke up with a thick head about seven.' The woman paused. 'I'm sorry I didn't see more.'

'You've been really helpful, Alice.'

'Did he burgle a house? There have been rumours up and down the street that Mr Jenkins was burgled. He's such a lovely man and his children are lovely too.'

Jacob closed his notebook, coughed and drank the rest of his water. Gina knew she needed to put Alice at ease. 'He wasn't burgled, luckily. If you see this person on your street again, could you please give me a call?' Gina handed her card to Alice.

'I certainly will, Detective Inspector. What a credit to your sex you are. I wished I'd done more than work in a deli.'

'You did do more. You and your husband were business-people; you worked hard. You have a lovely house and a beautiful family. You should be very proud of what you've achieved. Your great-grandson is adorable, too,' Gina said as she stood. 'We will now leave you in peace. You have my number.'

As they reached the car, Gina stood against the lamppost. It was the perfect vantage point. If he was seen, he could duck around the corner and head onto George Street. If he was undisturbed, he could see Luke Jenkins' house perfectly from afar. Her gaze turned to the house next door, near where the intruder had been sitting and watching Luke. 'He came from this direction both times. Maybe he parks up George Street,' she said. They had interviewed many people who lived on the surrounding streets, asking them whether they'd spotted any unusual vehicles that had been parked on the road, anything that had seemed out of place, but nothing had been said. Again, no one had CCTV on the surrounding streets. This area was normally trouble-free. It was a nice area, where people felt safe.

'Maybe, but I don't think that interview yielded much we don't already know,' Jacob said as he pulled out a tissue and gave his nose a good blow.

'It confirms he's stalking them. We have Luke's statement and we have Alice's statement. He's careful, wearing a scarf over his face. But yes, I had hoped for more. We should get back, see if O'Connor has made any headway with the farms.'

Jacob placed his used tissue in his pocket. 'I'm glad you're driving; my head is so thick with this cold.'

'A bit of hard work will soon clear it up,' Gina said as they got in the car.

'I didn't get my bed bath. In fact, she hasn't called again. I think my relationship with Abigail is over.'

'Did it ever start?' Gina asked as she pulled away.

'Plenty more fish and all that.' Jacob grinned.

Gina's phone beeped. It was a text from O'Connor. The information on all the local farms had been collated. Gina put her foot down as they reached the carriageway.

CHAPTER FORTY

Gina shivered as she wedged her office door open to try and disperse the condensation. Two cups sat on her desk, both containing the dried-up dregs of coffee from earlier. She switched the computer on and removed her damp coat. The interview with Mrs Lenton had added nothing new to the evidence they already had. Nothing that would help them catch this man and find Deborah. It did seem that Luke and his family were being stalked, but by who?

She couldn't shake off what she and Wyre had discussed before. This person was most certainly dangerous. Luke had been warned, and he had her number should the man return, but were they doing enough? Before the cuts, they would have offered Luke regular checks by PCs, but the money just wasn't there.

Gina grabbed her phone and dialled PC Smith. 'Smith, could we organise a regular drive-by past the Jenkinses' house? Yes, get it out on the briefing system.' She paused to listen. 'I know you're busy. I know and understand, it's the Christmas season and you're all busy. Please, make it happen.' She paused. 'Thank you.' If something happened to the family and she hadn't done everything in her power to protect them, she'd never forgive herself. She shuddered at the thought. Something was off, she could sense it; they could all sense it.

O'Connor tapped the door and walked in. 'You'll be happy to know that I did some training this morning. I cycled to the station.'

'You only live a mile away and the ground is flat,' Gina replied.

'It was piss easy though. Do one mile, you can do hundreds.' He placed a file on her desk.

Gina opened it. 'Well collated.'

'Thanks, ma'am.' Gina scanned the information in front of her. 'It looks like we have forty-three businesses that fit the brief in the area. Only twelve are operating and they are all farms that would be entitled to use red diesel. Eight of them farm animals and four farm vegetable matter, mostly asparagus and grains.

'Twelve is a manageable number, although I would like a drop-in on the other thirty-one that are not classed as operational at the moment. You never know. Our perp could have a business that is no longer going but could still have access to red diesel. And we can't discount the fact that some of these people might also be selling the odd bit of red diesel for their own gain. That would increase the legwork big time, so I hope it isn't the case. Start with the working farms and then move out to the others. Keep me posted all the way.'

'Will do. We're short on PCs but I'll do my best,' O'Connor replied.

'I know how hard it is,' said Gina. 'I've already put on Smith today. If the PCs can't go to them all, we'll need to. Go with Wyre and get this done quickly. We need to find Deborah.' Gina closed the file and placed her hand on her stomach as it grumbled. She looked up at O'Connor. 'Sorry, no breakfast.'

'I'll get on to the farms. It would be good for us to get out there too. We need to work hard on this one. If it takes all day, I'm in it for the duration, whatever the time,' O'Connor replied. 'By the way, Mrs O has made a Herman cake. It's in the kitchen. Go get a slice, you sound like you could do with some food.'

Gina smiled. 'What the hell is Herman cake? Is it a cake made of Hermans?'

'It's a Herman the German friendship cake. She spent days bubbling up some yeast mix on the worktop and she somehow turned it into cake. The house stinks of the stuff.'

As he left, Gina checked her phone. Still no word from Hannah.

Jacob entered, tapping on the doorframe. 'A long day ahead it is then. Farms to visit, leads to follow.'

'Don't make any plans. I've learned not to make plans, saves letting people down.' Gina stared down at the floor, deep in thought.

'You alright, guv?'

She nodded. 'Just being silly. My daughter's on one with me at the moment.'

'She'll come round, I'm sure.'

'You don't know my daughter. I've let her down so many times. Most other nans probably babysit occasionally or visit regularly. Me, I arrange for them to come over, or for me to go and visit them, and I inevitably end up letting them down.' Gina felt a lump in her throat. 'I should be seeing more of my granddaughter.'

'Not many people understand the demands of the job. No one cares that we're understaffed or that a major crime has just come in. You do a cracking job. I mean look at me – most of my relationships last a month, max. They get fed up of not being able to go out on weekends or evenings. They get fed up when you leave in the middle of a date. Balancing the job and relationships, it's a tricky one. Not all of us can find a husband or wife like O'Connor's. She certainly is one in a million.'

'She certainly is.' Gina paused. 'I've tried my best to be a good mother.'

'Listen to me, guv, you are a good mother. You rid the streets of dangerous people, the same streets that your granddaughter will be out on in a few short years. When that little girl is old enough to understand how cool her nanny is, you're going to be her hero.'

Gina smiled. 'Oh, you're smooth, Jacob.'

'I heard something like that on the TV – Jeremy Kyle, maybe. Those words aren't mine. And tell anyone about what I said and I'll blankly deny it, especially the Jeremy Kyle bit. Right, moving on. It sounds weird, Herman sourdough cake? I hear it's good.'

Gina laughed and nodded. She knew why she loved the job so much. Yes, it was satisfying to catch the bad guys, but it was also about the comradeship, the police family. 'Quick piece of cake and back to work,' she said. 'A starving body equals a poor mind.'

'Who said that?' Jacob asked.

'Me, I think, unless I just heard it.'

'Grab one of your mouldy cups. I hear mould tastes good with coffee.'

'Who said that?' Gina asked.

'Me. I always drink my coffee with mould in it and look how healthy I am. Police perk.' Jacob coughed, pulled a tissue out of his pocket and spat in it.

Gina pulled a mock grimace. 'I'm heading to the Jenkinses' in a short while, so I'll catch up with you later. Get on to the farms and bring me good news.'

CHAPTER FORTY-ONE

'Mother always said I was too kind for my own good. A sensitive, caring boy, she calls me,' he said as he held a cold compress against the lump on the back of her head.

Debbie remembered heading towards the door, but he'd grabbed her chain and yanked, then it had all gone dark. She flinched as she opened one eye. Since the tumble down the stairs, she'd been seeing a halo around objects and was struggling to adjust to any light. She had no idea how long she'd been unconscious. It could have been a few hours, it could have been a day. Fragments of strange dreams began to surface. Her head felt as though it has been smashed with a sledgehammer. Then she remembered: he had tapped her with a hammer. Not quite the sledgehammer that she was picturing in her mind, but it had hurt. As she shivered, gritty sweat gathered above her eyes.

'I can't believe you turned on me after I've been so kind.' He stopped dabbing the back of her head. 'Why? I keep you clean, I feed you, I do everything for you and you know it. You know how much I love you, but I don't feel loved in return.'

She looked away from his cold stare.

'Look at me,' he yelled, as he pulled out a knife, grabbed her hair and forced her to face him. 'Look at me or I'll slice through your neck.'

'I'm sorry,' she whimpered.

'You're sorry. Right. I'll tell you where I am with sorry. Sorry means nothing if you don't really mean it. I can see in your eyes that you don't mean anything you say. Where we go from here is anyone's guess. Slicing through your scrawny neck is sounding like a good option.' He stared into her eyes before placing the knife back in his pocket.

'Can I go home? Please let me go,' she begged as she leaned her head against his chest. She'd pleaded so many times. Why she thought that this time it might work, she had no idea. Hope was all she had in her mind. Hope that he'd see her pain. But the only pain he could see was his own.

He began to breathe deeply and quickly. Spittle emerged in bubbles through his partially closed lips. He flung the compress to the floor and stood. He paced up and down, as he often did. She looked into her lap and watched as her tears dripped from the end of her nose onto her cotton nightdress.

A sharp pain flashed through her head. She pulled the blanket over her knees. Sweat dripped down her forehead and she laughed out loud as she thought of the blow she'd delivered to his head. She'd only managed to strike him once with the kettle, but it had felt so good.

He stopped pacing and his face reddened as he began to seethe. Debbie continued to laugh. She'd laugh through the pain, through the fever, through the racing thoughts. In her mind, she relived the smashing sound over and over again.

A memory darted through her mind, one where she was reading a story about a magic frog to Max and Heidi. She laughed as tears rolled down her face. She was never going to see her children again, so why punish herself with any more misery. Whatever he did to her, she'd laugh. Maybe she'd antagonise him so much that he'd kill her. What difference would it make? She was already dead. If this existence was her life, then death would be a welcome change.

Luke had moved on. Her children were no doubt getting on with their lives. Did they call Luke's new woman Mum? As for Isobel, there was nothing she could do to protect her anymore. Her groin and stomach throbbed. She'd known she was getting worse when the burning pain had started to spread outwards from the wound. Every time she peed, it burned like hell. Her whole stomach was on fire. All night she'd been shivering but hot. Without antibiotics, her days were numbered. Living in filth after a traumatic birth wasn't conducive to a healthy body.

'This is your home,' he yelled. He grabbed her hair and dragged her to the ground. 'I give you a home, security, keep you safe and you laugh in my face. I give you a baby, one of life's most precious gifts, and you laugh. I give you my everything, my whole self, and I see it in your eyes. All you think about is him.' Debbie stumbled to the floor as he slapped the side of her head with the back of his hand. He kneeled beside her. She felt his hot breath on her cheek but she continued to laugh. 'Stop laughing. Stop fucking laughing!' he yelled as he brought his hand to her cheek over and over again.

'It's so funny though.'

'What is?'

Through bloodied teeth, she spat her words out. 'You. I'm dying, and you are not in control of my death. Unless you kill me, that is. You can still be in control, you can take my life.'

Debbie leaned up, grabbed his hand and forced him to slap her once again. In her mind, she was hysterical, the laughter never ended. She was ready to go. The pain was just pain, it was how she knew she was alive. When she ceased to be, the pain would stop. She would no longer be his prisoner.

He withdrew his hand and took a step back. She spotted something in his gaze that she'd never seen before. *He doesn't know what to do. He's scared.* He didn't know whether to hit her or leave. A mighty shiver travelled through her body. Sweat continued to seep out of her pores and the cold caused her teeth to chatter. He stepped forward and offered his hand to help her off the floor.

'You're sick. Mother said I was a kind boy. Mother would tell me to forgive you, you're not to blame for the feverish gibberish you spew. I shouldn't have slapped you in a temper. Be a kind boy,' he stuttered as he grabbed her arm and pulled her back onto the bed. 'I will fetch you some food. Soup, chicken soup. That will make you better and you'll forgive me.'

He walked towards the door. She tried to look up but the light caused a shot of pain to travel from her cranium to her neck. She rubbed the side of her head until the sensation passed. Light turned to darkness as the door closed. She lay flat on her back, listening as the chain that bound her settled with her stillness. She listened as he went down the stairs and out of the main door. Moments later she heard the dog barking. He was back in the main house now. Chicken soup. That was a result. Her body was screaming for some sustenance. It was rare that he brought her anything except honey on toast, but occasionally she did get something better. Her heart rate slowed down and she almost felt warm. She closed her eyes and let her exhausted mind and body rest. It was no use fighting it.

Debbie walked through the darkness of the street until she reached her house. Where was her shoe? No wonder her feet were bleeding; she'd just stepped in a broken bottle on the pavement. The wound didn't hurt one bit. Even the fact that the glass was still lodged in her foot wasn't bothering her. Maybe she'd become so cold that it had numbed the pain.

Why was she only wearing one shoe? A perfect little snowflake settled on her nose. She almost went cross-eyed trying to get a better view of it. She shivered and wrapped her arms around her body as she stared through the bay window. 'Right, time to go home and see the kids.' She needed to be sitting in front of the fireplace with a hot chocolate, watching Christmas films with Luke and their babies.

She tried to take a step forward but the glass that was stuck between her toes was burrowing deeper into her flesh. She leaned against the gate and lifted her foot up. She yanked at the green shard but it wouldn't budge.

'Luke,' she called, but he couldn't hear her from inside the house. She pulled again and the glass dislodged. As she yanked it out, a gush of blood oozed from the gaping wound and flooded the ground. 'Luke!' As if sensing her presence, he came to the window. She tried to hobble forward, but blood kept flooding out. Her leg was getting heavier and her mind felt woozy. Luke looked out into the night, beyond her and into the darkness. Tears began to fall. What was happening? Why couldn't he see or hear her? A featureless woman holding a baby came to join him at the window. He brushed her hair from her face and kissed her.

Heidi and Max ran over to them and they all hugged before closing the curtains. 'Luke!' she yelled, as tears flooded her face. She began choking as mucus ran down the back of her nose and into her throat as she sobbed. She couldn't breathe; she was choking on her own mucus. She tried to cough harder to move the obstruction. She tried to swallow to dislodge it.

'Luke, Luke, Luke. Why do you shout for him? It is not him who feeds you and cares for you.' He forced a spoonful of chicken soup down her throat. She prised an eye open and observed the frustration on his face. She gagged and spluttered as the warm liquid slid down the back of her throat, coughing the soup onto his chest. 'Eat it, you bitch,' he yelled. She swallowed. It was warm but flavourless.

Whether her fever was upsetting her taste buds or he had just given her some other warm liquid, she had no idea, but she needed it. Her body needed the calories. Or did it? Death wouldn't be so bad. She wanted this all to end, but her body and mind were still fighting. Why couldn't they just give up?

Tears rolled down her face as he placed the spoon in her mouth once again. 'Good, nearly finished, then you can have a sleep.'

Sleep, she wanted to sleep. Maybe she'd wake up, maybe she wouldn't. Maybe, all maybe, maybe nothing… It was getting harder to think. Maybe what? She lost her train of thought. What was she thinking? Something about a cut foot.

An overwhelming sense of loss flushed through her body and mind. She slumped back into the blankets and closed her eyes, and within minutes she was standing in the dark, staring in through the bay window. The curtains were closed but she could hear a baby crying. 'I'm still here,' she whispered as she sobbed outside their gate. 'Don't forget me.'

CHAPTER FORTY-TWO

Gina's stomach had finally stopped rumbling. She wasn't sure if Herman cake was her thing, but at least it filled the gap. She approached the door to Luke Jenkins' house and took a deep breath, brushing her fingers through her tangled hair. There was no avoiding another chat with Luke. He needed to be more vigilant, on alert and suspicious of everything and everyone, no matter how insignificant. In her heart, she didn't believe they were safe.

'Inspector Harte,' Luke said as he approached her from behind. He smiled and loosened his tie.

Gina stumbled back. 'Apologies. I was just about to... Look, I know yesterday was strained—'

'Sorry I made you jump. It should be me who apologises. It's not been good around here lately and I know that none of this is your fault. Admittedly, I've been cursing you all for not pursuing Deborah's disappearance more over the years, but I want to help things, not hinder them.' Luke paused and rubbed his temples. 'I had to talk with my children last night about all that's been happening. Heidi is devastated and Max, he doesn't understand. Either that or he's pretending and doesn't want to talk. But our family is made of tough stuff and we'll pull through it. Debbie is made of tough stuff. Wherever she is, I know she'll be fighting to get back with us. We have to be strong for her, and my job is to keep this family together.' Luke looked away, towards the wall. 'Whoever is watching us, he'll be back and I'll be waiting.'

Gina looked up at Luke. 'Whatever you do, call me immediately. Don't approach this person if you don't have to. I will come straight away.'

'I'll do everything I need to do to protect my children.'

As the front door opened, the baby's shrill screams escaped outside. 'Hello, Inspector,' Cathy said.

'Sorry I'm late,' Luke replied as he stepped into the house.

Cathy took his coat and hung it up. 'Not to worry, you know I never mind. The children have both eaten and are watching TV. Isobel is due for a feed, as you can tell.' Cathy grimaced as another wail pierced the hallway.

Gina followed the pair into the kitchen. Devina was sitting out of the way, in the corner. Cathy tested the bottle that was on the side and placed the teat into Isobel's mouth. The little girl sucked contentedly as Cathy stroked her brow.

'To what do we owe this visit, Inspector?' Cathy asked.

Gina undid the buttons on her coat. The house was exceptionally warm. She felt her cheeks begin to redden as she fanned her face with her hand.

'I know it's hot in here,' Cathy explained. 'I've kept it warm for Isobel.'

'Excuse me. I just have some calls to make. I'll be back in a few minutes,' Devina said as she stood and left the room, holding her phone.

Gina smiled as the social worker passed. 'I just wanted to personally pop by to see how things were going and to tell you that I have organised regular drive-bys. Every couple of hours a PC will drive by and check on your house. After the other night and with all that's been happening…' Gina paused.

'Do you know something you're not telling us?' Luke asked.

Gina looked up at him. 'Since the attempted break-in and your report of being watched by a stranger, we feel it would only be right to keep a closer eye on what's happening around here. We still don't know whether this person has anything to do with Deborah's disappearance, but we're working hard to try and get to the bottom of what's happening. We want to ensure that you are safe and that you feel safe. As you said yesterday, you have children in the house and we want to offer you some protection.'

'Thank you for being honest,' Luke said as he sat at the kitchen table. He grabbed the pack of nappies blocking his view and placed them on the floor. 'Are you any closer to finding Debbie?'

'Sorry.' Gina shook her head. 'There are several lines of investigation that we are following, but there's nothing new to report at the moment. We have officers out, looking at every strand of information that we receive. As you know, I can't promise you anything, but as soon as I find anything out, I will be the first to call you.' Gina knew it wasn't the answer Luke wanted. He wanted to know that the police were closing in on her whereabouts, that they'd narrowed down a list of suspects, that they were on a dead-cert trail that led to Deborah's return, but Gina had nothing concrete to offer them. Cathy eased the teat from the sleeping baby's mouth and held her towards Luke.

Luke stood and took the baby. 'This little one needs her mummy, and I'm sure her mummy needs her too. I know I sound ungrateful sometimes, but thank you. Thank you for the patrols and thank you for not giving up. If I see or hear anything, I will call you immediately.' He held the baby and paced the floor as the little one gently snored.

'I'll leave you both alone now.' Cathy followed Gina out and opened the front door.

'Please bring my daughter back home,' Cathy said as she held the door open. Gina looked sympathetically at the woman, not knowing what to say. She wanted to reassure Cathy that her daughter would be returned to her, that her children would have their mother back and that Luke would have his wife home, but she couldn't. She stood there ready to speak, but then closed her mouth and nodded before saying goodbye.

Dampness filled the evening air as she crossed the road and headed over to the wall. She stopped outside Alice Lenton's house and leaned against the lamppost, then she stared over at the Jenkinses' house. The suspect had been standing on this spot before the break-in, observing, planning his next move. Gina looked up at Alice's bedroom and then at her lounge window. The curtains were closed. She ran her fingers through her frizzing hair and a few drops of rain began to fall.

She sat on the wall and took her phone out of her pocket. Still no message from Hannah. She rubbed her forehead as she imagined being in Cathy's position. How would she handle things if Gracie had been the baby found on the library step? How would she sleep at night if her daughter had been missing for years? If a baby sharing her DNA had been abandoned? Would she obsess about the man who made the phone call that led them to check the baby's DNA?

She reached into her pocket and found a stray lozenge. She unwrapped it and popped it into her mouth as she contemplated all that was happening. She missed her daughter. She needed to hug her and hold Gracie and tell them she loved them. She flinched as a sudden clap of thunder filled the air. She sat on the wall as the rain fell.

Back then, on the night of Terry's death, as thunder clashed, she had stared at Terry's lifeless body at the bottom of the stairs as Hannah screamed from her cot. They'd tussled at the top of the stairs before he'd slammed her against the wall.

She wiped the tears and rain from her face. Deborah was going through much worse. Was she imprisoned by fear or shackles? Gina had known the power of fear.

She had to crack the case and bring Deborah home. Avery? Nelson? Who was the hooded man at the school? She'd looked into Avery's life thoroughly over the past few days. He had no connections to farms, no pets and she'd never seen him in a hooded jacket. He'd lived above the pub four years ago, and he still lived there now. It was his only residence. His parents still lived in North London, hardly rural, and he had a sister who had two children. She hit the wall with the flat of her hand. What was she missing? She would go over the notes from the Angel Arms once again and then look at Deborah's workplace.

A little further down the street, Devina stepped out of her car. She must have finished with her calls.

'How are the family doing?' Gina called as she walked over.

'Unbelievably well. It's so awful, what they're going through. Any news on Deborah Jenkins?'

Gina shook her head. 'No news.'

Devina looked sympathetic, and waved as she hurried back towards the Jenkinses' house.

Gina looked at her phone, at Hannah's name in her contacts list. She pressed the call button. The phone rang twice and was cut off. She tried again and once again the call was cut off.

As she walked back towards her car, she typed out a message on her phone and held her index finger over the send button. She needed some company. She needed Briggs. They could talk about the case, eat together and who knows. A message pinged back.

Come to mine. We can order some food while we work.

She replied.

See you in a couple of hours.

CHAPTER FORTY-THREE

She watched as Briggs slept beside her. His bedroom wasn't as comfortable as hers and she still couldn't believe she'd ended up staying. It didn't feel right. There was a bed and furniture, but there were no pictures, no cushions and only one flat pillow each. After they'd caught up on the case, they'd enjoyed a takeaway in front of the television. When they'd made love, her mind had been elsewhere. She was sure he could tell.

Briggs wasn't Terry, she had to keep reminding herself of that. She could leave his house at any time. She gasped and took a deep breath, trying to force her tears away. Deborah's case was affecting every aspect of her life. She couldn't get the images of baby Isobel out of her mind, and the scenarios that her mind constantly churned up weren't pleasant.

She took the crime book Briggs had been reading from his chest and pulled the quilt over his arm. She removed his reading glasses, leaned over and placed them on his bedside table. He stirred and half opened an eye. 'Are you sleeping over?' he asked.

Gina hit the shutdown button on her laptop and closed the lid. 'Do you mind? I'm too tired to drive home.' He shook his head as he rolled over and nestled into his pillow. She turned off the light. The case would still be waiting for her when she awoke. With heavy eyes, and a heavier heart, she allowed sleep to take over.

*

As she sank into a deep sleep, she dreamed she was standing on the landing in her old house. She knew Terry was in the house, but where? Then he ran at her, approaching at high speed. His dilated pupils told her all she needed to know about his current state. There would be no reasoning with him.

Hannah screamed. She needed to get to Hannah's cot before Terry did. She tried to duck under his arm but he grabbed her by the hair, yanking her back. She felt her head crash against the wall.

She smacked the side of Terry's head, but he didn't even flinch. A grin spread across his face as he pinned her against the wall and unbuckled his belt. 'Please, Terry, no. Please,' she said as she wriggled and twisted.

His zip became jammed. He let go of her for a second to tackle it. As he looked down, he stumbled at the top of the stairs. Then, with a gentle nudge, Gina shoved him over the edge. As he fell backwards, his eyes locked onto hers and his arms reached forward, as if he were pleading for her to grab him. But she didn't move. She just remained still and watched as his skull cracked against the wall, then his leg scraped the bannister and he finally landed in a heap by the front door.

Gina jolted up and ran to the bathroom. Acid began to climb up her throat. She turned on the bathroom light and kneeled in front of the toilet. Her heart was whirring. Sweat dripped down her brow as she shivered. As she stared into the bowl, the feel of cold tiles on her legs grounded her and her heart rate began to slow. She grabbed the sink and dragged herself up. She ran the tap and splashed her face with icy water then stared at her reflection.

Her reddened skin was slowly returning to its normal colour. She shivered until her joints ached. As she leaned over the sink, she allowed herself to quietly sob. Had she shoved Terry down the stairs that night? Even if it was just a little shove, did that make her a murderer? She felt a yearning to hold Hannah as a baby in her arms and tell her everything was going to be alright.

'Are you okay?' Briggs asked, grabbing his robe from the back of the bathroom door and placing it around her shivering body. 'Come back to bed. We need to warm you up.' He led her back to the bedroom and helped her back into bed. 'Are you ill?'

'I had a bad dream, that's all,' she said as she wiped her face and turned away.

'It's not real. Come here.' He placed his arm around her shoulders and pulled her closer to him.

She reached over and grabbed her phone, hoping that Hannah had texted her, but again there was nothing.

'Is there anything I can get you? Water?' Briggs asked.

'No. I'm fine.' She pulled away from his embrace. 'I'm going to head home. I shouldn't be here, we both know that.'

'It's the middle of the night.'

He was right. There was no point in leaving. She turned away from him. He turned off the light and they both lay there in the dark. 'I'm sorry. That was embarrassing.'

'Don't be daft.' He snaked an arm around her waist. 'Let's try and get some sleep. It's going to be a long day.'

As she closed her eyes, she thought of Hannah again. She owed it to her to be there on Saturday. She was going to attend the service. She'd do it for her daughter. She wiped her face on the sleeve of his robe and enjoyed his warmth as she closed her eyes and drifted off to sleep.

CHAPTER FORTY-FOUR

Thursday, 7 December 2017

Luke lay there, half asleep and half awake, thinking about everything that was happening. It had been a long few days, getting to know Isobel. His phone buzzed. He grabbed it and saw that he had a text from Brooke.

I miss you.

He stared at the words. His heart ached for Brooke, but he loved Debbie, he'd always loved Debbie. He began to type out a reply, then stopped. He had no idea how he felt. He placed the phone down and stared out of the window, at the stars.

He thought back to earlier that day. Max had complained that Isobel was noisy and had asked how long she was going to keep visiting for. Heidi didn't seem as annoyed by her presence and quite enjoyed playing peekaboo with her, but then the questions about Mummy came up. He'd tried to explain what he could, but Heidi wasn't stupid. He couldn't gloss over things the same way as he could with Max. She'd gone very quiet, and he'd found her crying into her little jewellery box, which had once belonged to her mother.

When Debbie had been pregnant with Heidi, he'd cursed himself many a time for thinking that the arrival of their daughter would ruin what they had together. He thought he'd always be second when it came to affection. But his little girl had stolen his heart. She was the most precious thing in the universe. Then Max came along and made their life complete. It broke his heart to see their children so confused and upset. He thought it had been hard when they were little, but any hardship back then was nothing compared to what they were all going through now.

It hadn't always been easy, especially in the early days when Debbie was on maternity leave. Babies were expensive and the property market was up and down. One month they'd be celebrating with a bottle of bubbly, the next they'd be eating mostly beans on toast in the run up to payday. They would both laugh through the uncertainty and make light of it. It was part of what he loved so much about Debbie – she was an eternal optimist. She'd originally not wanted to leave the children in day care, but needs must, and Cathy had helped out a lot. The children actually loved it and thrived being around other children.

Luke smiled as he reminisced about the good times. He would eat nothing but beans on toast for the rest of his life if it meant he could have his Debbie home. He wiped a tear from his cheek as he stared into the darkness of his bedroom. He wondered if Debbie still held on in some small way to her optimism, or if she'd changed beyond repair. Would they be reunited? And if they were, would she reject him? Would the trauma she'd gone through mean the end of what they'd had?

If she came home, he would make it work. He'd be there in his entirety throughout her recovery. He wasn't naive to the prospect of what he might have to face, but he loved Debbie more than anything and he wanted her back with him and their children. They would make it work. He sat up and rubbed his eyes. How could he be this exhausted and not be able to nod off?

Did he just hear a trickle? He held his breath and listened. The letter box clattered and a few seconds later a whooshing sound followed. He jumped out of bed in his pyjama bottoms and T-shirt and ran for the bedroom door.

'Max! Heidi!' he yelled as he threw their doors open. He ran towards the top of the stairs and watched as the orange flames flickered in front of the main door. The fire spread along the hallway and began licking the wooden bannister of the stairs. The sound of the smoke alarm filled the house.

'What's happening, Daddy?' Heidi asked, looking confused, with one eye open. She coughed as she inhaled a lungful of smoke.

'Go to my bedroom and wait by the window.' He ran into Max's room and snatched the quilt off his sleeping son's body.

'Dad?' Max rubbed his eyes. 'What's that noise?'

'We have to go.' Luke grabbed the little boy's arm and dragged him to his own bedroom. Debbie and he had carefully planned their escape in the event of a fire. There was a small ledge below his bedroom window, where the kitchen had been slightly extended by the previous owner. He needed to feed Heidi and Max onto the ledge and follow them. From there, they could jump down. As he passed the landing, he saw that the flames were making their way up the stairs.

He helped Heidi through the window first. Max obediently followed. 'It's cold, Daddy, and I haven't got my shoes or coat,' Max cried, tears falling down his cheeks.

'Come on Max. We have to get down,' Heidi said in a calm manner. If he'd had time to stop and talk, he'd have told her how proud he was of her for being such a help amongst the chaos.

He grabbed his phone from the bedside table and stepped out of the window. 'Right, kids, I need you to be strong and brave. Can you be that for me?' he shouted. Heidi nodded; Max was still crying. She grabbed his hand and hugged her brother.

'I'm going to hold you by the arms and lower you on to the grass. Can you be ready to jump when I say?' Heidi nodded. 'You're going first because you're the tallest and then I can pass your brother down,' he said to her. Max let go of his sister and starting bawling. Tears filled the little boy's eyes as he stared out at the garden, confused as to how he'd got there and what was happening.

Luke grabbed Heidi's hands and lay on his stomach as she wiggled over the edge. He lowered her as far as he could. 'I'm going to have to let you go. Can you land okay?'

'I think so, Daddy?' she said as she looked up at him with teary eyes.

'Get ready on three,' he shouted. 'One, two, three.' He let go of his daughter and heard her yelp as she landed on the grass below. He looked down. She waved back at him.

'I'm okay, Daddy. My foot just hurts a bit but I'm okay.'

Luke grabbed Max. 'Right, I need you to be a big man for me now, son. Can you do that?'

The boy sobbed into his father's chest. 'I'm scared, Daddy. I don't want to jump.'

'I need you to be a brave boy. Remember, we spoke about what would happen if we had a fire. We have a fire in there and we need to do this.' Luke heard the roaring of the flames coming ever closer. He grabbed Max's arm and lowered him over the ledge. 'Daddy, no. I can't jump. I'm too short.'

'You can do this. Heidi will be there to lower you down.'

He lowered the boy as far as his arms would reach. 'I have your foot, Max. I'm here,' Heidi shouted.

'After three. One—'

'No, I don't want to do it. Please, Daddy.'

'Two, three.' He dropped Max and hoped that Heidi had managed to assist his fall. In the distance, he heard a fire engine approaching. Someone must have called the fire brigade. He looked down and saw Max and Heidi sitting on the grass. Heidi was comforting him as he cried into her neck, but they both looked fine. Smoke began to billow out of the bedroom window. He had to get down, away from the building.

Within seconds a firefighter had run around the back. Another followed with a portable ladder. 'We're coming to get you, just hold tight.' She placed the ladder against the wall. 'Is there anyone else in the house?'

'No, it's just us,' Luke shouted as he climbed down and ran towards his children, relieved that Isobel was still only with them for short visits 'I'm so proud of you both, so proud,' he said as he hugged them closely. They were gently ushered out to the front, where a crowd had gathered. A large hose was pumping water into their hallway. The door had been bashed in. Smoke filled the air as they extinguished the last of the flames.

'You're very lucky. With your quick thinking and your good fire-resistant carpet, your family is safe and the damage is minimal,' the firefighter said.

Pulling his phone out of his pocket, Luke selected Cathy's number. The children needed somewhere to go for the rest of the night, somewhere safe.

As he stood to the side of the road to make the call, the drive-by patrol car pulled up. If only they'd been there a bit earlier, they might have caught the person who set the fire and prevented this whole mess. Luke shook his head as the officer got out of the car. 'I just heard on the radio. We passed here only an hour or so ago.'

'The fire is under control and everyone is accounted for and safe. We've checked the house,' said the firefighter. 'It looks like the blaze started in the hallway by the letter box, but it's too early to be sure. However, there is a smell of accelerant hanging in the air. We need to survey the damage more thoroughly, which we'll begin soon.'

Luke turned to face them. 'I was lying in bed and I heard liquid being poured through the letter box. I heard it. Someone tried to kill us. He tried to kill us!'

Cathy answered his call and he sobbed as he relayed to her what had happened. He needed her to just turn up and take them to her house. As he ended the call, an ambulance pulled up. Heidi started to weep as he led her towards the first paramedic and up the ramp, into the ambulance. With the attempted break-in and now the fire at his house, Luke knew the hooded man would stop at nothing to harm his family.

CHAPTER FORTY-FIVE

With closed eyes, Gina reached out in an attempt to grab her phone. It vibrated off the bedside table and landed somewhere on the floor. The ringing stopped. She prised her eyes open and leaned across Briggs to see the time on his radio alarm. Two thirty in the morning. She sat up and leaned over the side of the bed. Eventually, she located her phone. She rubbed her eyes and noticed the missed call from Jacob.

'Is everything alright?' Briggs asked, as his phone beeped too.

She fumbled in the dark for her clothes, which she'd left in a folded pile by the door. The moonlight coming through the bathroom window flooded the landing and seeped into the bedroom as she nudged the door further open. Her phone went again, and she jogged towards the bathroom and answered. 'Jacob.'

'There's been a fire at the Jenkinses' house.'

'Are the family okay?'

'All are safe. I don't know what would've happened if it wasn't for Mr Jenkins' quick thinking. Apparently, he lowered the two children from the extension ledge off his bedroom. It all sounds very dramatic but everyone is safe. It definitely looks suspicious. And get this, there's a witness. The witness called the fire brigade. He didn't see the fire being set but he did see someone suspicious before turning into the road and seeing flames. I don't know any more than that at the moment.'

'Head straight to the station and interview the witness. I'll head to Luke's house.'

'Will do, guv. See you in a bit.'

Gina began to shake with excitement as she paced the bathroom. A witness was just what they needed. She forced her legs into her trousers and quickly buttoned up her shirt. She dabbed her hair with some water and smiled as she grabbed the new toothbrush that Briggs had left out for her.

'Fire at the Jenkinses' house. I'm heading over now.'

Briggs was getting out of bed and battling with his trouser legs while half asleep. 'See you at the station,' he said.

CHAPTER FORTY-SIX

As she pulled up on Luke's road, she spotted the ambulance outside the house. She turned the ignition off and walked over to him. 'I just heard.'

'We're all safe, thankfully,' Luke said, clutching a blanket around his shoulders. Max was sitting on a seat in the ambulance while a paramedic was tending to Heidi's ankle. 'Slight sprain but she's okay, aren't you, sweetie?' he said as Heidi looked over and wiped her teary eyes.

'She's been very brave,' said the paramedic.

'I jumped out of the bedroom window,' she said with a slight smile.

'It sounds like you all did really well,' Gina replied. She lightly pulled Luke away from Heidi's curious ears. 'Did you see anything?'

Luke rubbed his tired eyes. 'I've already spoken to an officer, a few minutes ago, but no, I saw nothing. At approximately half one, I heard a trickle through the letter box and then the fire started. From then on, well, the rest is a blur. My only priority was getting the children out of the house.' Luke's hands trembled as he brought them up to his mouth. He let out a sob. 'He's trying to kill us. Whoever has Debbie is trying to destroy the rest of my family. Not content with what he's done to my wife, he's out to get the rest of us.' Gina looked down.

She'd have loved to reassure him, but she knew he was more than likely correct. This was a vindictive attack by someone intent on burning the house down with the family in it. She watched as forensics carried their kit bags towards the front door and began their work.

'I'm so sorry this is happening to you, Luke. Do you have somewhere to stay tonight?'

'Yes. We're okay. The kids like staying with their nan anyway. I don't know how I'm going to deal with all of this. I don't know if I can go back in there with what's happened.' He wiped his teary face with the blanket and stared into space.

'Daddy. The lady gave me a sticker for being a brave boy,' Max shouted as he bounded along the pavement and hugged Luke's legs. 'Are you crying, Daddy?'

Luke smiled. 'Just a bit.'

'I left my dinosaur in the house.'

'Max,' Cathy shouted from the other side of the road as she crossed over. She hurried over to Luke and hugged him before bending down and ruffling Max's hair. 'Where's your sister?'

Luke nodded towards the ambulance, and Cathy bustled off to sit with Heidi. Gina watched as Cathy bent down and kissed her granddaughter on the forehead.

Gina's phone beeped. 'I'm needed at the station,' she said, reading the text. 'I have your number and I know where you'll be staying. Any news or updates at all, I'll let you know immediately. I really am so sorry this is happening to you.'

As she turned to go, Luke grabbed her arm with his shaking hands. 'Please. I can't live like this. This is too much. I don't know what to do anymore.'

She placed her hand on his arm. 'You *can* do this. See your children over there, they need you to be strong for them. You are doing the right thing. Tonight, go to your mother-in-law's house and stay there. You'll be safe with her and we'll continue patrolling.'

Luke nodded and began to weep.

'It's okay, Daddy. I'll look after you,' Max said as he hugged his father. Luke kneeled beside him and wrapped his small frame in his arms.

Gina hoped more than anything that this witness was going to be the one. Just one clue was all she needed, one good clue. It was obvious that they were close – the perp was becoming desperate. He had to slip up soon. Maybe tonight he had.

CHAPTER FORTY-SEVEN

'Fill me in,' Gina said as she strode across the incident room towards Jacob. She threw her coat over a desk and sat next to him.

'What a nightmare for that family. I don't envy them at the moment.' Jacob rubbed his dark eyes. She noticed that his shirt wasn't properly tucked in and he was wearing odd socks. His fine hair was mussed at the back where he'd been separated from his pillow; he'd obviously rushed in without combing his hair. Consequences of being called out in the middle of the night. She then reflected on her own appearance and grimaced at the thought.

Briggs entered and sat down, trying to flatten his hair. 'I hear we have a witness,' he said.

Jacob threw his pen down. 'We certainly do, and we have a description. A twenty-seven-year-old local by the name of Elliot Cooper was on his way back from a friend's house. He's also the one who called the fire department. Anyway, the suspect passed him with a holdall that could easily have contained an empty fuel can of some description. Cooper said the suspect was muttering to himself and didn't even notice him as he passed. He was wearing some sort of hooded top but the hood was down. He said he wouldn't have ordinarily taken much notice but the man's behaviour was exceptionally odd and it was so late.'

'How close was he to the suspect?' Gina asked.

Jacob pulled out the typed-up statement and began to scan the information on it. 'The suspect bumped into him. That was another thing he said – there wasn't even an apology. Our man shouted at the suspect. As per his statement, he called him a wanker, but he was completely ignored. Mr Cooper stated that he knew he'd had a couple of drinks so he didn't pursue the incident any further, which is when he continued on towards Herring Crescent, where he lives. Of course, he never got home as he spotted the Jenkinses' front door alight and called the fire brigade.'

He handed Gina the statement. She was immediately drawn to one piece of information, though she couldn't work out why. 'Dark messy hair, about five nine or ten. Average build. Mr Cooper said that he watched the suspect rubbing his neck and left shoulder as he approached, as if he were in some discomfort.' Gina stood and began pacing the incident room. She stopped and closed her eyes. 'Where's my mind going with this?'

'Are you okay, ma'am?' Wyre asked, entering with a mug of coffee.

'Shh.' Briggs held a finger up to his mouth.

'Yes, there's just something…' Gina trailed off as she stared into space.

'What are you thinking?' Briggs asked.

The room was silent as she tapped the statement and smiled.

'I've got it. I know who we're looking for. Briefing in the incident room in two minutes. I want everyone there.'

CHAPTER FORTY-EIGHT

'Get all the information we have on Jeffrey Wall – now.' All the old notes flashed through her mind. Luke, Deborah's workplace, the pub, the school. His car had been in the Angel Arms car park all that night; it hadn't moved. He'd been in the office – or had he? Did the staff just assume he was in the office, therefore providing his alibi without thinking? He must have left by foot, avoiding the cameras. As the person who was watching the CCTV that night he'd certainly know where he could walk to avoid detection. Clever, not even a shadow on the footage. So where the hell had he left the van?'

Jacob stood and walked over to Gina. 'The barrel man at the pub?'

She turned to face him and her smile turned into a grin. 'He's about five ten with brown hair, but there's an even bigger giveaway…'

'Guv?' Wyre said.

'The day we went back to the pub, I watched as he brought the barrel up from the cellar. He placed it down for a moment and I noticed him rubbing his neck. Imagine carrying barrels like that, for years. It would do me in. He was carrying the barrel on his left shoulder. It's him. Paula, put a warrant out for his arrest and let all departments know. We need to get to him before dawn. Surprise the bastard.' She grabbed her coat.

'Did you just call me Paula? I think that's the first time you've ever used my first name,' she said with a smile.

'Indeed I did. Now quick, we need to apply for a search warrant on Wall's property. I'll call our lovely magistrate Daniel Berwick and let him know we're on our way to get it signed.'

'On it now, guv.' Wyre turned back to her computer and began typing away.

Jacob took the statement from Gina, held it to his lips and kissed it. 'Thank you, Mr Cooper.' His phone rang and he smiled as he listened to the other person on the line. 'Add a chipped tooth to the description.'

Briggs stood. 'Nail the bastard and keep me updated on everything.'

CHAPTER FORTY-NINE

As they charged through Wall's door, led by the enforcer, Gina called out, 'Jeff Wall, this is DI Harte and DS Driscoll. We have a warrant for your arrest and a warrant to search the property.' She crept a few steps closer to one of the closed doors. She wriggled in her stab vest and realised it was a little bit tight. Her breath was ejected with force every time she exhaled. She felt for her truncheon and pepper spray, which were all accessible and in their rightful place. She flung the door open as officers flooded the other rooms in unison. She pulled out her torch as she entered the dark kitchen-lounge. 'Bloody hell, it stinks in here,' she said as she covered her nose.

Jacob brushed past her. 'Fortunately, it only smells of old bin,' he replied. The curtains were drawn on the old split-level cottage. Wall lived on the ground floor.

'There's no one here,' one of the officers shouted.

'Where the hell is he?' Gina whispered. She stepped around the room, flashing her torch into every corner and crevice. The seventies' brown and orange wallpaper had peeled in strips off the walls, revealing the damp plaster beneath. The old tiled fireplace was devoid of any waste and the room was freezing. Hardly any furniture occupied the space in the small room. A floral two-seater sofa was pushed against the back wall. An old teak coffee table sat in front of it. She flashed her torch a little closer to the table. There was a single coffee cup containing a mass of mould that resembled mushrooms. An old box-style television filled the corner of the room by the window. Gina walked over to the fireplace and got a closer view of a photo in a frame. 'He has a photo of Deborah. Was this taken outside the school?'

Jacob walked over to her and stared at the photo. 'That's definitely the school her kids attended.'

The photo had been taken from a distance. Deborah had been standing there, unaware that she was being watched. Gina felt a wash of nausea spreading through her body. Fanning her face, she took a step back.

'Guv?' Jacob said.

'What?'

'You look a bit peaky, are you alright? I know it whiffs in here but we've smelled worse.'

Gina shook her head. 'I'm okay, it's just the remnants of this virus.' She knew it was a lie. It was the smell of rot and the thought that Deborah was somewhere out there, still being held by this monster. The hairs on her neck prickled as she thought of Terry. She imagined his filthy hands all over her naked body as she wept. She hoped that Wall's filthy hands weren't all over Deborah while they were here.

'Tell me about it. When I awoke in the night, I had to spend several minutes coughing my guts up.'

'Thank you, Jacob,' she said, taking a deep breath. She turned back to the photo. That photo confirmed everything.

Wyre entered and headed straight to Gina. 'Is that who I think it is?'

'Certainly is. Now we need to figure out where he's keeping her and where he is now. We need to get hold of him quick. We don't even know if Deborah's okay after everything she's been through. I don't know what I'll tell her family if the outcome isn't good.' Gina adjusted her stab vest and turned away from Wyre.

'We've obtained his current vehicle registration from the DVLA and we have officers on the lookout for his car. We'll catch him,' Wyre replied.

'I know we will,' said Gina. 'I just hope it's not too late for Deborah.'

Jacob had stepped out to check on the rest of the flat, and now he popped his head back into the musty living room. 'They're bagging and tagging a few items in his bedroom but he seems to be a man of very few possessions. There really isn't much, apart from a shoebox containing a pile of old photos. Looks like childhood portraits of him with his parents. He has no computer, no other electronic devices, hardly any clothes. It's as if he's just using this place as a cover and for the storage of random junk. We've checked the bin and there's only takeaway leftovers in there. What you can smell is half a mouldy portion of fish and chips and what looks like a curry. He doesn't have any bills or identification on the premises.'

'Sounds about right. Looks like it is just a cover. Why he's left a photo here is beyond me. Maybe he can't bear to be anywhere without Deborah. He's one dangerously devoted arse wipe,' Gina replied as she walked away from the fireplace. 'He'd been watching her for months at the school, after work, at the pub, even at home. He finally saw his opportunity on that cold winter night. He'd been prepared for a long time.

He must have a van. I know there isn't one registered to him, but... The night he left the pub, he must've used one then, leaving his car in view of the CCTV. He'd probably done that on many occasions, and his colleagues never noticed. He isn't the life and soul of anything. He quietly comes and goes, tending to paperwork and his barrels in the cellar. He's purposely invisible. The van had always been ready, as was his method of getting her into it, leaving only her shoe behind. He'd waited and waited for her to leave that night. Driving up and down, he waited for her colleagues to leave and, finally, he spotted Deborah. His patience had been rewarded. Deborah wasn't the type of person who was often alone in the dark, but that night she was, and he was ready.'

Wyre looked back at her from the kitchen area, nodding. 'I think you're right, gov.'

'We'll nail him,' said Gina. 'We need to get back to the station. Make sure everything's bagged, tagged and loaded onto the van. We need to book these items into evidence and work on this like we've never worked before. I'm going to task Smith with cordoning off the flat. I need him to be here on sentry duty. If Wall turns up, I want him arrested immediately.' Gina patted Jacob on the shoulder. 'Right. We need to find out from O'Connor how the door-to-doors are going on the farms, and get out there ourselves. There's still something in the red diesel clue. Call him now and get him to start looking for a possible connection to Jeff Wall and any local farms.'

'He's not in for another hour,' Jacob replied as he looked at his watch.

'Call him and tell him to come in earlier. We need all the resources we can get and O'Connor's the one who's been working on the farm leads. He's the best person for this. Oh, and I look like crap, as do you. We need coffee. I'm exhausted and I've got a feeling it's going to be a long day.'

'Speak for yourself, guv, I always look good. You're just trying to make yourself feel better.' Jacob laughed. She knew full well he wouldn't normally come out with uncombed hair, looking like he hadn't washed and wearing crumpled clothes. Wyre, as usual, looked amazing. No one looked good in a stab vest, but Wyre somehow pulled it off. 'How does she do it?' Jacob asked, as they both stared at Wyre.

'What are you both looking at?' Wyre asked.

'Nothing,' Jacob said, blushing. 'We were just saying what an asset to the team you are.' He cleared the tickle in his throat. 'Excuse me. Damn cold.'

'I see,' she replied as she left the room, Jacob's gaze following her all the way.

'You like her, don't you?' said Gina.

'She'd never give me a second look. Besides, it wouldn't be professional, really, would it?'

'I wouldn't know,' Gina replied, as she felt her cheeks burning up. 'Come on, Eros, back to the station. The other officers can continue with the collection of evidence. Today is going to be hell. I'm half hoping that O'Connor turns up with baked goodies, but my stab vest tells me I need to cut back. Now make that call to O'Connor and be prepared for a long day. I want Wall caught.'

As they turned to leave, Gina spotted a tiny corner of laminated paper under the curtain. 'Wait.' She bent down and saw it was a driver's licence. Staring at the photo, she felt there was something familiar in the features. The broken nose. Where had she seen this woman before? 'I recognise this person. The woman we found in the river just after Deborah vanished, is this her?' The woman in the photo had a crooked nose just like the woman they'd found in the river.

'It looks a lot like her, from what I remember. She had a very distinct nose.'

'We'll need it verified, but it looks like we've identified our corpse. Nicoleta Iliescu. Romanian and young. Poor woman. We need to get the bastard now! I want him in custody yesterday.'

CHAPTER FIFTY

Friday, 8 December 2017

He whistled 'You Are My Sunshine' as he drove away from the farm and headed towards his flat. He only needed to pick up a few bits, but he had to be quick. Deborah would need breakfast soon. She was his fallen angel, just like Satan himself, there to deceive, trick and entice. He needed to cast her out permanently. There was no room for a rabid demon in his life. It would be hard giving up on the relationship, but it had come to an end.

His mother had insisted that she wanted the old photos from his flat. It had been weeks since he'd been there and he couldn't remember if he'd taken the bin out. Why she wanted the photos he had no idea, but she'd been going on and on about the past, refusing to allow him to sleep at night while she persistently rambled on about the good old days.

His mother was a supposedly infertile woman who got lucky once and bore a son. A son she doted on her whole life, at the expense of any friendships. His father had died in his thirties, and after that she'd worked their asparagus farm just outside the Vale of Evesham with a few helpers, providing a living for her precious boy. Her boy would never go without. Her boy was her entire reason for being. Her boy could do no wrong.

He knew he was a good boy, really. Deborah just hadn't appreciated him, and now she would pay.

He continued to whistle his tune until he passed a rabbit on the verge. The scared creature scurried away as soon as the headlights caught its line of sight. 'Why? Why? I wouldn't hurt you. I'd never hurt you.' As he pulled up at a junction, he slammed his hands on the steering wheel repeatedly. 'I still sing your song. I loved you, but what do you do? You give me nothing. I hate you. I know Florence survived, but she is an extension of you. She will never be me, will she?' He pummelled the steering wheel and the passenger seat. 'You're not my sunshine, you're my morning gloom. My dark oppressor, like the skies above. Everything. I gave you everything.' He punched the dashboard as hard as he could. 'I hate you!'

He drove with a face like thunder all the way to Cleevesford Village. As he crawled along the road behind the shops, he spotted a police car at the other end. He pulled up on Holland Street and turned off his ignition. 'Why are you lot out at this time of the morning?' he whispered.

'They're coming for you, son.' His mother's voice echoed through his mind.

'Shut up. Shut up.' He massaged his aching head.

He turned his headlights off and stepped out of the car. He sniffed his fingers. The smell of petrol still lingered on his hand. He'd definitely wash and change before he saw Deborah. The last thing he needed was her having a crazy fit on him like the other day. And the time before that, she'd chipped his tooth with a cup.

Holland Street was devoid of human activity. He looked at his watch; it was just past six in the morning. A generator purred from one of the shops. He heard a loud thump as someone shouted. The words were unrecognisable from this distance. He continued walking along the back of the shops until he reached Primrose Lane.

The three-storey terraced buildings blocked out the light. He crept towards the edge of the main road, peeked around the corner of the building and saw the police. His heart felt as though it were in his mouth. 'Why are you in my flat?' he whispered as he turned and walked away.

He had to get back, decide what to do next. If they found him, they may eventually find the farm. What would happen to Mother if he had to leave quickly? Maybe she'd end up in a home. She was never going in a home, he wouldn't allow it. He always knew what was best for her.

He had to do something, but he didn't have much time. They'd never understand the depth of his love and devotion for Deborah – no one would.

Now that they'd fallen out and Deborah was in a mood, he had no idea what she'd say. He'd only chained her up because he wanted to keep her. He loved her so deeply, so passionately. She had to love him back. She'd given birth to their child. She stroked his hair on the nights when he was upset. She told him she loved him to outer space and back. He never hurt her, except when she attacked him first. Admittedly, she'd purposely angered him many times and he sometimes had to give her a scare, but she drove him to it.

With shaky hands, he managed to get the keys in the ignition and drive away with his lights off, passing the Angel Arms and the Cleevesford junction before heading back along the country road to the farm. There was only one way out of all this. One way.

CHAPTER FIFTY-ONE

Sweaty. She was sweaty but cold, then hot, then sticky and sick and tired – so tired. As she gave in to sleep, shapes danced in the darkness beyond the end of the bed. Was it a bed? She had dreamed that she was floating on a blanket, a magic blanket that Aladdin would use. One that took the traveller anywhere they desired to go. Debbie had chosen Andalusia in Spain, where her mother had once had a villa. She and Luke had gone there a few times before the children had come along. They'd enjoyed many a week alone as a new couple. The children would've loved it, but her mother had sold it before they were born. She had needed the money for her retirement.

The blanket took her there and landed in the garden. 'There's only one catch,' the blanket said. 'You have ten minutes. Use your time wisely. After that, I will depart and you will have to make a choice: go back to your reality or stay in the villa garden forever. You can never move forward, you can never leave. You can never dream, you can never come back.'

Luke spotted her emerging from the shrubbery at the end of the garden. Holding out a large glass of red wine, he waited for her to arrive at the table. She smiled and took the glass. She sipped the wine and leaned into Luke's chest, waiting for him to embrace her and tell her everything was going to be okay. But though he coldly allowed her to lean against him, there was no warmth. She pulled away and swigged the rest of the wine. Why wasn't he pleased to see her? Was it the new woman? Had she been brought here so that he could end their marriage?

She took the last gulp of wine and placed her empty glass on the table. Her body normally responded quickly to alcohol, but she felt nothing. Her stomach rumbled. Little dishes of tapas were spread out on the table. She reached down and grabbed a handful of *croquetas de jamón* and rammed them into her mouth. It had been such a long time since she'd enjoyed good food. If the wine wasn't doing it, then maybe the food would. She chewed what was in her mouth, waiting to savour the ham and cheese, but there was nothing. She tuned to the side and spat the mulch onto the ground. 'What's going on, Luke?

He looked at her, no smile, no reaction, and no answer to her question.

'Tell me why I'm here.'

'Five minutes,' said the blanket.

'Why am I here?' she asked.

Luke picked up a plate of fried chorizo and held it in her direction.

'Say something.' She grabbed the plate and smashed it on the slabs in front of her. He picked up the bottle of wine and proceeded to top her glass up.

'Three minutes,' the blanket called.

Luke, please.' She placed a hand on his arm, but he didn't respond. He didn't pull her into an embrace, or stroke her hair with affection, as he'd always done.

'One minute,' the blanket cried. You can stay forever or come back with me, but you have to choose. If you stay, you can never leave.'

The world she had entered had no substance. What was a world without warmth, aroma, taste and love, devoid of everything to which humankind was so beholden? She stood and stepped back towards the blanket, staring at Luke as she got further away. The centre of his chest vanished, revealing nothing but the back of the garden fence. This world had no heart. Luke had no heart. He'd left her; he'd moved on. She was alone.

'Ten seconds.'

She turned and ran back to the blanket, jumping onto it as she reached its edge. 'I want to go back. Take me back now,' she yelled as tears flooded her face.

The blanket soared immediately into the clouds. Blue became grey, warm became cold and safe became stormy. As she lay in the middle of the blanket, it dipped and rose in sharp bursts, threatening to throw her off.

'You left him and passed your test. The test had no reward. There is no prize, no points, no certificate, just a sense of satisfaction that you chose me,' Jeff said.

'I didn't choose. I had no choice,' she yelled through the blanket covering her face. She struggled to move, as he'd rolled her tightly up in it.

With every bump down the stairs, the pain in her stomach and groin intensified. He was moving her, but to where? Was this the end? Was he going to release her, or release her to death?

'Everyone has choices and everything comes to an end. You are at your end. They're coming for me and I can't let you go.' All she could see was darkness. She inhaled the grey material that was threatening to suffocate her. 'You're not going to a better place, my little demon. You're going where you deserve to go.'

'Jeff? My Jeffrey? Did you get the photos?' the old woman shouted as the main door burst open, releasing a gust of cold air through the barn. Deborah remained still, the musty blanket covering her head as she listened to the woman shuffling closer to her.

'Go back, Mother.'

'I need bread.'

'You don't need bread. You have two loaves.'

'Help!' Deborah called through the blanket's fibres, hoping that her weak voice could be heard.

'Is that my blanket?' the old woman asked.

'Shut up, Mother. I said leave me alone.' He turned the frail woman around and pushed her towards the door.

'Please help me,' Deborah called, feeling suddenly light-headed. The pain in her groin burned through her body. Sweat began to pour from her brow as she fidgeted in the blanket, trying to find a way out. 'Let me go, please!' She felt a boot dig into her stomach. She coughed until she almost vomited.

'I heard someone. Who's that?' the old woman asked. 'Who's in my blanket?'

'I've had it with you, Mother. I can't do this anymore,' Jeff said.

The old woman began screaming, her voice hoarse and weak. She let out a final yelp as he dragged her away, out of the main door, towards the house. The voices got quieter until she could no longer hear them. She pushed her arm out of the top of the blanket that was rolled around her body and began to painfully wriggle out. There was no sound of the chain that had kept her prisoner for so many years. As she tried to stand, she stumbled forward, hitting her shoulder on the white van, the van that had brought her to her doom. She slumped over the bonnet, exhausted.

The dog began barking in the distance. She had to move quickly. He was coming back. She grabbed hold of one of the window wipers and dragged her weary body to a standing position. As she straightened her body, she felt a trickling down her legs. She looked down and noticed that drips of blood were following her every move. As the barn spun, she closed her eyes, trying to maintain her balance. She started to heave and her stomach contracted as nausea swept over her.

She swayed as she tried to focus. The world was like a stormy ship and she was battling a storm to stay upright. She stared down at the blanket.

'I'm going home,' she said, as she placed one foot in front of the other. She reached the door and pushed it open. Stepping out into what looked like a grey morning, she breathed in the damp air. Air had never smelled so clean after the staleness of urine, excrement, sweat and blood that had filled her life over the past few years. How many years, she couldn't remember. With each step, pain burned from her groin, stabbing into her lower stomach and kidneys. She flinched as her head pounded to a sickening beat.

The dog barked again. She had to go. She wanted to be with her children, be there on Christmas day and watch them opening their presents. She staggered across the yard, away from the house. Maybe she could hide in the woodland out the back, stagger through the trees and wave for a motorist to stop.

Her cold feet soon became numb to the sharp stones and grit that dug in every time she took a step. She laughed as she staggered forward. She was going home – wherever home was. She was going to her mum and she was going to see her children. She didn't know if her captor had told her the truth about Luke's new woman, but it didn't matter. She just wanted to see him again.

'I'm going home,' she repeated with every step.

'You're not going anywhere.' She turned around and saw a needle full of clear fluid in his hand. He stabbed it into her arm and within minutes she was on the floor, seeing double.

CHAPTER FIFTY-TWO

Gina stared at her computer screen. Photos of Nicoleta Iliescu's waxy face and body filled her screen. One eye was missing, but the freezing water had mostly preserved her features. The report stated that she had drowned, and the diatoms present confirmed that. Gina flinched and grabbed her coat.

'O'Connor. What have we got? And make it brief,' Gina said as she entered the incident room, where O'Connor, Wyre and Jacob were hard at work.

'There are five farms left to investigate. None of them have been matched to Jeffrey Wall. About the farms. Three of them produce asparagus. The closest one is run by a Mr and Mrs Wallis. They've had the farm for over twenty years, live there with their five teenage children. Second one belongs to a Trevor Tucker. Trevor is in his sixties and barely produces anything. He's a sixth-generation farmer. No children and lives alone. Last one on the asparagus list is Julia Benson. Julia is in her seventies and the farm is no longer a working one and the land isn't being farmed anymore. She lives alone and ran the farm for many years before retiring about fifteen years ago. The other two produce fruit. A couple in their twenties, Sophie and Will Stanton, run one. They have a little shop where they sell jams and chutneys et cetera.

They've only been there about a year and have twin girls aged four. Finally, there's a chap called Joseph Gittins. He's in his fifties and the farm is still fully operational as he has staff. He's never been married and lives alone. We cross-referenced the results from the vets and none of them are registered as owning a black dog.'

'Great work.' Gina picked up the list and gazed at the names. 'Right, you and Driscoll can visit the Stanton's, Mr Gittins and Mr Tucker. Wyre and I will head to see Mr and Mrs Wallis and Ms Benson. If you catch sight of a dog with black fur, call it in immediately. It might not be registered with a vet. We're also looking for a white van, any suspicious activity and outbuildings. Keep your eyes and ears open at all times. Deborah's life may depend on us doing a good job today.'

'Yes, guv.' Jacob nodded.

'One more thing. Wall is dangerous – remember that. For those who weren't there, whilst searching Wall's flat, we found a photo driving licence belonging to a Nicoleta Iliescu. From this photo and the autopsy report detailing the cadaver's age and the fact that she had a previously broken nose, we believe there is a high possibility that this woman is the body we discovered in the river just after Deborah's disappearance. We need Wall in custody now. I want to know exactly what happened to Nicoleta and I want Deborah brought home safe.'

O'Connor stood and put his coat on. 'Let's go.' Jacob grabbed his car keys off the desk and followed him out.

'I've printed the addresses out for the Wallis and Benson farms. Where first?' Wyre asked.

They weren't looking for a couple. What could their suspect have to do with a couple? Unless he was residing in a part of their estate that was unused. Or maybe he rented a lockup or another type of storage unit from them. Their investigation into the farms hadn't thrown up any storage rental activity but she also knew farming worked on tight margins and subsidies didn't always cover their needs. Maybe they were renting out some space for a cash sum.

Then there was Julia Benson, a woman of mature years, living alone. Maybe Wall had befriended her and was using some sort of space on her land. Due to her age, her senses may not be quite as sharp as they could be. If that were the case, Wall might be able to falsely imprison a woman on her land. Perhaps she wasn't very mobile, making parts of her estate impossible to check. Gina had noticed that O'Connor had found very little information on Ms Benson when he'd compiled the notes. She'd lived at the farm for over fifty years and had never married. There was barely anything about her on record. 'We'll start with Julia Benson.'

'Good move,' said Wyre. 'Although, I'm wondering if the other two will find anything on their visits. Mr Gittins, man living alone in his fifties. Plenty of farmland. Possibly in cahoots with Wall.'

Gina felt her heart rate speed up as adrenalin pumped through her body. Today might be the day. She had to find Deborah. Reuniting this wife, daughter and mother to her family was all she wanted. Christmas was fast looming. If anyone deserved a good ending, it was the Jenkinses.

'If we find her, things will never be the same again for the family,' said Wyre. 'How do you get over years of captivity and pick up where you left off? How as a husband do you fix things? How as children do you attempt to feel close to someone you can't remember that well? How as a mother do you look at your child and not think about what she went through? How long does that take to subside?' Wyre looked down and placed her hand on her forehead.

Gina placed her arm on the young woman's shoulder. 'I know we all put a face on when we deal with awful cases, but we're human at the end of the day.'

Cold air blew through the door as Smith walked in. 'I've left one of the team outside Wall's flat. You know you're using up all our PCs on sentry duty and tracking your perp? We have drunks in the cells that need processing and barely anyone to do the paperwork. I don't know how long we can offer this level of support for, I mean, we can't—'

Grabbing the address list, Gina did up her coat and brushed past Smith. 'We're on it now. I'm really sorry, but we're all under-resourced. We have worked all night and now we are working all day. O'Connor has been called in early. It's the way things are. I wish it wasn't like this but I don't know what to say. All I can say is that this man is dangerous and we need to find him. We need your support.'

Smith exhaled and stepped aside. 'I know, it's getting to us all. Lack of staff, lack of everything. We haven't even got any bog roll in the men's,' he said with a smile. 'It's bad when you have to bring your own bog roll in.'

Gina smiled. 'I wish we had more, I really do, but, this is the way things are at the moment.'

'Just go. We'll back you up with everything we have. I'm heading down to the drunk tank to deal with the piss and vomit. Could be here all day and all night too at this rate. Go and find him and bring her home. We may gripe but we're all rooting for Deborah's safe return.'

'Julia Benson's it is then. Let's go,' Wyre said as they left the incident room.

CHAPTER FIFTY-THREE

They drove up the bumpy mud track, watching as the unkempt farmhouse in the distance got nearer. Ivy grew up the left side of the building, covering all the windows on that side of the house.

They pulled up at the gate. Wyre got out of the car and unlatched it before jumping back into the passenger seat. Magpies pecked at what looked like the carcass of a rat. The road narrowed. They'd have to walk the rest of the way. Gina pulled up on the grass verge and they both stepped out of the car. 'There's tyre tracks in the mud.'

'Maybe Ms Benson has gone out,' Wyre replied.

'Maybe,' Gina said, trying to avoid the rain-filled potholes. 'She certainly wouldn't walk out of here easily.'

Her phone buzzed in her pocket. It was a message from Hannah, saying the memorial service was at ten the next morning at St John's. She took a deep breath. The whole thing was a farce. Terry hadn't even been religious, and in her mind, he wasn't deserving of any form of remembrance. She ran her fingers through her knotty hair as she tried to reign in her unusually mixed emotions. Her hand got stuck in a tangle. 'Get lost,' she muttered, as she snatched her hand away from her head and ripped a few strands out.

Wyre stopped beside her. 'What's up?'

'Nothing. Family problems.' She'd said it. No more blaming the virus or brushing past it. 'I'm going to a memorial service tomorrow for my ex-husband, Hannah's father. Thing is, we had an awful relationship. I'm doing it for her, and if I'm honest, I'm absolutely dreading it.'

The young woman placed a hand on her arm. 'Family is a funny thing. I don't get on with my dad, he left us when we were still in nappies, but the other year, I had to attend his bloody wedding. Not only is he close on being a member of the EDL, he's a sexist, racist and… What can I say, I just don't like him and I resent the abuse he showered on my mother. Anyway, sometimes we have to do things we don't want to do. I didn't want to go to the wedding, but my fear of future regret was so great that I still did it. I suppose I hoped he'd changed. Am I glad I went? I have no idea.'

'I had no idea about your dad.' Gina smiled and they carried on avoiding the potholes as they neared the front door.

Wyre knew that her father was an unsavoury character, but Hannah didn't have a clue about her father's shortcomings. The father Hannah had created in her mind was so different to the real person. He'd died when she was two. Gina had been twenty-five – such a long time ago, though it still haunted her everyday memories. One day she would share her past with her grown-up daughter. Maybe secrets were a bad thing. Though perhaps the circumstances around his death weren't for sharing. After all, she still wasn't sure what had happened. Did she help Terry down those stairs or was he going anyway? That uncertainty would stay with her forever.

The black paint on the front door was mostly chipped away, right down to the hard wood. Gina knocked and the flimsy door rattled in its frame. She gazed at the front window, trying to see beyond the dirty yellow netting. She spotted something that looked like a sideboard with a lamp on it. Gina walked around the corner and saw a two-storey barn in the distance. The woodland behind almost reached the back of the barn. As with the road, the approach to the barn was defined by trodden mud and wild shrubbery.

'I wonder if she's gone out,' Wyre said.

Gina walked back to the front door. She rang the bell several times and followed it with a loud knock. 'We'll try again. If no one answers, we'll go and take a quick look at that barn behind the house.' Gina walked back over to the window and stared hard through the dirty netting. She could just about make out the back of a white-haired woman, a crocheted blanket draped over her shoulders. The wind picked up, blowing a gale around her ears. She shivered as she began tapping on the glass, hoping that the hunched woman in the chair would notice, but there was no response. She stared for a moment longer; there was no movement. 'There's someone there. Shout through the letter box.'

'We're police detectives. DC Wyre and DI Harte. We need to ask you a few questions.'

'We need to get in. She's not moving.' Gina pushed the door and heard it rattling against the lock. She rammed it with her shoulder, breaking the flimsy lock and almost falling into the hallway.

She slid in her damp shoes along the tiled hallway, which was scattered with old, matted rugs, and entered the living room.

The smell of excrement and urine hit them as they saw the woman. She was sitting stiffly in a chair, propped up by cushions. Gina almost heaved as she leaned over and checked the woman's pulse. She was gone. Her eyes were drawn to the woman's bloodshot eyes and the large mole on her cheek. A pillow lay in her lap. She thought of the woman struggling for breath as Wall held it over her face.

'Call it in.'

Wyre stepped out of the room to get a signal.

Gina stared at the birdcage in the corner. A large, dead bird was lying on the bottom of the cage. Wrappers from sausage rolls and pies filled the other corner, next to the orthopaedic chair the woman was sitting in. Two settees and several wall units filled the room. One wall unit was crammed with porcelain dolls; the other was piled up with Royal Doulton. The tops of the units were stacked with old newspapers.

'Deborah, Debbie, are you there? Just shout or bang,' Gina called as she began walking around the house. Her heart pounded with every step. Was Wall behind a door, ready to pounce?

As she reached the kitchen, Gina noticed the full ashtray on the worktop. A collection of straw hats spilled out of the cupboard doors. Clutter and cobwebs filled the room. She could just about make out that the work surface was pine underneath all the oddments and dust. It was strewn with money boxes, empty bottles and tins and more old newspapers.

Gina darted up the stairs, careful not to touch anything. 'DI Harte,' she called as she reached the top. She was met by silence. All she could hear was the blood thundering through her veins. She quickly checked the four bedrooms and the old-fashioned avocado-coloured bathroom. Cobwebs, damp, mould and decay were all she could find. She ran back downstairs. 'Clear,' she called.

'Backup is on the way,' Wyre replied, meeting her in the hall.

A scratching noise came from the back of the house. 'I think there's someone in the kitchen,' Wyre whispered.

The two detectives left the room and crept along the hallway. The scratching got louder and was followed by barking. 'A dog,' Wyre said. They hurried towards the back door and opened it. A black spaniel darted past them, wagging its tail.

The cupboard door under the stairs blew open slightly as Wyre pushed the back door closed. Gina pulled her phone out of her pocket and used its torch to see. On an old bookshelf was a family portrait, a bit like the photos that were bagged from Wall's flat. She picked up the photo and stared at the woman. She had a large mole on her cheek, and was standing next to a young boy who bore a striking similarity to Jeff Wall. Ms Benson was Wall's mother. They'd been looking for someone going by the name of Wall. She'd never married Wall's father.

'Let's check out the barn,' Gina said, sprinting out of the house.

'Shouldn't we wait for backup?'

'We might not have that long. I'm going up there now.'

CHAPTER FIFTY-FOUR

Four years had gone since he'd taken her and she still remembered that night like it was yesterday. 'Please, don't hurt me. Let me go. Let me go!' Those had been her first words when she'd first set eyes on Jeff Wall after he'd taken her, all those years ago. Back then, she had no idea where she was. She'd been asleep. Her head had ached and she'd been possessed by an overwhelming thirst.

She'd gone over it constantly, thinking of how she could've handled it differently, how she could have avoided becoming his prisoner. That day still seemed like yesterday; it never left her mind.

'Where am I?' she asked, trying to swallow. He stared back at her, seemingly unsure of what to do next. When she moved, she felt the draw on her ankle from the chain that was imprisoning her.

She remembered being the last to leave work after making up time. She had been walking through the industrial estate. It was dark and wet and Jeff had pulled over, offering her a lift in his van. She remembered politely declining – but what happened after that? One minute she was standing on the roadside, talking to him through his van window, the next, she was in some cold room, chained up by the man who worked at her local pub.

He paced up and down, muttering words she couldn't decipher. She knew him from the pub where she played pool. In fact, she'd been there only three nights before. They'd recently lost to the Spinster and she and Lottie thought it might be a good idea to get a bit more practice in. Jeff had always been a quiet man, never really socialised much. He managed the cellar, as far as she was aware, and covered paperwork duties, but he rarely worked the bar. Why had he taken her? Questions ran through her head. Was it some sort of revenge thing?

'Has Samuel set you up to do this?' she asked.

He stopped pacing, turning to look her in the eye. He darted over to the bed and sat beside her. He leaned in and kissed the spot where he'd slapped her, before tracing her cheek with his trembling fingers. 'I'm going to take good care of you. You are my love and I will do everything for you. That Samuel will never come near you again.'

Tears ran down her face. 'Jeff, I have to get home to my children. My family are expecting me. Please take this thing off me,' she said as she lifted her ankle, revealing the chain.

'You are home.' He wrapped his arms around her body and breathed deeply into her neck. 'I have waited so long for you to be here. So long. I kept you safe out there, and now I will keep you safe in here.'

What did he mean? Had he been watching her? She'd never seen him around, apart from at the pub. There had been no warning of his feelings towards her. She'd never noticed any lingering looks.

His hot breath on her neck made her shiver as he continued to speak. 'For years, I watched you leaving work and getting home. I wanted to make sure you were safe, but it got too hard. I couldn't be there all the time. The only way to make you safe was to bring you here. You will be safe forever. You are too precious to me.'

Too precious. She barely knew the man, but apparently to him, she was everything. She was precious. And that meant he needed to trap her in some hellhole of a room.

'Jeff, please, I have to go home. We won't say any more about what has happened this evening. Just open the door and let me go,' she spluttered.

He drew back. Spit bubbles emerged from the gaps in his teeth as he exhaled. 'I've done all this for you, so that we can be together, and this is how you repay me. Don't you dare say a word about going home or I will make sure you never speak another word, ever. This is your home. Do you hear me?'

'Jeff—' Her sentence was cut off as he punched her hard in the face. Then he stood and marched towards the door, taking the oil lamp with him. The door closed and she was left in darkness, sobbing into the night, hoping that she'd soon get to leave. But it was only the beginning.

She gasped for air and opened her eyes. Something was jabbing into her back and tongue was furred. She grimaced as she realised she was in the boot of a car.

Her hands were bound behind her back but her feet were loose. The car clunked as they went over a humpback bridge. A horn honked and the car jerked to the left and skidded a little.

She stretched her legs out to try and brace herself against the side of the car. Where was he taking her? She reached for the object that was jabbing her in the back, felt its form with her fingertips. It was solid and thin and had a handle. A screwdriver. Her hands were bound with what felt like duct tape.

The car turned sharply right and she let go of the screwdriver. Maybe she should try to kick the brake light out and shove her foot through. Someone had to see her. She brought her foot out towards the corner of the car and kicked. As she stretched, the pain in her stomach and groin seared through her body. Sweat dripped down her face, trickling around her left ear. She kicked again and screamed. Tears streamed down her cheeks and her stomach burned. The light wasn't budging.

He took another turn and she felt the tyres bumping over a rough track. He was off the main road. Was he taking her to another rural location? She gasped and yelled as she kicked the light again. She reached around for the screwdriver, felt the handle and grabbed it. She had to get out. She had to hurt him, kill him, whatever it took. He was taking her to her end.

She cried as she remembered begging him to end it. Thinking that Luke no longer wanted her and that her children may have already found her replacement had been too much to bear, but now the notion of an end seemed too final. No one would ever know what had happened to her. She might be on the missing persons register forever. And her baby, what would become of her baby? Would her mother look after her little one? Would she end up in care? She would never know her real mother.

She sobbed as the pain intensified, but she battled through it. She managed to turn the screwdriver around and then inwards and began jabbing at the tape. As she gasped for breath in the dark box that was the boot, her vision began to blur. She needed to calm down, take a deep breath and think carefully, without panicking.

The car rolled up on a gravelled surface. She held her breath and listened to the ducks quacking outside. They were by water. Why had he brought her to the water?

The car door opened and then slammed. She heard each of his footsteps dig into the gravel as he whistled 'You Are My Sunshine.' Her heart almost stopped. She wanted to yell and scream, but instead she remained still. Was it best to pretend to still be drugged? Had he heard her crying?

She lay there with closed eyes. Whatever he had planned, she wasn't going to make it easy for him. He stopped whistling. She held her breath.

CHAPTER FIFTY-FIVE

'We're just at Gittins' farm. The guy has carers in most of the day – he can barely get out of his chair,' Jacob said on the other end of the phone.

'It doesn't matter anymore. You need to get to the Benson farm immediately. Julia Benson is Wall's mother. We've called it in, she's dead,' Gina replied as she caught her breath and continued running along the bumpy path, towards the barn. 'I'm just checking out the barn.' A gust of wind howled through the bushes, propelling a twig towards Gina's face. She moved to the side just as it passed her. An almighty storm was brewing.

'Wait for backup to arrive.'

'It's okay, Wyre is here. Besides, there are fresh tyre tracks on the road, leading out. I think he's gone out and Deborah might be in the barn. Just get here and make it snappy.'

There was only one entrance to the barn: an old wooden door that was slightly ajar. There were no windows. Mature oak trees stood tall behind it, stretching their bare branches towards the shabby walls. The tip of a large birch looked like it was ready to burst the rain cloud above. Gina shivered as a bitter gust almost pushed her back.

'What if they're not his tyre tracks?' said Wyre. 'It could've been a post van. He could be in there now.'

'More of a reason to get in there and get Deborah out. We can't wait for the others. If anything happens to her and we could've prevented it, I'll never forgive myself. You could wait here and let backup know where I am.' Gina stared into Wyre's anxious eyes and felt her own apprehension reflecting back at her. Wyre's neatly pinned hair had escaped and was now blowing freely in the breeze. She wiped a thick strand from her mouth.

Whatever was behind the door wasn't going to be pleasant, but it may well be the answer to everything. Gina's heart pounded in her chest as she felt the thinness of her coat and shirt against her breast. She had no stab vest for protection, no truncheon, no pepper spray, no Taser, nothing. It was her, Wyre and whatever situation was waiting behind the door. They were vulnerable, and they both knew it.

'Wait here,' Gina said.

'And let you go in alone? No way. We're in this together,' Wyre shouted over the howling of the wind, taking the last few steps towards the barn.

Gina slowed down and crept towards the door. She held her finger to her lips. 'Don't make a sound,' she whispered. She held her ear to the door and listened for any sign of life. A further gust of wind caught the door and it flew open, revealing a metal staircase and a white van.

Wyre gave Gina a glance as she pointed at the vehicle. Gina nodded. The large space behind the van and stairs was filled with tyres, an old dismantled tractor, water butts and a wall-to-wall workbench. General tools adorned the walls, providing plenty of things for spiders to spin their webs on. Gina spotted a petrol can on the floor and wondered if that particular can had been used by Wall to set fire to Luke's house. The air was thick with the smell of damp. As Gina began the silent walk up the stairs, the stench of human waste hit her. She gagged and turned around. Wyre held her sleeve over her nose.

'DI Harte and DC Wyre. We're coming up the stairs,' she called. She was tempted to walk on in silence, but something told her she needed to call out and listen for a reaction. If Deborah were there, maybe she would call out. Or maybe she'd startle Wall and his movement would reveal where he was. But there wasn't a sound, apart from the creaking of the main door as it swung back and forth on its hinges. 'I don't think they're here,' Gina whispered. As the main door banged once more, a gust of wind billowed through the building. Gina grabbed the stair rail as the black spaniel bounded up the stairs, stopping to yap and wag its tail when it reached the top. She exhaled as she continued to the top of the stairs and looked right through the open door and into what she knew had been Deborah's cell. She held her hand over her nose as she passed the small kitchenette and entered the dark, damp room.

'Where's that bastard taken her?' she yelled as she kicked the doorframe. 'Where's he taken her?'

She watched as Wyre continued along the corridor and checked out the other room. 'There's an old bathroom here, that's all, and a cupboard,' she said as she closed the door. The dog continued barking and jumping around Wyre as she walked.

Gina stared at the filthy quilt and almost wept for Deborah. She removed her hand from her nose. The smell of urine overpowered her, but she didn't cover her face this time. Deborah had endured the awful conditions and stench for years; she could endure it until the others arrived. She stepped over to the bed and gazed around the room. The only light came from the tiniest air vent, and as the breeze whipped up, it made a clicking noise. Next to the bed, a metal ring was fixed into the concrete floor. Gina shuddered as she thought of Deborah lying in the dirty bed, giving birth in the dirty bed and enduring whatever he forced upon her in the dirty bed. The coldness of the room was beginning to penetrate her clothing. She had no idea how Deborah had survived the winters.

Gina wiped away a tear and exited the room. In the corner of the kitchenette was an open bag of dirty linen. Gina kneeled, catching the stench as she leaned forward. Amongst the mangled sheets were obvious clues that Deborah had given birth a few days ago. All the mess was displayed for her to see. He'd made no attempt to get rid of it. Was she even still alive? There was so much blood and dirt. Maybe he'd taken her body to dispose of her.

'Why isn't she here? I was so sure she'd be here,' said Gina. Wyre stood behind her, mouth slightly open as she surveyed what was in front of them.

Wyre pulled out her phone, and Gina listened as she relayed what they'd found and requested once again that they hurry. They needed a team, and quick. The dog nudged its head under Gina's arm, seeking affection.

Gina heard the sound of a siren approaching. 'They're here,' she said as she stood. The dog jumped up onto its hind legs and rested its front paws on Gina's waist. 'I wish I knew what you'd seen,' she said, as she gently lifted the dog's paws and placed them back on the ground before giving the spaniel a final pat on the head. 'Where's he taken her?' He must have known somehow that they were coming. Maybe he'd popped back to his flat and seen the officers guarding his door. What would he do with Deborah? Her mind flashed back to Nicoleta Iliescu. She grabbed her phone and called Briggs. 'We need to check the waterways for Wall now, and check the fisheries too. We found Nicoleta in the river. He's probably heading towards water. He knows we're on to him and he's cornered.'

CHAPTER FIFTY-SIX

Was he making her wait on purpose, delighted at the thought of her increasing anxiety? He stopped whistling, and the sound of his lighter flipping open made her flinch. She was jolted a little as he sat on the boot, making the car bounce. She suppressed a cough as she inhaled the cigarette smoke that flooded through the crevices.

'I gave you everything, but my all wasn't enough. It was never enough.' He slammed his hand on the boot. Debbie let out a scream. It was no use pretending to be out of it anymore. He knew she was awake. 'Mother's gone too, and guess whose fault it is? If only you'd kept your loud mouth shut. You killed Ma.' He started gibbering to himself. 'I know you forgive me, Ma. It's just Debbie and I and little Florence now, but you won't be alone for long. We'll join you and we can all be together.'

She frantically jabbed at the tape with the screwdriver, trying to ignore his ramblings. She flinched as the sharp tip pierced her back.

'The end has come. We all reach our end one day, and for us, that is today.' He paused. 'Our family will go together and we'll be at peace. One day our story will be a legend. The greatest love story ever told.'

Tears soaked Debbie's face. These moments, in the boot of his car, were probably going to be her final ones. She trembled violently, almost dropping the screwdriver. By family, did he mean her baby too? Her heart thumped against her ribcage.

She kicked and wriggled, trying to free up any part of her body, but with every movement her energy dwindled. Occasionally the darkness of the boot would spin around, confusing her more. What had he drugged her with? A flash of pain darted through her head.

'We will never be at peace,' she yelled. Do you hear me?'

The boot clicked open, and she flinched as the light of the day sent pains shooting though her head. His gaunt face stared down at hers, showing his sickly grin and chipped tooth. 'You're angry, but you'll be fine. I'm going to get Florence after this, and she will join us.' He took a final drag of his cigarette and flicked the butt onto the rubble.

'No! I hate you. I've always hated you. They won't give my baby to you.'

'Your baby? Let me tell you something – she's mine. I made her. My blood runs through her veins and keeps her little heart pumping. I gave her life and I can take it away.' He leaned over and placed his hand on her cheek. 'It'll be fine, you'll see. We'll all be a family again in another world. Together forever.'

'Leave her alone. She doesn't belong here. This is between me and you.'

'Florence is my sunshine,' he said. 'I hoped you both would be, but you soured that one, didn't you? I'm a family man at heart. That's all I wanted, a family, and that always included children. When I first saw you at the pub, clumsily trying to pot a ball, I knew you were the one. I knew then that I'd die for you, and today I'm going to prove that, despite all that you've put me through. We are all going together, as a family, and you're first.'

He leaned in, grabbed her under the arms and dragged her out of the boot, dropping her onto the ground. She gasped for breath as the pain in her stomach throbbed through her entire body. The wind whipped strands of hair into her mouth. Gravel dug into her wrists and legs, but she gripped the screwdriver with all she had. She tried to pull her wrists apart, hoping to rip the tape, but it was too strong.

'You don't have to do this.' She looked up at him, pleading with her eyes.

'You don't understand. They have come for us, and we have nowhere to go. This is the end.'

'There's always somewhere to go. You can put me back in the boot and we can drive far away,' she said, crying. If it meant saving her baby, she would happily be his prisoner for life. The sweat from her brow trailed down her face. He walked away, holding his head in his hands, pacing, as he always did when he felt conflicted. She gazed around. He had parked on a small gravelled area and his car was the only one parked next to the murky pond, in the middle of nowhere. They were surrounded by trees, with what looked like acres of fields in the distance. 'Help!' she yelled.

He reached into the car, grabbed a rag and stuffed it into her mouth. The dry cotton material made her gag. She coughed, managing to push it slightly forward. Tears welled up once more in her eyes. He stared at her; she shook her head. She wanted to yell, 'no, stop, please stop.' Then he began to drag her to the lake.

Hail began to fall from the sky, bouncing off her bare legs and leaving marks where they'd so violently landed. Her legs scraped across the gravelly ground as he tugged her towards the grass.

Grasping the screwdriver, she tried to fix it into the ground, hoping that it would slow him down, but it was no use.

Finally, they reached the water's edge and he let her body fall. She flinched as her head hit the frozen ground. 'Don't feel you are alone. We will be joining you soon.' She watched as hailstones landed in his messy hair, settling on the top of his head. 'I love you. I love you both.' He bent over, lifted her up and began walking into the pond until the water was at his waist. She shivered uncontrollably, her teeth chattering into the rag, as the cold wetness soaked through her nightdress. Then he lowered her into the water. She shook her head and allowed her teary eyes to linger on his gaze. She wanted to beg him not to let her go, not to leave her, not to let her die, but she couldn't. All she could do was look at him and shake her head.

'You're beautiful, like Ophelia herself. I'd hoped we'd go out to Stratford to watch a play one day, but not now, not ever.' He bent to kiss her on the cheek. She felt her hair splay out, framing her face as he lowered her further into the icy arms that were hungrily awaiting her arrival.

She began jabbing at the tape once again as he let her go. She sank into the icy pond. Scum enveloped her and the trees disappeared from view and very soon the light vanished. Water soaked through the rag that was in her mouth and she gagged as the air in her lungs was replaced by water. She tried to bring her legs downwards to stand but they had stiffened with the cold. She felt the bottom of the pond with her toe. Weeds entangled around her legs, pulling her down. Her grip on the screwdriver loosened, and she finally let it go.

CHAPTER FIFTY-SEVEN

Larry peered around the tree. The car had gone. He sprinted to the water's edge, flinging his boots off as he ran, keeping his eye on the spot where the lady had been drowned. He had to get her out.

As he entered the water and it passed his waist, his breath was almost taken away. It would be a miracle if she survived not only the drowning but the icy temperature. He reached down, feeling deeper and deeper into the pond. He'd never been a brilliant swimmer, but he loved sitting by the water. It was part of the reason he loved fishing so much. But this was no time to think about his hatred of being in water. A woman's life was at stake.

He reached down again and still he couldn't feel a thing. He lowered his head under the water, held his breath and kept his eyes open. The brown water gave no clue as to where she was. He slipped off a rock and was plunged into darkness. He continued holding his breath until he came across what felt like the flesh of a person. He grabbed a limb and stepped back, pulling her at the same time. As his hand slipped further down the limb, he felt fingers. He linked his fingers into hers, steadied his feet and burst through the water, taking a huge breath of fresh air.

He leaned back in, grabbed the woman under her arms and lifted her head out of the water. With shaking hands, he felt for a pulse. He couldn't feel anything, but he wasn't sure. He needed to perform CPR. Grateful that his workplace had just sent him on a first aid course, he pinched the woman's nose and sealed his mouth over hers, exhaling a lungful of air into her. He needed to do chest compressions. Dragging her to the water's edge, he placed her on the grass and began to pump her chest. Nothing. He continued with what he'd been taught, over and over again, just like he'd been shown with the doll.

'Come on!' he shouted, wet and shivering and with only the ducks to bear witness to all that was happening.

The woman coughed and spewed out a stream of murky pond water. He rolled her into the recovery position and ran back to his fishing peg. He grabbed his phone and dialled 999 before returning to her side with his knee blanket and flask.

'We'll all be together soon' – that's what the man had said. The words ran through his head as his teeth chattered. It's not every day a person witnesses someone trying to murder a woman. Was the killer coming back? The woman opened one eye and tried to scream.

'It's okay, there's an ambulance on its way.' He pulled the blanket over her shoulders and held a cup of hot coffee towards her. Debbie burst into tears and placed her hand on his as she lay back down. He smiled as he saw flashing lights coming down the long winding road.

Deborah continued to sob. 'I'm Deborah, Deborah Jenkins,' she croaked.

'And I'm Larry,' he replied.

'Thank you.' Her smile turned into a frown as she became more lucid. She reached for his chest, knocking the coffee down his front. 'Please tell them, he's going for my baby next. They need to stop him.' She tried to sit up, but fell back in a heap. 'They need to stop him,' she whispered, as the police car crunched to a halt in the car park. Her heavy eyes finally closed.

'Deborah!' Larry called.

'PC Smith.' The man removed his coat and placed it over the woman. 'I've just heard on the radio, there's an ambulance on its way.'

'Her name is Deborah Jenkins,' Larry said. He watched as the policeman took the woman's pulse before radioing for the ambulance to hurry.

CHAPTER FIFTY-EIGHT

Gina watched as two officers dodged the undergrowth while trying to reach her and Wyre at the barn. She brushed away the droplets of water that had gathered on her sleeve from the hail shower. Her phone rang. She pulled it out of her pocket and stared at the screen. It was Hannah. 'Why do I always get calls I need to take at the worst of times? It's my daughter.'

'You should talk to her,' Wyre replied.

Gina smiled and accepted the call. 'Hannah.'

'Tomorrow at ten. You got my message, didn't you?' she asked with no pleasantries. Gina smiled as she heard Gracie cooing in the background.

'Yes. I'll be there. Look, I'm sorry I've been a little off lately. After tomorrow is over, can we have a chat? I need to talk to you.' Gina's hands began to shake and her face flushed with heat.

'Chat. What about?'

'It's not a good time now, I'm at a crime scene, but you must know that I love you and Gracie dearly. I really do. Please don't shut me out,' she said, her voice cracking with every word.

The two officers reached the barn and walked over to Wyre.

'Okay, but I need tomorrow to be about Dad. Maybe we can meet for coffee next week. Take Gracie to soft play and have a chat there. Can we do that, Mum? And can you promise to turn up, whatever happens?'

'I can. See you tomorrow, love.'

'Bye, Mum.'

Gina ended the call and placed the phone back in her pocket.

Wyre walked over and placed her hand on Gina's shoulder. 'Everything alright, ma'am?'

'I think so.' Her phone rang again: Jacob this time. In the distance, she saw him get out of O'Connor's car and wave at her with the phone pressed against his ear. She accepted the call.

'I've been trying to call you. You were spot on about the water. They've only gone and found her!'

'What?' Gina replied. He hung up and she watched as he ran towards her, past the house, past the two officers until he reached her side, gasping to get his breath back.

'Tell me then,' she said.

'I just got the call this second, as we pulled in. Deborah Jenkins is alive. A man saw some commotion up at the fisheries. He was there, trying to catch carp, and called in as he'd seen a man drowning a woman in the pond. He'd been scared and waited behind a tree until our perp drove off. Thankfully he knew a bit of first aid and managed to revive Deborah. He said he'd heard the man shouting that they'd all be together soon or something like that,' Jacob said as he wiped the sweat from his brow.

Gina grabbed the barn door, almost stumbling as she took in the news. 'Well blow me over with a gale – literally,' she said, as a twig flew past her head. She began to shake as Jacob's words sank in. O'Connor finally caught them up, and Gina looked his way. 'Get a unit over to the Jenkinses' house now. He's going for the baby. If he said they'd all be together soon, he means the baby too.'

'On it now, guv.'

'We need everything in this barn and house sealed off.' Wyre picked up her phone and made the call. 'We need to get to the Jenkinses' house. Now.' Jacob nodded. '

We'll take your car,' he said as they hurried down the mud path towards the house. The dog ran after them, wagging its tail and yapping all the way to the car. It jumped up Gina's legs and cocked its head to the side as she reached the car. She stroked the dog's head before opening the door.

'Call the RSPCA to deal with the dog and then message Briggs. Tell him what's happened,' Gina said as she accelerated the car down the muddy path, past the gate and onto the country road. 'Shit!' she yelled as she sped over the humpback bridge. 'Call Luke Jenkins. Tell him to lock the doors and not answer to anyone. Tell him we'll be ten minutes.' She put her foot down as they turned onto the main road, heading straight to Cleevesford.

CHAPTER FIFTY-NINE

Luke flicked through the channels on the television, settling on a morning news show. Then he walked over to the window and stared out. He didn't really feel like celebrating Christmas, but he had made a bit of an effort for Max and Heidi. The children wanted the tree up and Cathy had been excited to decorate it with them. Devina was sitting in the kitchen, making notes whilst Isobel slept. She had been concerned about the planned visit given what had been happening, but he and Cathy had put up a good argument. They needed this time to bond with Isobel.

The smell of smoke still filled the hallway. Luckily, on the night of the fire, the kitchen and living room doors had been closed, but the hallway was in a state. A cleaning crew had come by and sorted out the worst of the mess. The temporary front door was okay for now, but it would need replacing when he had the chance to deal with it.

He'd never normally be at home alone in the week. Today was an exception, as Cathy had seemed tired and he'd been given compassionate leave to sort out the mess that was his life. He'd insisted that Cathy have a lie-in and come over at lunchtime instead. They'd argued the morning after the fire when Luke had decided to return home. He'd never argued with Cathy before.

He clenched his fists as he fought the urge to slam them on the windowsill, knowing Devina might hear. The last thing he needed was children's services deciding that he was unstable. For his and Cathy's sakes, they needed Isobel in their lives.

He turned to the fireplace and picked up the photo of Debbie. He missed her so much. He held the photo close to his heart. His thoughts flashed back to the moment he'd shared with Brooke at the window. They'd been good friends, and he was sure they'd have been happy as lovers. In that moment, he'd almost been ready to move on with his life, resigning himself to the thought that Debbie was never coming home. How had a few days made such a difference?

The wind howled through the shrubs in his front garden, dislodging the bare branches and sending them hurtling into the sky, and the side gate banged against the wall. 'Bloody thing,' he said, placing the photo on the windowsill and hurrying out of the temporary front door. He walked around the charred carpet that had been dumped beside the house. Rain trickled down his face as he fought with the breeze to close the gate. He was sure he heard the phone ringing. Shivering, he ran back in through the front door, but the phone had stopped.

'Luke,' Brooke called as she ran down the road, into his garden. 'Can we talk?' She brushed her tangled hair from her face. 'I've missed you.'

'I'm sorry, Brooke, but I can't... I need some time.'

'Just a quick coffee, please?' A tear escaped down her cheek. He wanted to hold her but he couldn't. So much had happened. He pushed the temporary door open and showed her in. He ushered her into the living room and closed the door.

'I heard what happened. You should have called me. I could've helped.'

'There's nothing anyone can do. Besides, we're fine.'

She wiped her face. 'I thought I could handle this, but I can't. I think about you all the time. I miss you so much. I miss our chats, I miss the kids. Joe misses them.' She turned to face him, her gaze meeting his. He reached out and wiped the tears from her cheek. She leaned forward to kiss him.

He turned to the side. 'We can't do this.'

'We were doing it alright the other day.'

'Brooke, I don't want to argue with you. Besides, the social worker is in the kitchen. I thought you understood,' he whispered.

'I do, I do. I just… I don't know why I came. It was stupid.'

'Look, a lot has happened…' He pushed back his wet hair with his fingers, wondering what to say next. On the TV, a mid-morning debate was in full swing about whether further cuts to the NHS budget would cost even more lives. He grabbed the remote control and turned it down.

'I should go.'

'Shh—' He stepped in front of Brooke as he heard a cry, followed by a thud, coming from kitchen. Was his overtired mind playing tricks on him? 'Hello?' he called. The house was silent. 'Devina?' His heart rate sped up with every step he took through the hallway. He felt Brooke's trembling hand on his back as she followed.

He pushed the kitchen door and inhaled with a force that almost made him faint. Brooke gasped. Standing in front of him was a damp and dishevelled man, gripping Isobel in his arms. Devina was slumped beside the chair she'd been sitting on, unconscious, with blood dripping from her head.

He recognised the man, but it took a few seconds to place him. The pub. He'd seen the cellar keeper on only one occasion, all those years ago, when he'd made his own enquiries into his wife's disappearance.

'She's mine. I've come for her,' the man said as he took a step closer to the back door. As he turned, Luke spotted the knife pointing directly into Isobel's stomach. Luke took a step forward, and the intruder stepped back, squelching as he did. A trail of wet footsteps led from the back door to the baby basket.

'You work at the Angel, don't you?' Luke said as he stared at the man. 'I know you don't want to hurt her. Please, just pass her to me.'

'Hurt her! She's going to a better place. She belongs with her mother and father.' Isobel stirred in his arms but didn't wake. Luke trembled as he watched Debbie's baby in the grip of this madman.

'Where's Debbie? Where's my wife, you prick?' he yelled as he took another step forward.

'I'll take her now if you come one step further,' the man shouted. Luke stepped back and exhaled as the man moved the knife away.

'Why have you done this to us? Where's my wife?' he said, his voice cracking with emotion. He'd become attached to little Isobel over the past few days. He stared at her innocent face. All he wanted to do was walk over to her, take her away from him and protect her.

The man headed towards the door, smiling his revolting smile. 'I loved her more than anything, more than you did. I treated her like she was a princess, but she was an ungrateful bitch.'

'Loved,' Luke said. 'What have you done to her?' He stood helplessly in front of the kitchen door, his gaze on the knife.

'Luke?' Brooke reached for his arm and began to sob.

The man began pacing by the door. 'I've done nothing but the right thing. I loved her and you didn't. She knew about your other woman. Your whore. I once knew a whore, you know. She was the first girl. She got what was coming to her.' Jeff stared at Brooke and grinned. 'Debbie knew everything before she died, I made sure of it. I'm the only person to have ever loved her wholly and truly.'

Luke ran his shaking hands through his hair and wiped a tear from his eyes. He placed his hand on the worktop to try and regain his balance. Deborah was gone. His wife's killer was standing in front of him, threatening the life of his wife's baby. He had to do something, but what? The man was pointing the knife towards Isobel's heart, muttering to himself as he stared out of the window.

'The time has come. Try to stop me and little Florence will die here without her mother. Let me go and they will be together forever. Get back.' Luke took a small step back into the doorway. 'Out of the room!' the man shouted. 'Now. Both of you.' Luke took another step back into the hallway and Brooke ran behind him.

Luke knew he'd have to leave by the garden gate. Maybe he could stop him out the front. He heard the kitchen door open, then he heard the sound of sirens fast approaching. The back door slammed shut. Luke peered into the kitchen. The man was still there. Isobel began to scream as he paced up and down, holding the knife to her little chest. The phone in the living room rang.

'Answer it,' the man yelled, sweat dripping down his face.

He dashed to the phone and held it to his ear. As he waited for someone to speak, he watched as several police cars pulled up and a police van arrived. An ambulance followed. 'Listen to me, Luke. Is he there?'

Luke nodded at Detective Harte, who was standing in his front garden with her mobile to her ear. Isobel's screams filled the house.

'Tell them to leave or I will kill her, I swear,' the man said from the kitchen. 'Shut up!' he yelled at the baby.

'He said you need to leave. He has a knife held against Isobel's chest and Devina is lying unconscious on the kitchen floor. He will kill Isobel if you don't all leave.'

Gina placed her hand on her forehead as she paced in the garden. 'Can you put him on the phone?'

'The detective wants to speak to you. Can I bring the phone to you, in the kitchen?' Luke called.

'Tell them to leave, now!'

Luke shook his head at Gina. 'He won't talk. He said leave now. I'm scared he'll hurt her. Please leave.'

Gina held up her arm to the others and Luke watched and listened as she instructed them to leave. One by one, the cars left until the road was clear. 'They've moved to the next road. I'm going to end the call. Tell him we've all gone.' He watched Gina's trembling hands as she ended the call and headed to the side gate.

'They've gone,' he called as he went back to the kitchen and waited by the door, with Brooke sobbing behind him. Devina had stirred and was trying to sit up.

'I didn't want it to be like this. I know they're close by. We were all meant to go together, but it looks like Florence and I will be going here.' He placed the screaming baby back in the basket. As he lifted the knife above her, he closed his eyes. 'Goodbye, Florence. Daddy will be joining you soon.'

Brooke screamed as she covered her eyes.

Luke dashed across the room and jumped against the man, catching his hand on the blade. The baby basket tipped over, flinging Isobel under the kitchen table. 'You bastard. This is for my wife,' he yelled as he brought his fist onto Wall's nose over and over again.

As he brought another punch down, he felt his arms being restrained. 'Get all units here now,' Gina yelled into her phone. Within seconds the place was stormed by several officers. A young paramedic walked over and attended to Devina, who was crying and holding her head. Baby Isobel was lifted off the floor by an officer and Wall was restrained and read his rights by DS Driscoll. Luke lay on the floor, bleeding and exhausted. He cried for the wife he knew to be dead as her killer was dragged from the scene.

'I loved her,' the man shouted as they dragged him out of the door and along the slabs, his nose showering blood all over the garden.

Devina was being helped out the door. 'The baby, Isobel. Is she okay?'

'We're just going to check her over now,' said the paramedic, as she took the wailing baby from the officer. 'She looks very lively and responsive though. Let's get you checked over. That looks like a nasty bang to the head.'

'You saved the little one,' Gina said, as she slid down the wall and sat next to Luke on the kitchen floor.

'My Debbie's dead. He told me. He killed Debbie.' Luke was sobbing so hard he couldn't breathe, his injured hand wrapped in a blood-soaked dishtowel.

'No, Luke – we've found her. She's been taken to Cleevesford Hospital. She's alive and she wants to see you,' Gina replied.

Luke dragged himself to a sitting position, and his tears turned to sobbing laughs. He saw a tear slide down the detective's cheek. He grabbed her and hugged her with his good arm. 'Thank you,' he said as he sobbed into her hair.

Brooke walked over and kneeled in front of him. DI Harte looked away. Luke opened his mouth to speak but nothing came out.

'You don't have to say anything. I know.' Tears filled her eyes and she began to sob.

'I really am sorry.'

She leaned forward and kissed him on the cheek. She now understood it was the end.

'You alright, guv?' Jacob asked as he came back into the kitchen.

'No one is seriously hurt, thanks to Mr Jenkins,' she replied. Officers and detectives bustled around the scene, but Gina remained on the floor. The case was solved and Wall was going down. She picked up her phone and called Briggs. 'We have Wall and Deborah is safe.'

'Yes!' he shouted. She knew he'd be punching the air.

A paramedic helped Luke to stand and led him out of the back door towards the ambulance. Jacob offered Gina a hand up. She needed to be there when Luke saw Deborah. 'Come on, we'll take my car to the hospital,' he said.

'What a day,' she replied as she followed him out. And it was going to be an even longer day, with interviews and evidence – and she wanted to be the one to interrogate Wall. They'd finally solved the case of missing woman Deborah Jenkins. She was now free of Wall. There was no doubt that she and her family would need ongoing support, and Gina had no idea what the future held for them, but that evening, she was going to celebrate with the team. Pizzas delivered to the station were on her.

EPILOGUE

Saturday, 9 December 2017

Gina shivered as she trudged through the muddy graveyard. A gust caught her umbrella, turning it inside out. Within seconds, her hair was damp. She turned the opposite way, trying to get the wind to catch the umbrella and fix it. Just before she could declare herself officially drenched, the umbrella turned in again, protecting her face and body from the storm.

She glanced at her watch. In half an hour, the rest of Terry's family would arrive for the service. She passed the little graves and noticed a headstone for a baby. Her mind wandered back to little Isobel and Deborah. How Deborah managed to give birth to a healthy but small baby was beyond her comprehension, given the conditions she had been living in.

The previous day, Gina had gone back to the hospital and seen the reunion between husband and wife, a moment that had confirmed that all the sacrifices she'd made for her career were right. Days like yesterday made it all worth it – the danger, the calls in the middle of the night, the ruined baths, all of it. The sight of Luke running over to his wife and hugging her, both of them sobbing and holding each other, would stay with her forever.

Deborah had been lucky. Diagnosed with hypothermia, a serious infection and severe malnutrition, her road to recovery would be a long one, but with the help and strength of her family, Gina felt that she would be fine. The hospital was keeping her in until the infection was under control, but she was away from Wall. She was safe.

Jeff Wall had been taken to the station and charged. There was clear evidence of him mistreating and falsely imprisoning Deborah, and he'd be banged up for a long time. They'd listened to him wailing all night long from his cell, screaming that he loved her to the moon and the stars and everything in between. He'd continued by conversing with his dead mother and throwing his mattress around his cell. He'd been easy to crack and his interview had been one of the most satisfying of Gina's career to date. Knowing he'd lost everything, he'd also confessed to killing Nicoleta Iliescu. His mother's death, as per his confession, was apparently the fault of Deborah, who wouldn't shut up. He'd also worked alone. No evidence had pointed to Nelson or Avery colluding with him.

As for Briggs, he'd been pleased that the case was closed. He'd smiled for a second when she'd told him of Deborah and Luke's reunion. They'd enjoyed pizza at the station while getting through the mountain of work.

She continued walking until she reached Terry's plot in the graveyard. 'Terry Smithson, loving husband to Gina and father to Hannah, taken tragically but never forgotten and always in our hearts.'

She swallowed. Taken tragically, that much was true. But was it a tragic accident or self-defence or maybe even manslaughter? Her shoes became sodden as she stood in the muddy puddle beside the grave and closed her teary eyes. Her hand had touched his arm just before he fell down the stairs. She may have pushed him. She was certain she nudged him. She delayed calling an ambulance. Paramedics may have been able to save him.

She closed her umbrella, allowing the rain to mix with her tears. The last thing she wanted was for people to see her crying. They'd assume her tears were for Terry, when they were for herself this time, for the years he'd taken that could never be replaced, for the piece of her that she would never find again and for the years of guilt and angst.

She flinched as she felt a rough hand rubbing her neck. 'The widow sobs. I see you're still being a bitch, but it's good you decided to actually come to your deceased husband's memorial service.' It was Steven, Terry's brother. He reached over and stroked her hair.

'Get your hands off me,' she said as she turned and pushed him away.

'Assaulting a civilian.' He swayed back and forth, rain dripping down his pathetic face as he almost slipped in the mud beneath his boots. 'What ever became of meek little Gina? *Yes, Terry. No, Terry*,' he mimicked. 'After he died, you took Hannah from us. You took her away.' He moved forward and went to touch her face.

She blocked his hand, almost knocking him off balance. 'You smell of weed. Just leave me alone.'

'*You smell of weed.*' His nose was nearly touching hers. Steven reminded her so much of Terry. Her heartbeat quickened. No one had yet arrived, and if they had, they'd probably head straight into the church with the weather being so bad. 'What's the big bad copper going to do about it?'

'Get away from me or I'll have you arrested for assault,' she said.

'Go ahead.' He smirked as he went to stroke her hair.

She stepped forward and pushed him into the mud. 'That was way more satisfying than getting you arrested,' she said, laughing at the pathetic man lying in the mud. She looked up as she saw Hannah walking down the path.

'Terry was right about you being a bitch,' he replied.

'Uncle Steven,' Hannah called as she ran over to help him up.

'Thanks, Hannah,' he said as he grunted and walked back towards the church.

'What happened?' Hannah asked.

Gina laughed as she watched the mud-sodden man stagger towards the arriving party. 'Your uncle has had one too many and stinks of weed. He just lost his balance and fell, that's all.' Yet another lie to go with all the others she carried around.

'Thanks for coming. It means a lot to me, Mum.'

'Come here,' Gina grabbed her daughter and embraced her, taking in the delicate smell of her perfume and the feel of her soft hair. 'I'm here for you, remember that.'

Hannah pulled away after a moment. 'I saw the news before we came out. I'm proud of you, Mum. And I'm sorry. Shall we head into the church? It's starting in about five minutes, we don't want to be late. Besides, I've left Gracie with Nanny Hetty. You know what she's like. She's probably already fed her full of sweets.'

'I'll catch you up.'

'Okay. Five minutes.' Her daughter jogged towards the church, where she was greeted by Terry's family.

Gina's phone beeped. She opened the message. It was a photo of O'Connor covered in mud with a red nose and cheeks. He was holding a piece of paper with 'I came 167th' written on it. So much for romping the race. Gina smiled.

She noticed another text that must have arrived just before O'Connor's. It was Briggs – Chris.

Shall we have a real celebration tonight? You, me, a real date.

She smiled as she headed up the muddy path and entered the church. She took a seat near the back, turned off her phone and waited for the memorial service to start.

As the church went silent, Gracie wriggled in her mother's arms. 'Nana,' she shouted. Everyone turned around and looked at Gina. Great, she was now the centre of attention. The toddler began laughing and cooing.

'Shall I take her?' Gina mouthed as Hannah turned towards her. Her daughter smiled and nodded. Gina walked briskly down the aisle and took the little girl from her mother, bouncing her up and down on her hip at the bottom of the church.

'Nana,' she cooed as she played with Gina's soaking wet hair and giggled. She kissed the happy toddler on the head. A loud crash filled the church. Steven had fallen off his pew, dragging a stack of bibles with him. It was going to be one of those days.

A date with Briggs would be totally unprofessional. He'd been unprofessional to ask. Was she unprofessional enough to accept? She'd think about it.

A LETTER FROM CARLA

Dear Reader,

I'd just like to say a massive thank you for taking the time to read my first book in the DI Gina Harte series. I hope you enjoyed reading it as much as I enjoyed writing it. Gina's character has been close to my heart for such a long time now and it's exciting to share her story, finally releasing her from the confines of my imagination and presenting her to the crime-reading community.

As a writer, this is the part where I bite my nails and hope for a good response. If you enjoyed *The Next Girl*, I'd be hugely grateful if you could take a moment to write a review, letting other readers know what you thought.

Please feel free to connect with me on social media. I have an author page on Facebook and I'm on Twitter, too. I'd love to hear from you.

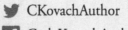

🐦 CKovachAuthor
📘 CarlaKovachAuthor

Once again, many thanks for reading *The Next Girl*.

Carla Kovach

A LETTER FROM CARLA

ACKNOWLEDGEMENTS

I'd like to start by sending thanks to my editor, Helen Jenner, at Bookouture. Your advice, your suggestions and your enthusiasm for *The Next Girl* has meant so much to me. Your input has been invaluable and has made the book what it is today. It has been a pleasure working with you.

Thank you, Bookouture team. You have been a delight to work with at every stage. Special thanks to Kim Nash, who works in publicity. You work so hard to send our books into the big wide world. Also, thank you to the other Bookouture authors. Your support during the process of publication and long after is much appreciated. Thank you for making me feel so welcome.

I'm very lucky to have a splendid group of beta-reading friends and I'd now like to offer them huge thanks. Thank you so much, Su Biela, Brooke Venables, Vanessa Morgan, Derek Coleman and Lynne Ward. You all give me so much encouragement and I'm very lucky to have you all in my life. Some of you are authors too and it's a privilege to know you and to have read your work. May we continue to chat, meet up to talk writing or just meet up to eat cake. The future's always bright when there's cake involved and it's even brighter when we talk about books.

Writing a crime novel can be a little technical for us mere mortals who don't work in policing. We have procedural books and Google, but there's nothing quite like having a real detective to ask. DS Bruce Irving, you have been brilliant in answering all my police-related questions, and I'm so grateful for the time you've given me. I know your time is precious so thank you so much. I look forward to our continued working relationship.

Lastly, I have to thank my husband, Nigel Buckley. You always encourage me, even when I've lost belief in myself. Writing is like riding a rollercoaster. One day you can be filled with confidence in what you've written or published, and another you can be crippled with the darkest of self-doubt. Nigel has seen all aspects of me during my journey as a writer and he's always been there to support me, give me a pep talk and replace my doubt with self-belief. Without that self-belief, I wouldn't be where I am today. Thank you so much, Nigel.

Read on for the beginning of
Carla Kovach's next novel, *Her Final Hour*

PROLOGUE

Saturday, 14 August 1993

It had been a sticky night – so sticky, she had constantly been wiping a drizzle of sweat from her brow. She inhaled the smell of beer mixed with body odour and smiled. Turning eighteen had been brilliant, better than she'd ever imagined it would be. She went out to a pub or club most weekends and this weekend it was the Angel Arms in her hometown of Cleevesford in Warwickshire. Her friend Sarah had left her alone after pulling Jake, the boy Sarah had been after for months. No doubt they were down some alley, making out.

As last orders were called, *he* walked over to her, insisting on paying for her last drink, a pint of lager. The disco was still going through the decades and had just about reached the nineties. She'd intended to leave after the eighties had played. Jake would probably walk Sarah home after finishing up in the alley and she hadn't wanted to hang out alone for too much longer.

'Don't think because you paid for the drink it means anything,' she said. The man laughed. There was something striking about him. His piercing blue eyes felt like they were already stripping her naked. 'I mean it.'

He laughed and passed her the beer. 'It's just a beer. The rest would be up to you.'

'There is no rest,' she said as she took a swig and almost fell off the stool. She'd already had far too many and would never hear the end of it from her dad when she returned home drunk. 'Can you watch my drink while I go for a piss?'

'Of course,' he replied.

On her return she smiled and took a large swig of the pint, reaching the halfway mark. She'd show him she could handle her drink. 'What do you do?'

'I'm studying accountancy in London. I'm just back for the summer,' he replied.

She looked up, almost falling as the room took a quick turn sideways. The room hadn't moved, she'd just had too much to drink. 'Aren't you a bit old to be a student?' she slurred.

Then his sickly grin turned into a predatory look as the sound of 'All That She Wants' by Ace of Base played.

The music was quieter as he escorted her away from the pub, into the darkness of the car park. 'Get in the car, I'll drive you home,' he said in a robotic voice, or did he say that? She hadn't told him where she lived. As she stared up at the stars, she lost her balance and stumbled. It was okay, the man from the bar had her and he was taking her home. As her limbs deadened, she gave up and nestled into his neck as he took her weight.

She opened her eyes and a shot of pain flashed through her head. Birds sang and the rising sun caused her to squint. The sour taste in her mouth almost made her gag as she realised she was lying next to a pool of sick in the car park. The intense headache made her flinch.

A scruffy collie scurried towards her and began licking her face, soon followed by its owner. 'Stupid slut,' the middle-aged woman said as she put the dog on a lead and pulled it away.

Ace of Base, the robotic voice, the beer, the blue-eyed man – her mind filled with everything that had led up to her being in the pub car park, looking worse for wear. But the man was taking her home. That much she remembered. Her heart quickened. She reached down, her skirt was on but her knickers felt damp and cold. She'd urinated, or had she? Why couldn't she remember leaving the pub? Her cheeks burned. What had the woman with the dog thought? Had she had sex with the blue-eyed man in the car park of a pub? The smell of oil came back to her as she tried to stand. She remembered the creaking back and forth. Where had she been? What had he done to her? What had she done? Why couldn't she remember anything that had happened after she left the pub? She flinched, feeling a deep throbbing pain below as she got to her feet. She wanted to cry with each step. She'd never have agreed to doing that – never. What had he done to her and why had her mind gone blank?

As she stumbled towards the path home, tears fell down her cheeks. She couldn't hold them in any longer. She tried to think back, bridge the gap between her memories of being in the pub to ending up on the pavement. Her memories were gone, nothing. A car drove past, blasting out 'All That She Wants'. All that she wanted was to remember what had happened. Who was the man? She was going to find out.

CHAPTER ONE

Thursday, 12 April 2018

Melissa grappled with the duvet until she poked her head out, reaching the cool air of the bedroom. She gasped as she rode the strengthening palpitations, fighting the waves of nausea back with a few deep breaths. The wine had gone down far too well and now it was getting its revenge. She should have stopped at one glass. Staring into the darkness of her bedroom, she rubbed her sticky, sleep-filled eyes. Same story, different day. Her relationship with Darrel was slowly killing her. She needed out.

They had a lovely house in an exclusive part of the Warwickshire countryside, savings, and an investment portfolio – whatever that consisted of. She could get her divorce settlement and make a new start with their two-year-old, Mia. She could go back to working as a customer service agent in insurance, earning a living, something Darrel had never approved of in their six years of marriage, even though they'd met when she started working for his company. He'd never approve of her lover Jimmy, either, if he ever found out, but that was another story. Things were getting harder; Jimmy wanted her all to himself. Why had he complicated what they had? She checked her phone, making sure all Jimmy's messages were deleted and, as always, they were. Even after hitting the wine, she always tried her best to delete any traces of what she was up to. She tucked the phone away in its secret place. Darrel could never know.

During their marriage she knew there had been others in his life. He was forever in the pub, or attending courses and conferences that needed overnight stays. Then there was his insatiable sexual appetite, to which she knew full well she wasn't attending. Credit card receipts showed meals for two in cosy restaurants. He certainly wasn't taking the staff to those types of places. He'd never even taken her to those types of places since they'd married.

Dating had been different and so had their four years premarriage. He'd given her everything, taken her on last minute romantic escapes and bought her flowers. He'd been perfect in every way. Handsome, intelligent, successful and considerate. What happened? That was the only question she'd been unable to answer. After their wedding, their relationship declined. She thought that having Mia would bring him back to her but it had driven him further away. Her needs and wants were no longer a part of his reckoning.

She stared at the fluorescent clock. It was only nine thirty but the quietness of the house made it feel like the middle of the night. The television had been on when she'd gone to sleep. It had obviously turned itself off due to inactivity. The other side of the bed was empty and the house was silent. Darrel probably wouldn't come home until closing time at the Angel Arms. He'd taken everything he'd needed from her earlier that day and, after, he'd gone to the pub without so much as a kiss goodbye, leaving her alone, tending to the pain while looking after their child. She clenched her thighs together and wiped a tear away.

She'd originally gone along with all the things he wanted to do, hoping the fad would pass. He'd hurt her, but it had also been over quickly – and, quite often, he wouldn't bother her again for a few days. Maybe she hadn't been enough. It certainly felt that way. She'd wanted nothing more than to keep him happy. Having an affair hadn't been part of her plans. A solid marriage, a child and a nice house were all she'd originally craved. She hoped that when he was happy, he'd then think of her and her needs, but that never happened. He blamed her for not making an effort. Maybe she just didn't want to make an effort with him – maybe that was it. She brushed her fingers over her nipples and winced.

She flicked the lamp switch on and ran her fingers through her matted hair. The taste of sour wine reached the back of her dry throat. She rolled her tongue around her furry teeth. Why had she drunk the whole bottle again? It was so easy to have a couple, put Mia in her cot and finish the rest – far too easy.

She flinched as she got out of bed. Reaching between her legs, she dabbed the torn skin, almost bringing tears to her eyes. Pulling on her dressing gown, she padded down the stairs in need of a tall glass of cold cola – the only thing that helped quench her thirst after being dehydrated from wine. The wine had soothed away the pain he'd left her in but its soothing properties had soon worn off, leaving her with a sandpaper throat, a deep ache inside and a thirst for cold pop. As she reached the hallway of their large, four bedroomed, detached house she heard a chair scraping behind the kitchen door.

'Hello.' She paused and listened – silence. 'Darrel, is that you?' Her quivering fingers gripped the door handle. A shuffling noise startled her. Darrel didn't normally come in through the back door when he returned home. She went to call his name again and hesitated. Her heart began to hammer against her ribcage. If it was Darrel, he would have answered. It might not have been the most welcoming answer; it never was when he'd come home from the pub. They'd argued a lot lately, not today, but most days they argued.

The silence was broken by Mia's cries. She had to get her child and get out. Her mobile phone was in the bedroom. She ran back towards the stairs, fighting the light-headedness that threatened to knock her off balance. If she could get her phone and run to Mia's room, she could shut them both in. She could push a chest of drawers against the door and call 999.

Footsteps thundered behind her and the sound of her beating heart whooshed through her head. As she stumbled forward, the well-built intruder shoved her face into the stair carpet with ease. She went to scream but a blow to her head rendered her world dark. As she drifted into unconsciousness, the only thing she heard was her daughter's cries.

She awoke to the sounds of her little girl screaming, woozy from the blow to her head. The chair she was sitting on was being scraped across the kitchen floor. The pain to the right side of her head flashed through her neck, then finally calmed to a dull ache. The light from the cooker hood was all that illuminated the room. As the masked intruder dragged the chair again, it screeched across the floor until it stopped in front of the cooker hood. She tried to reach out but her wrists were bound to each armrest of the carver chair. She could feel the binds that tied her feet together as they rubbed the skin on her bare ankles. She tried to yell but the cloth in her mouth just shifted further back. Her heartbeat revved up, almost making her gag as she gasped for air through the fibres. *Breathe through the nose*, she told herself.

A large figure stepped into the shaft of light in front of her, casting a long shadow across the stone kitchen floor. Tears slipped from her eyes. There was no way she was going to be able to get out of the binds. All she could see was a thin gauze covering the man's eyes. She couldn't see him but he could see her perfectly. The man stood tall and broad, his red mask reminding her of the devil. Covered from head to foot in a white crime scene suit, she knew he wasn't planning on leaving any evidence behind. As her heart battered her chest, sweat began to trickle from her brow. The figure moved closer. She flinched as his gloved hand reached forward and slapped her across the face. He was so close, she could smell a hint of his musky aftershave.

'Please,' she tried to yell through the gag. She wanted to be able to speak, to reason with the intruder. Why? What had she done? Who was he? What was he going to do with her? He stared as she wriggled in the chair. She bowed to the side as he struck her again. A flash of pain shot through her head. Blood trickled past her ear. She trembled as it dripped into her lap, dotting her pale green dressing gown. His gaze moved from hers, to the top of her head and beyond. She wriggled, fighting the binds. She needed to stand, to fight back but the cord around her waist snatched her back. A flood of tears streamed down her face as her daughter's distressed cries filled the house. Was there another intruder up there with her daughter? Would they hurt Mia? Forcing her weight forward and back, she managed to build up to a rocking motion. She had to free herself, get Mia and run. The man grabbed the chair and firmly held it.

'You're finished,' he said as he held his fist to his heart before nodding. She tried turning, but it was no use. It was as if her neck was locked into place. She swallowed down the nausea as her head flashed with pain once again. As the room started to sway another pair of gloved hands brought a cord down, laying it gently under her chin. She trembled, writhed and wriggled. Panicking, she almost choked on the rag in her mouth as she inhaled it further. Tears dripped off her chin and mingled with the blood in her lap. Mia – what would happen to Mia? Her body trembled as the intruder standing behind her wrenched the cord.

As her body jerked in its confines she thought of Mia, her little brown-haired girl and the love of her life. She tried to inhale and to butt her head back. The man before her remained still as he watched her struggling for her life. She could sense his grin under the red mask as her vision became peppered. After no more than a few seconds, the world went black to the sound of Mia's cries. A final tear rolled down Melissa's cheek as the cord's pressure continued to constrict her arteries until she reached her end.